I0627942

A love story

Matt & Zoe

Charles Sheehan-Miles

www.sheehanmiles.com

Published by Cincinnatus Press
PO Box 814
South Hadley, Massachusetts
United States of America

Copyright © 2016 Charles Sheehan-Miles

All rights reserved. No part of this book may be reproduced in any form or by any electronic or me-chanical means, including information storage and retrieval systems, without permission in writing from the publisher, except by a reviewer, who may quote brief passages in a review.

This is a work of fiction. Names, characters, places, and incidents either are the products of the author's imagination or are used fictitiously, and any resemblance to actual persons, living or dead is entirely coincidental.

ISBN: 9781632021427

v02142016

CHAPTER ONE

MISS ANNOYING (ZOE)

THE BRAKES ON Nicole's patrol car squeal as she brings it to a gentle stop in front of the unmarked building. It's an old three-story white house with black shutters, with three cars parked in the gravel driveway. From the outside, there's nothing to indicate this is an emergency shelter for children.

South Hadley is well outside Nicole's jurisdiction, but all the same, I'm glad she's here with me. The sunlight flashes off her badge as her shoes crunch in the gravel. We walk to the front door, and I feel tension in my chest. Nicole knocks, and I cross my arms. The sunlight is glaring down, hot against my shoulder, but I've been in much worse heat. My tension isn't from the heat out here, it's from what I might find inside.

The front door opens. A tired looking woman stands there, forty or so, with ill-fitting clothing.

"Can I help you?"

"I'm Officer Banks. This is Zoe Welch; she's here to pick up her sister."

The woman's eyes dart to me, scanning over my uniform—rumpled from forty-eight hours of travel—then to Nicole—then back to me. "Miss Welch... my name is Linda Whitney. Come in, please. You're ... younger than I expected. I was led to believe you're a Sergeant in the Army?"

I shrug. "I am. Or was—the Army discharged me yesterday."

She leads us into an entry room. It's bare, with refinished pine flooring, white walls and plain furniture.

"Please, wait here, and I'll go get her. Um... do you have any identification?"

I open my functional purse and pass over my Army Reserve identification. I don't have a current driver's license. I'll have to take care of that soon.

Linda frowns, looks at the photo on the identification, then back at me, as if she doubts I'm the person in the photo. I don't know why—my Army Reserve ID was printed yesterday—the photo is clearly me. Without a word, she passes the ID back and I tuck it away. She walks out of the room, shutting the door behind her with a loud thump.

"Wicked friendly, isn't she?" Nicole asks. Her tone is dry.

"I guess." Another time I might have laughed, but right now it's hard to have any kind of sense of humor. I've slept little since Captain Wilson awakened me in the Hardy Barracks in Tokyo forty-eight hours ago.

Sergeant Welch. I regret to inform you your parents were killed in an accident.

I have to hand it to Captain Wilson and the Army—they moved quickly. My first question when I learned my parents were dead was: *where is Jasmine?* Mom and Dad didn't have any siblings, and our nearest relatives are some distant cousins in California.

The initial answer terrified me: nobody knew where she was. Within a few hours I learned that Jasmine was in an emergency shelter. The Army granted me an immediate hardship discharge and flew me home. I skipped the normal out-processing—Captain Wilkins and my First Sergeant stepped in and took over everything so I could be on a plane as quickly as possible.

I sway a little on my feet as the door opens and the sourpuss woman walks back in. Jasmine enters the room next. She's downcast, hair hanging in her eyes, and wearing a clean but threadbare dress. At eight years old, Jasmine is about four and a half feet tall and weighs sixty pounds. Her wispy, dirty-blonde hair looks limp and lifeless.

"Jasmine," I whisper, dropping down to one knee.

Her face whips up and her blue eyes widen, then in a blur she runs toward me, crying out the word, "Zoe!" in a choked, grief-stricken wail. She hits me hard and I almost fall backward. She begins to sob.

"It's okay," I whisper. "It's okay."

It isn't okay.

The accident was bizarre enough it made the news all over. I'd read the details. A truck full of premium commercial ovens hit a pothole, swerved across the road and rolled, throwing a one-ton stainless-steel gas range at my father's 1961 Austin Healey Sprite, a car that was probably smaller than the oven that hit it. Mom and Dad were killed instantly.

I don't know if things will ever be okay again. I lie to Jasmine and hug her tight, squeezing my eyes closed because, if I don't, I'm going to start crying.

"We'll need you to sign some paperwork…" says Miss Annoying.

"I'll take care of that," Nicole says.

"I'm afraid you can't, she has to sign the papers."

"Is this necessary?" Nicole's tone is exasperated.

I look up. "I'll sign. Whatever you need." I stand, lifting Jasmine with me. Moments later, the woman shoves papers in front of me, including one indicating I'll have to have a guardianship hearing in four weeks.

"Why is a hearing necessary?" I ask. "She's my sister."

The woman says, "Of course. It's a formality, but the state has to formally make you her guardian. Don't worry about it."

Nicole mutters something unpleasant under her breath. I finish signing the papers, then wait until Linda goes off to make copies. Minutes later, we're back in the sunlight and getting into Nicole's cruiser.

INDECENTLY NORMAL (ZOE)

Nicole's dad grew up in Boston, but ended up living and working in Western Massachusetts because that's where he was able to find a job. Every once in a while the harsh nasal tones of Jamaica Plain come out in her speech. He's a cop. She always wanted to be a cop. Thinking about him makes me feel warm—we spent much of our childhood at each other's houses.

"The Lieutenant gave me a couple days off so I could help out, I'm switching some hours so I can cover the Big E clinic in a couple weeks anyway." She drops the r in hours.

I shake my head. "The what?"

"Ah, well you know, basketball."

"Right," I say. I forget—even though Nicole was a giant nonconformist in high school, she inherited two things from her dad. She always wanted to be a cop, and she loves UMASS basketball. When she got out of the Army, she got to combine the two—she's the newest member of the UMASS Amherst Police Department. Most campus police departments are tiny, but with a student population of more than 30,000, UMASS needs a larger one than most of the nearby towns.

As Nicole drives out of South Hadley Falls toward my parents' house, my eyes keep drifting off the road and blurring. I haven't been home yet—my flight got in at 9 am. Nicole picked me up at the airport, then we drove to get Jasmine. and I went straight to meet Nicole and pick up Jasmine. I don't know what to expect when we get home.

Despite the balmy weather, I feel like February. Cold. Lifeless. I ignore the traffic on College Street until we approach Mount Holyoke College. The house is on the left.

It's a two-story Colonial with a wraparound porch and sagging foundations. Nine acres of horse pasture sprawl behind the neighboring properties. I have no idea where the horses are, or if anyone has taken care of them, or if they're just on the property, hungry (or dead?). I don't know if the house is locked, or if Jasmine has a key (I don't have one) or anything much at all. I can see the house up ahead on the left, nestled in the shade of a stand of trees. The gravel driveway doesn't look any worse than it did when I was on leave last January. I missed Christmas by a few weeks last year, but Mom and Dad made up for it, including cutting down a fresh tree and decorating it. When I walked in the house, exhausted from two solid days of travel, I saw the tree and almost burst into tears.

When my mother saw me, she did burst into tears.

I'm having trouble keeping it together today. It's been months since I've been here, months since I've seen my parents, and I never expected to be coming home an orphan.

I don't like the way the way word feels.

Nicole seems to sense my shift. She's quiet as we approach the house. The left turn signal clicks as loud as helicopter blades when she slows down in front of the house. Traffic, oblivious traffic, flows by in the opposite direction. None of them know my parents are dead.

None of them know that I am going to have to figure out how to be a parent to an eight-year-old girl.

Nicole turns left. The tires hit the deep ruts of the driveway and a splash of mud flies away from the car. She comes to a stop behind my mother's minivan and switches off the ignition. I can't help but wonder if the accident would have been—not as bad—if they'd been driving the van. Or *anything* other than my father's tiny hobby car.

We're blanketed in an uncomfortable and unpleasant silence. A bird chirps in the distance, and somewhere closer, a horse snorts.

I smell the pungent tang of a skunk. Not close, but close enough. You can often smell them in the area in the summer time.

I open the passenger door and slide out, my combat boots slipping half an inch into the mud. That's okay. After today I won't be wearing them much, unless it's for working around the house and grounds.

As always, the house looks like it needs work. Mom and Dad loved the idea of fixing up an old house, but in practice it had always been more of a dream than practical reality. I love this old house. I also associate it with unfinished drywall, cracked and dry flooring, and drafty windows. Mom gardened sometimes, and often spent hours riding the horses, but Dad's idea of enjoying the outdoors was sitting on the old rocker on the side porch or tinkering with his car. Staring at the house now, I'm left with an empty feeling. I can't imagine the place without them.

I take a deep breath and listen again. I can hear the horses, for sure. As soon as we get into the house, I'll walk over to the stable and check on them. In the meantime, I look down at Jasmine, who meets my eyes with an uncertain smile.

"You ready?"

She nods. But from the expression in her eyes, I don't think she is. She's an orphan too, and she's never been in this house without our parents being alive. I pick her up and put my arms around her, and she squeezes her arms around my shoulders. Then I walk up the side stairs and onto the porch.

The gray paint on the porch deck is peeling underneath the rocking chairs. A glass, still half-full of sweet iced tea, sits on the table between the two rockers. It has to be sweet tea, because that's all he ever drank. The tea has mold growing on the top. Dad must have left it when they went out.

I approach the side door and reach out to open it.

No luck. It's locked. Of course. The keys are probably at the morgue, and I'm not going there, not with Jasmine. Maybe another day. In the meantime, I need to check the front and back doors and maybe the windows. Worse case, I can push one of the window-unit air conditioners in through the window and climb over it.

"Let me put you down. I gotta check the front door."

I slide Jasmine to her feet, then walk to the front door. She hurries along beside me.

It's locked. Damn it. I check under the mat and along the top of the door frame, but no luck.

"I'll check the back," Nicole says. She knows the way as well as I do—when we were in school, Nicole spent as much time in our home as she did in her own. In the meantime, I start checking for unlocked windows. Even if the windows aren't locked, they'll still be difficult to open. Many layers of paint combined with the heat of summer tend to seal windows shut.

"Do you know where Mom and Dad have been keeping the key?" I ask Jasmine.

She shakes her head. I look over toward the garage. I haven't been in there in a long time, and I don't want to go in now. Some of my happiest memories of my childhood are in that garage. I want to go in there, but not right now. Instead I want to wait. I want to go slow, take my time, peel it back like a band-aid. It seems that if there's any place Dad might have left a house key, it would be on a hook in there.

"Stay here," I say.

I walk toward the two-car garage. It's detached from the rest of the house, a white building with a shallow angled roof and no windows. Dad always keeps the Austin Healey parked in here, and the van stays in the driveway.

Rather, he kept it in there.

I shuffle toward the garage. My feet weigh a hundred pounds.

Nicole comes back around the corner. "I found the key," she says. "It was under the loose brick in the back stairs."

I close my eyes. There's no way I can express the relief that floods through me. I follow Nicole back up the stair onto the porch. Jasmine is leaning against the front door, turning the knob. Nicole says, "Hey, honey, let me unlock it."

We enter the house.

The living room looks the same as always. The wide plank flooring has needed refinishing since before I've been alive. A mix of antique and thrift-store furniture surrounds a broad coffee table. The curtains are drawn back and light streams into the house. It all looks so normal it's indecent.

The floor creaks a little as I walk down the hall toward the kitchen. The hallway smells, and the odor gets stronger as I approach the kitchen. It's been three days since anyone has been in the house—it smells like something went rank in the trash can.

The kitchen is dazzling, the sun glaring through the window. The blue flowery wallpaper is peeling in the corners, and fruit flies buzz around the trash can. I brush the lid open and see a banana peel crawling with fruit flies. I shudder, then begin to gather up the garbage to take outside. I need to fix this right now.

Nicole is in the living room with Jasmine. I can hear Nicole's voice but can't make out the words. She's speaking in almost musical tones, and I realize as I pull the bag out of the can that I'm crying.

Dad takes the garbage out at night. Took. He took the garbage out at night.

I can't think of them in the past tense. But he won't be taking any garbage out ever again. As I pull the bag out, the stainless steel can falls over with a crash. I stagger toward the kitchen door and open it up, then walk to the trash can out back. Flies buzz around the can.

I swipe my hands at my face and eyes. I need to hold it together. I have an eight-year-old sister in there who's been through hell. And she needs my help. I turn and walk back into the house.

When I enter the living room, Nicole looks up. Her eyes narrow a little bit. "You okay?"

She could always see right through me. I shrug and say, "You know."

"Yeah," she says. "Let me get your duffel bag. Why don't you and Jasmine check out upstairs? She was asking about her stuffed bunny, but didn't want to go up alone."

I smile at my little sister. Jasmine's usually not afraid of anything. "Come on, Jasmine. Let's both get changed and we'll go check on the horses."

I stand up and take her hand.

CHAPTER TWO

MONO (ZOE)

"**C**—CA—CAN I COME with you to the stable?"
Jasmine looks frustrated and unsure of herself when she asks the question—as if she's afraid I'll say no—or maybe she's just unsure of me. Either way, I tell her to come. She tags along beside me, a solemn expression in her face.

The stutter is new. I think. At least, she wasn't doing it last time I visited home, and my parents certainly never mentioned it.

My sister doesn't know me, and I know nothing about her. At least nothing that matters now. She doesn't care that I used to mash up bananas and spoon feed her when she was a baby, or that I cried when I learned she'd been born, or that I used to blow on her feet to make her squeal with laughter. That's ancient history, and well before anything she can likely remember.

As we walk down the back steps toward the stable, I rack my brain trying to remember her favorite color. What kind of ice cream she likes. Whether she likes ponies or unicorns or what.

I don't have a clue. I know some things. Mom and Dad sent me pictures, and I always saw their updates on Facebook. I've seen a hundred pictures of Jasmine riding horses, including Mom's giant Shire horse Mono. At 18 hands high, Mono looks fearsome, but he's a gentle giant. The name was Mom's little joke. He's called Mono because he was sick for most of first year after Mom bought him. Mom said it was because he wasn't getting decent nutrition, she got him from a divorcing couple in Hadley. When I was home on leave the summer after she bought him, her eyes were glassy with tears when she talked about the condition he'd been in. The first two months she'd had him, he had thrush in two of his hooves—from standing around in a soggy and filthy stall.

Mom's Facebook page displays hundreds of photos of Jasmine with the horses, and especially riding Mono. She'd ridden him during the Memorial Day parade this year, a tiny girl on top of a giant horse.

As we approach the stable, I hear the horses nickering through the open stable door. A deep voice croons something to the horses. Who is it?

"Stay back." Jasmine ignores my order—instead, she runs for the door and into the stable. I'm right behind her, but I come to an instant stop as I walk in the door.

It's Paul Armstrong, owner of the adjacent horse farm that runs behind the line of homes on College Street for a solid half mile from here. I haven't seen him since my senior year in high school. He's somewhere in his late thirties, I think, or maybe a very young forty. As always, he has red skin and ruddy cheeks from working outdoors. Paul and my Mom have always been rivals, but friendly rivals. Right now he's chatting with Mono as he brushes him. Mono looks restless, and when he sees Jasmine he lets out a loud whinny.

Jasmine runs straight to him and without hesitation slips between the slats of the stall. My chest tightens with immediate tension—Mono was Mom's favorite, and I know Jasmine rides him all the time. Still—he's enormous. His black fur glistens from the light streaming in the door of the stable, and his hooves stamp at the ground, raising clouds of dust. Jasmine doesn't hesitate, climbing up the slats to sit on the top rail. Mono nuzzles his face against her and she wraps her arms around his head.

Paul grins. "He adores her. Welcome home, Zoe."

I nod. I'm not discourteous, just unsure why he is here. "Thanks. I didn't expect to be here."

"I'm so sorry about your Mom and Dad. I've been coming over here to keep an eye on the horses when I could—I was hoping you'd be back soon. Are you home on leave? How long are you staying?"

That was a lot of words all at once. I open my mouth, unsure of myself.

"I'm sorry, honey," he says. He moves straight to me and wraps his arms around me. I stiffen at first—who the hell does he think he is? Then I almost collapse inside. The tension in my muscles slips away as if it had never been there.

"I think I'm here for good," I whisper. "I'm out of the Army."

"Ahhhh," he whispers. "So you'll be taking care of Jasmine."

"Yes."

"That's good," he says. "That's good. I didn't know if she was with relatives or a foster home or what. I just knew no one was feeding the horses."

"Do you have time to be over here feeding Mom's horses? What about your teams?" Paul's horses often win national prizes in shows around the country.

He releases me and waves a hand in dismissal. "Husband's covering for me."

My eyes widen. "You're married now? When did that happen?"

He says, "Four years ago, honey. Blake quit his job two years ago to work with me."

I smile.

Then I remember that four years ago I was in Iskandiriyah. I missed a lot of what was going on back home then. "I'm so happy, I just didn't realize."

"It's all right." I will say this: he looks happy, and that's a change. I remember seeing him at competitions on the circuit the summer before my senior year in high school—when Mom and I were arguing all the time. Paul was never relaxed. In fact, he looked like the most stressed out human being I had ever seen. He was stocky, with a thick muscled neck and sometimes awkward movements. He always used to look like he was thirty seconds from a heart attack. Now, he still looks red in the face, a little parboiled, but the stressed-out look in his eyes has melted.

"Marriage seems to agree with you."

His smile reveals orderly gleaming teeth. I think they're new... I don't remember that unnatural smile.

"How long have you been watching them?"

"Ever since the accident, I've been coming over twice a day. Although Mono needs more attention. I've been riding him in the morning, but he missed Jasmine."

Jasmine hugged Mono again. "Can I ride him now?"

Paul looks at me, and it takes me a fraction of a second longer than it should for it to sink in that he's looking to me for permission. Because I'm in charge, both of the horses... and of Jasmine. I shiver. I'm not ready for this.

"Go get your boots." The words feel awkward coming out of my mouth.

Jasmine plants a huge kiss on Mono, then jumps down from the rail and runs for the house.

"I've never ridden Mono." I'm eyeing the horse as I say the words. He's huge. I know Jasmine rides him all the time, but it still makes me a little nervous.

"Jasmine handles him like a pro," Paul says. "She'll be fine. Nettles is out back with Eeyore. Wasn't she yours?"

I nod. Mom always wanted me to be into horses, just like Dad wanted me to be into literature. Neither got what they wanted. "They're doing okay?"

"Yeah. They've all been moody. They miss your mom."

I swallow, unable to reply to his words. I do too.

My Fault (Matt)

When my phone rings, it's two in the afternoon and I'm already late. I've spent the day driving from place to place, buying supplies for my classroom for the year. Dry-erase markers, paper, crayons, construction paper, glue—the staples of elementary education. Every year the school provides fewer materials and I buy more. I'm used to making do with even less, so it's fine. At least the supplies are tax-deductible.

I take my right hand off the wheel and fumble to pick up the phone. It's Tyler Norris, a fellow elementary school teacher. There are very few men teaching in the lower level grades, so the two of us form a sort of fraternity, even though we're nothing alike. Tyler is … exuberant. He's outgoing, muscular, a guy's guy. He's an assistant coach for the high school football team and drinks like a fish. Beer, mostly. I'm pretty sure he was the guy chugging Jägermeister from the bottle in college while his frat buddies shouted, "Chug! Chug! Chug!"

He's also my best friend, though it would be impossible for us to be more different from each other.

I lift the phone to my ear. "Hey."

No fancy Bluetooth or electronics for me. My Toyota is twelve years old. My flip-phone and the eight-year-old Mac I bought my freshman year at Boston University still work just fine. I love technology, but I love being out of debt more. I'm trying to pay off my student loans before I turn sixty.

"Yo, Matty, what up? Where are ya?" Tyler's voice is boisterous with an undercurrent of gravel.

"I'm on my way, I got held up in traffic in Hadley. It's chaos from the students coming back at UMASS."

"Right, right. They're ready to start without you."

I mutter a curse. "I'm ten minutes away. Stall them, please." As I say the words, I pull out into the traffic circle. Everything goes black as a minivan comes out of nowhere and crushes the front of my Toyota. Force yanks me toward the steering wheel, but the seat belt locks me in place. With a loud bang, the airbag deploys right into my face.

It takes a few seconds before the shock lifts. I turn off the car and just breathe.

Steam pours out of the front of my car, and Tyler is shouting in my phone "Matty? Matty? You okay?"

I groan. Then I say, "Tyler, I just got into an accident. Tell them I can't make it today."

"You all right? Oh, man—"

"I'm fine," I say. I need to get him off the phone. I flip it shut and gingerly reach for the door handle.

The door opens. I step out, still disoriented. The front of my car is crumpled in, but the minivan doesn't appear to have sustained any damage. Sitting behind the wheel is a young mother with bleach blonde hair and wide blue eyes.

She opens the door and slips out of her seat. She's wearing a UMASS t-shirt, and as I stand up next to my car, I revise her age downward. She's not a mother, she's a college kid driving her mother's van. I don't know if her almost white hair is bleached or naturally blonde, but it's cut longer in the front than the back. Her t-shirt is a little too tight. Not that I'm complaining.

"Are you all right, sir?"

"Yeah, I'm fine, are you?" *Sir? Do I look like a sir?* I look down at the steaming front end of my car. The white cloud is not encouraging.

"Looks like you ruptured the radiator. You shouldn't talk on the phone while driving."

"Pot, meet kettle. You hit me, kid."

"First, I'm not a kid. And second, I had the right of way. I hit you because you raced out into the rotary without looking."

Just what I need. A twenty-year-old college sophomore patronizing me about my driving. "Lady, I've never had an accident in my life. How fast were you going? There's no way I pulled out too fast for you to stop."

She shakes her head, a grim look on her face. I'd have thought she was completely emotionless—her facial expression is remote—but her hands are shaking. "We'll let the police do their report. I'm just grateful neither of us was hurt. You got insurance information?"

I shake my head in disbelief. "Yeah, yeah, let me get my insurance card. Unbelievable." I lean into the car to open the glove box. Traffic is moving again, inching around us. Her van is partially obstructing traffic. I hear sirens in the distance. Amherst Police, probably. Christ. This is going to end up costing me if the ticket gets blamed on me. Meanwhile, some over-privileged college kid walks away from the accident with no repercussions at all.

I retrieve my insurance card and stand back up. "Here. And you've got yours?" I dig out my driver's license and hand both to her.

She hands me back an expired driver's license. Not recently expired either, but expired more than a year ago.

Who lets their license expire for more than a year?

I write down the insurance information and her license number. The address is in South Hadley, right around the corner from the school. That gives me pause, but not long enough to make me shut up.

The insurance card, of course, is in her parents' names.

"Out for a spin in your mom's van, huh? With an invalid license? That's grown up, about what I'd expect from a college kid." I'm working myself up into a near rage.

She looks at me with a vicious expression and says, "You're an asshole."

"Well, that's mature, too," I mutter. I'm frustrated and stressed. The meeting with the school board is happening right now and I'm supposed to be representing the union. And I can't if I'm here dealing with some twenty-something-year-old who was probably texting and didn't see me as I entered the traffic circle.

The police pull up. Not one, but two Amherst Police sports-utility-vehicles, blue lights flashing. One comes to a stop on the grass behind me and the other parks behind the college girl's van. I go back to writing down her information.

Zoe Welch. College Street, South Hadley. She's 24 years old--older than I thought. 413-555-1200.

Where do I know that name from? Welch? I've only been in South Hadley for two years—it's a small town, but not so small that everyone knows everyone. Whatever, it doesn't matter where or if I know her from. What matters is that we get this over with, that I get the meeting rescheduled, and that I move on from this as quickly as possible. I am so frustrated.

Police officers descend upon us. I hear one of the cops say, "Zoe Welch? You're back? I'm so sorry about your parents."

The girl's response is too quiet for me to hear. I've got a sick feeling in my stomach. *I'm so sorry about your parents.* What does that mean? Where is she back from? And what happened to her parents that the local police know both her and them?

I let those questions roll around my head while one of the cops walks me away from the scene and asks me my version of the accident. I follow, my brain still on the girl and the *I'm so sorry about your parents.*

I give my name and particulars to the police officer, who introduced himself as Officer Cavendish. He's chewing gum, wearing mirrored sunglasses, and wouldn't look out of place on a football field.

"You want to tell me what happened?" Cavendish says. It must be a slow law enforcement day because I've got his full attention. His partner is wandering over too.

I want to stay silent. I start to say, I'm not sure what happened, it's possible she was going too fast. I want to shift blame away from me, because my life experience hasn't taught me to trust the police, but my mouth, as always, has a mind of its own. Instead of saying something sensible, or asking for my lawyer, or remaining silent, I gawk at myself as I say the words, "It was my fault."

What? *Seriously?* Who says that?

"I was late for a meeting and got distracted when my phone rang, and I rolled too far into the intersection. I didn't see her until it was too late because I wasn't looking."

Cavendish stops chewing his gum and looks at me under raised eyebrows. "Your fault?"

"My fault. I pulled out right in front of her."

He grunts. "All right. Stay here, I'll be right back." He started to walk away and I put a hand out. "Quick question... one of the officers said sorry about your parents to her... what was that about?"

Cavendish shook his head. "I think you need to mind your own business," he grunts. He's cranky. I wait as he walks off.

I call Tyler. He answers on the first ring. "You all right, Matt?"

It's an indicator of how concerned he is that he doesn't butcher my name. "Yeah, I'm fine. Listen, any chance you can take a ride up toward Atkins Farm? I'm going to have to get the car towed, it's not going anywhere."

"Yeah, yeah. After I told them about the accident, Barrington rescheduled the meeting."

"Well, that's a minor miracle."

Tyler chuckles. "You aren't kidding Matty. All right, I'll be there sometime tonight."

"Tyler..."

"Twenty minutes."

"Thanks."

We hang up just in time for me to get a ticket for improper entry into the traffic circle. The girl is getting back in her van as a female UMASS cop talks with her. All the local jurisdictions getting in on the act. Must be a slow day. I want to walk over there and apologize, though I'm not sure what for. I'm too late. She starts the undamaged minivan, fastens her seatbelt and drives away.

Thirty minutes later a tow truck is hauling my Toyota away and I'm in Tyler's car, headed back home.

"So who hit you?" Tyler asks. "Was she pretty?"

Tyler's real subtle.

"Yeah," I say. "A real knockout, she ran me right over."

He gives me a strange look, then it hits him. He lets out a surprised guffaw. "That's pretty good! Matty, when did you get a sense of humor? And more importantly, did you get her number?"

"Shut up, Tyler."

"You did! High five!" He raises his right hand for a high five, even as he steers up the winding road with his left. We're halfway up the hill to the Notch, a pass just east of Bald Mountain and the primary road from Amherst to South Hadley. I see another car coming down the highway as Tyler swerves.

"Tyler, watch the road for Chrissake!"

He laughs and returns his right hand to the wheel. "Christ. Always serious. Is this why they appointed you to do the negotiations with the school board?"

"Yeah. It's because I have no sense of humor, Tyler. You know that."

"What'll you do if people ever learn the truth about you, Matty?"

"What truth?" I ask.

He laughs. "Like I'd know. I do know one thing though."

"Yeah? What's that?"

"I know we're going out for drinks tonight! Nine o'clock at McMurphy's."

I frown. McMurphy's Tavern is tiny and often packed full of college kids from Amherst and UMASS on the weekends.

"Tyler, we're not twenty-one anymore," I say. Never mind the fact that tomorrow is the first day back at school for teachers.

"Who cares? The girls are!" He laughs and I shake my head.

CHAPTER THREE

WHAT ARE YOUR PLANS? (ZOE)

"**A**RE YOU SURE she should even start school yet? It seems so soon." Nicole's voice sounds a little tinny on the phone. She's out on patrol I think, so she's probably using a headset. The sun glares off the glass in the minivan, right into the house—it's going to be another hot, humid day. The light streaming through the windows looks wavy where it lights up uneven rectangles on the bare floor. Some of the windows are original handmade glass. All of them are dirty. Mom and Dad were both always too busy with academics or their personal pursuits to worry about the fine details of housework.

I sigh. In some ways Nicole is right. Maybe. Part of me feels like it is too soon for Jasmine to go back to school. But there is no right answer for Jasmine. "I'd agree, but she asked to go back. Which is a lot coming from an eight-year-old. I think she needs some normality in her life."

"I get it," Nicole says. "I just wish I could go back in time a week, and … well, you know."

"I know," I whisper. "I do too."

"What are your plans?" She asks.

I shrug, even though she can't see me. "I don't know. I've got a meeting with the Veterans Services office at UMASS tomorrow. It's too late for this semester I'm sure, but maybe I'll go back to school."

Nicole's response is predictable. "You know, there's an opening in the department. I'm sure you would be a shoe-in for the academy."

"Nicole, I'm not interested in being a cop."

"Why not? You were a great MP."

I snort. "Bullshit. I went along with it because that's what you wanted to do. I liked the civil affairs work. Riding around in a patrol car and dealing with traffic violations and drunk college kids? No thanks."

"So what's your plan then?"

"I don't know," I snap. "Right now it's to get settled and get Jasmine back into school. I haven't even buried my parents yet, all right?"

"Jesus, Zoe, I'm sorry." Nicole's voice is low and repentant.

"It's going to take me a little while. Three days ago I was expecting to have a career in the Army. I liked what I was doing. Tokyo was gorgeous, and I was good at what I did and it just… everything's turned upside down, all right?"

Nicole's sigh is drawn out. "I get it, Zoe."

"Anyway," I say. "I've got a meeting with the counselor and her second grade teacher in about an hour. Jasmine's going to come, so she can see the classroom and get a little comfortable before school starts."

"It's a good idea. You want the school to be paying attention to her."

"Yes."

"Okay, now—I won't nag you about your plans. Talk to me, okay? Why don't we go out and grab some drinks tomorrow night?"

I feel relief settle on me at the thought. That sounds wonderful. "I'd love to, where?—wait—"

"What is it?" she asks.

It hits me there, yet another way my life has irrevocably changed. "I don't have a sitter, and … Jasmine needs me here. She hasn't slept through the night yet. How about you come over here for drinks?"

I can hear the hesitation in her voice. Or maybe I can't. Maybe I'm just imagining it. She says, "Sure, that sounds great. Should I, uh… bring anything?"

"No! Unless… maybe something to drink."

"You got it. And Zoe?" She sounds tentative.

"Yeah?"

"Get some rest. I know you're taking care of Jasmine. But you gotta take care of yourself too. She's not the only one who lost her parents."

I close my eyes. She's right, of course. I do need to take care of myself. I need to rest. I need to find time to grieve. But I don't have that kind of time. Right now Jasmine's needs override everything else.

MISTER P (MATT)

The dream always begins the same, with the sound of the crowd. The screams and catcalls, the rising applause, the rise and fall like the breath of a dragon, an organism all on its own. There's a certain lifecycle to that sound. It's born in relative quiet, with the bleats of the animals and the trainers, the managers and dancers the only accompaniment.

The sound of creaking ropes, palms slapping the bars, and the shouts of my father as he counted the rhythm... *One two three four five One two three four five.*

The quiet doesn't stay long, because the birth is coming with the opening of the gates. First dozens, then hundreds, then thousands stream into the arena, and the voices rise and rise and rise. The smell changes, no longer the smell of oil and sweat, now it's the smell of tobacco, body odor, perfume. The crowd is alive, waiting for the show to begin, and in a rush quiet the labor pains begin. The lights go down, followed always by the roars of approval. In the dream I'm swinging in the trap, my legs wrapped around the bars, hands outstretched. The anger is still rushing through me, pulsing in my veins. I can still hear father's shouts in my ears.

You'll do as I tell you, boy! For three generations our family has flown. You'll do the same, as long as you live under my roof.

I shouted right back. *You don't control me! You don't own me!*

The fight was loud. Everyone heard. Well everyone but Carlina and her father, Nick, but that was because they weren't with the circus anymore, thanks to my dad. Papa was the star of Ringling Brother's Circus, and we were his satellites. You don't cross the star. Except maybe I was wrong. Maybe Papa had nothing to do with it at all.

I'd been dropped back in the ring kicking and screaming, but even I didn't dare cross him once the show had begun.

So there we were, swinging back and forth, as my father began his most difficult cross, a quadruple forward somersault. In the dream I still feel the sickening terror as his hands slipped out of mine.

My eyes jerk open. I'm bathed in sweat, the bellows of my lungs expanding and contracting painfully. I sit up.

Oh, man. That was a bad one.

I continue to sit there, breathing, trying to get a handle on my surroundings. I'm not on the road. I'm in my apartment in South Hadley.

I look at the clock.

Almost 5 am.

I'll be getting up soon anyway. Might as well get started with the day.

***

The day before school begins is always hectic. You spend your summer in continuing education courses, or working another job to cover the permanent pay shortage, or trying to write a PhD thesis, and suddenly you have to shift gears. This is my fourth year teaching, and the setup is the same. Come in, get your classroom. If you're lucky, you're assigned to the same room as the year before.

I wasn't lucky this year. Just the opposite, in fact. They moved me from second to third grade—not a bad move—and down the hall to the third grade pod. That is where the good news ended. Principal Blunt assigned me to the least desirable classroom in the school, the only one in the entire building which has the windows partially blocked off by a not-well-thought out addition to the building. Lauren Blunt is a thoughtful boss, but somebody had to get *"the cave"*, which is what the other teachers call this room. Naturally it would be the newest third grade teacher. Why would the others move?

The room is clean, at least. In fact, it's so clean that the scent of ammonia stings my nostrils a little. I walk to the back of the class and open my one functioning window in hopes of getting some fresh air into the room. I wonder what it will be like in here once it starts getting cold.

It'll be fine. Because what choice do I have anyway? I haven't been here nearly long enough for tenure. I walk back to my new desk and open up the backpack into which I'd stuffed as many classroom supplies as I could. Without the car, I'd walked to work this morning. Luckily, it isn't all that far, a little bit less than a mile going south past Mount Holyoke College. I carried Mabel Stark in her cage, the tiny hamster running around, nose twitching, as she checked out the surroundings during the walk.

Inside the backpack I have construction paper, printouts, posters and other materials. I begin taping up the posters. I like teaching, and I like the kids to have fun and be engaged in class. I'm looking forward to taking on third graders this year. They're high energy and interested in school, and they're not jaded yet like the older kids. I treasure the enthusiasm.

It's a little after lunchtime and I have my back to the door, taping up a poster in the back of the room, when I hear a knock on the door. I look back—it's Sarah Higgins, the school secretary. She's a sweet lady of indeterminate years, somewhere between forty and sixty. Laugh lines around her mouth and eyes, and graying hair.

"Hey, Miss Higgins—what can I do for you?"

"Intercom's out," she says. "They're working on it. In the meantime, I wanted to let you know that you've got an appointment later on. Jasmine Welch and her older sister."

"Oh Jasmine! I saw she was in my class this year. Why her sister?"

Her face clouds immediately. "Oh, my. You didn't hear?"

How would I know if I heard? "Heard what?"

She sighs. "Jasmine's parents were killed in an accident last week."

Oh, no. Poor Jasmine. I remember her parents well from our parent-teacher meeting's last year. Doctor Welch was a bear of a man who lumbered into my classroom in a way that made it seem like he had to stoop to enter the room. My overall impression of Jasmine's parents was kindness, aliveness ... they were people who loved their daughter, loved their lives. It's hard to imagine them dead.

And Jasmine's coming back to school right away? "Last week? And she's coming back to school already?"

"I wondered the same thing—I can't imagine what her family is thinking, putting her sister in charge. They must have grandparents or something. Her sister hasn't even lived in South Hadley in years, she went off to be in the Army or something. Anyway, she called wanting to talk with Jasmine's teacher, so they'll be here in about twenty minutes."

I mutter a little under my breath as she leaves. Twenty minutes. Fine. I finish taping up the poster and walk to the desk. I still have a significant amount of paperwork to complete—lesson plans and timetables—but I barely have time to even get started. Five minutes later, there is another knock on my door.

My eyes widen a little and I feel my fists clench when I see a woman standing in my doorway.

Her hair is blonde, almost white, cut just shy of shoulder length. I'd guess she's five foot six inches, and instead of jeans and a t-shirt, today she's wearing a blue knee-length skirt and a black tank top. I'm male and human and heterosexual, so my eyes drop to her well shaped breasts, but I force them back up to her eyes. She has intense blue eyes.

Angry looking eyes. And I don't have time to deal with her crap today, I have an appointment in just a few minutes with a student who lost her parents. I can't remember the woman's name... Chloe? I've always been terrible with names.

"I'm sorry, I've got an appointment in a few minutes. I don't know how you found me at work, but you need to go through your insurance company—"

"Stop."

"I don't have time to—"

"Mister P!" The voice comes from behind the blonde woman. A four foot tall blur races into the room—eight-year-old Jasmine Welch.

Jasmine *Welch*.

Oh, dear God. The woman who wrecked my car is Jasmine's older sister?

Jasmine flies into me, head-butting my stomach. I'm caught by surprise, and I gasp, suddenly winded. "Jasmine," I croak. I lift her up and hug her.

"Mister P, I missed you so much."

This little girl lost her parents? Just a few days ago? She was the kindest girl in my second grade class last year. Ahh, crap. I have to blink my eyes to keep them from watering and spilling over. I look up at the blonde girl—Chloe?—and meet her eyes.

She looks mortified.

CHAPTER FOUR

MABEL STARK (ZOE)

MISTER P.

I should have realized. But how would I? The signs said Mister Paladino and that's his name, of course, but I just didn't make the connection. But there he is.

Matt Paladino is about twenty-eight. He's just shy of six feet, with dark brown, almost black hair, and his tanned face has a neatly trimmed beard along a square jaw. It's a teacher workday, I realize, so maybe he's dressed more casually than usual, or maybe he just doesn't care about looking professional. Right now he's wearing blue jeans and a dark gray t-shirt tight enough to see that he's an athlete of some kind. Not a weight lifter—he has more the look of a gymnast or dancer, with powerful biceps. I look away, almost as annoyed with myself as I am with him.

He stands the moment he sees me, his face just a little red. "I'm sorry, I've got an appointment in a few minutes. I don't know how you found me at work, but you need to go through your insurance company—"

What the hell? The moment the self-important bastard starts to brush me off, I reach for Jasmine's hand. We can go straight to the office and demand a different teacher. Jasmine doesn't need this—

I don't get a chance. She evades my hand, shouts, "Mister P!" and runs right around me and into the classroom. He throws his arms out and hugs her as she buries her face in his shoulder.

I sag, confused and—well this is crazy—jealous. Except for the brief hug she gave me when I got her out of the emergency shelter, Jasmine has been pretty standoffish. She looks at me a little sideways, as if she doesn't think I'm going to stick around—or that I might do something dangerous and unexpected.

It sticks in my throat a little bit that she runs to this guy.

When he looks at me, I can see that however much of a prick he might have been to me, he feels for her. His eyes are glassy, not running with tears but definitely a little watery.

He eases her to the floor. He coughs, covering his mouth with a fist, then says, "I'm Matt Paladino. I guess you—" Damned if he doesn't get this self-effacing grin on his face. "I guess you knew that."

I reach out and shake his hand. "This is a little awkward," I say.

"Hey Jasmine," he says. "You remember Mabel Stark?"

Her eyes widen. "Is—is—is she here? Can I f—f—feed her?" As she stumbles over the word, her face scrunches up in frustration.

He points to the back of the room. "She just ate a little while ago, but you can see her. I bet she's on her wheel right now."

Jasmine runs to the back of the room.

"Mabel Stark?" I ask.

"White dwarf hamster," he says. "She was sort of a mascot last year."

I swallow. I roll my eyes up toward the ceiling and say, "Maybe we need to start over."

He raises an eyebrow.

I'm a little tongue-tied. "I mean—"

"Pretend like yesterday never happened?" he asks. Maddening.

I grit my teeth. Then I say in as calm a voice as I can muster, "For Jasmine's sake."

"Look," he says. "We don't have to pretend anything. It was my fault, and I was an ass. I apologize."

I blink. In my experience, men don't apologize for anything. "I accept."

"Have a seat," he says, gesturing to a chair. He sits down at the desk across from me, and I relax enough to get a look at the room.

It's cozy in here. A little stuffy, if you want the truth. Mister Paladino has started to decorate the room with an assortment of school stuff—maps and books. A row of computers are arrayed along one wall, and posters are above that—cats on a flying trapeze, motivational posters, and one huge, colorful poster from the Ringling Brother's Circus that looks like it was printed fifty years ago. Other materials are piled on his desk, ready to go up on the walls.

Jasmine is still in the back of the room, her face jammed up against the glass of an aquarium turned hamster cage. She's cooing to the hamster, a half smile on her face for the first time since I've been home. Well, except when she was riding Mono.

I wish I had some idea how to help her have a full smile again. I don't even know where to begin.

"I have to ask you one thing right up front, Chloe," he says. Chloe? *What?*

"Zoe," I say, unable to hide the annoyance in my voice. It's not like he hasn't had a chance to learn my name, since we spent all that time exchanging insurance information yesterday.

He flushes. Well, at least he has enough self-consciousness to be embarrassed about not remembering my name.

"My apologies. Zoe. What I wanted to ask you was… are you sure it's a good idea for her to come back to school so quickly? She … well, you both… have had a horrible shock."

I find myself blinking my eyes to force back tears. "We have," I say. "Sitting at home moping isn't going to help Jasmine. Look at her. This is the first time I've seen her smile. She needs some routine… some normality."

He nods. "Okay. Got it. Normal. I'll do the best I can. And please, can I offer my condolences? And my apologies, again?"

I nod. "Of course." I glance back at Jasmine. She's wandering the classroom now. Looking at books on the shelves. She picks a wooden puzzle off a shelf, and I start to say something to her, but Mister P reaches out and touches my hand to stop me.

I jerk my hand back.

"Sorry," he says. "I was just…maybe let her look."

I nod, taking a deep breath. "Yes. Yes, you're right. I guess I don't know her very well." I don't mean to sound wistful as I say the words, but I guess it's unavoidable. And it kills me to say it to him, but I need an ally here.

"I don't understand—"

"Mister P, I was in Tokyo until a few days ago. When our parents were killed they rushed me out of the Army and sent me home."

His eyes widen. "You were in the Army?"

I'm instantly defensive. I get so tired of people looking at me—blonde haired, blue eyed, I must either be an airhead or a slut. "You find that difficult to believe?"

He gives his head a slight shake. "I find few things difficult to believe. But... I had assumed you were a student at UMASS."

"I'm hoping to become one," I say. "I haven't even had a chance to get my feet under me yet, but I can't sit around and do nothing. So I was thinking I'd at least try to get enrolled in school. Or find a job... or ... or ... something."

The more I talk, the more I want someone to gag me. For the moment I just keep vomiting words. "The thing is... I wasn't in love with my career. But I loved the travel. I loved Tokyo. I never expected to come home on such short notice. I never expected—"

I stop talking. Because I was about to say I never expected them to go and die. I can't say that because Jasmine is walking back toward me, and for her, I have to keep my strength up. I need to show her strength, and compassion, and let her know that I can carry her too.

"All right," he says quietly. "Do me a favor. Let's talk via email over the next few days and weeks. A lot. I want to know how she's doing and how I can help support her, okay? Do you guys have any other relatives in the area? Grandparents? Cousins?"

I shake my head. "No one. That's why the Army sent me home so quickly. When the county couldn't find the next of kin, they sent Jasmine to an emergency shelter for abused kids until I could get home."

He winces and begins scribbling on a loose piece of yellow construction paper. "All right. Here's my number and email address. Call or text any time. I'll do whatever I can. Are you all sorted for the school bus and everything else? This must be all new for you."

I close my eyes. Despite myself, I feel relief. "I was planning to drive her to school."

"I want to take the bus!" Jasmine says, an edge to her voice.

My eyes pop open. She has an annoyed expression on her face, and one of her feet is set slightly in front of the other and turned out to the side. I feel a laugh start to burble up, because I do the same thing when I'm annoyed.

"You sure, Jasmine? It's up to you. If you want to take the school bus, you can."

"I did last year," she says.

"Okay. Bus it is."

I stand, and so does Mister P.

"Thanks," I say.

He nods toward Jasmine. "I'm happy to do anything I can to help."

Let's get to business (Matt)

At one in the afternoon, Tyler shows up at my door.

He chuckles as he walks in. "Man, you got screwed with this move. Look at that." He's referring to my window-wall of brick.

Perversely, I want to argue with him. "It's fine," I say.

He laughs and coughs out a garbled version of the word *bullshit*. "You got stuck with this room because you're representing the union. I guarantee it."

I shake my head. "It was the only third grade room open."

He smirks. "You ready to go?"

"Yeah. Is Peggy meeting us there?"

He nods. "If she's still alive."

I shake my head. Peggy Young is the head of the English Department at the high school, my high school counterpart with the South Hadley Education Association. In truth, the high school teachers have more to lose than we do if the contract negotiations fail. The school committee wants to eliminate extra pay for coaches and phase out department heads in favor of curriculum coordinators who will do the job of a department head but with no extra pay. That, along with increases to the cost of our health insurance and a freeze on pay raises for another year have pitted the teachers union against the school board.

Tyler and I step out of the room and I close and lock the door, then we head for the parking lot. Of course I have to get a ride. My car insurance doesn't cover rentals, which may be the dumbest decision I've made lately.

I get in the passenger seat of Tyler's Hummer. I can't imagine how he affords to drive it, unless it's fueled by surplus testosterone. He drives us out of the parking lot, crushing lesser vehicles under his wheels—well, that's not true—as he turns out of the school and toward Newton Street. I find myself thinking back to this morning's meeting with Zoe and Jasmine Welch. Zoe is nothing like I assumed when we had the accident. My first assessment was irresponsible college student. I couldn't have been more wrong—she was stepping into the role of mother after her parents were killed. Which makes me … a jerk.

I'm pretty sure it is too late to erase that first impression. But at least we're on board and in agreement on how to best help Jasmine.

Still… it's hard to set aside the sad look in her blue eyes. She's a damned attractive woman, with exquisite features. And clearly overwhelmed with grief and the weight of her new responsibilities.

I try to imagine how I would have felt at twenty-four? How would I have felt if my parents had been killed and I'd suddenly been the sole guardian of an eight-year-old sibling? When I lost my father, I had no one to worry about but myself, and even that was more than I could handle. I find myself feeling admiration for how well she's holding up.

Tyler comes to a stop at the light at Newton Street. It's the main thoroughfare through South Hadley, running from the bridge to Mount Holyoke College, where the name is changed to College Street. Tyler turns on his left turn signal and taps the steering wheel. I glance over to my right and my eyes fix on Zoe Welch.

She's a hundred yards away, on the other side of College Street, getting the mail from an ancient mailbox in front of an old worn-down colonial. The house looks impoverished, in need of a paint job and probably a lot more. A UMASS police car sits in the driveway, along with her minivan, and Jasmine is sitting in a rocker on the porch next to a female cop.

That explains how the Amherst cops knew Zoe—this woman must be a friend.

"Check out that chick's butt," Tyler says. "*God* I'd love to get a piece of that."

"Don't be a dick," I say.

"Why the hell not?" He asks, chuckling.

I shake my head. "Light's green."

He jerks a little, taking his eyes off Zoe, then steps on the gas and turns left toward South Hadley Falls, the area that passes for a downtown in this sleepy little town.

After a couple of thoughtful minutes, Tyler says, "*Smoking* hot."

I ignore him. Five minutes later we're parking in front of the town hall, a three-story structure across from a park and field that butts up against the Connecticut River. This part of town doesn't have the bucolic feel of the rest of South Hadley. A number of derelict homes compete for space with several condemned buildings. The liquor store, gas station and police department line one side of the street just around the corner, right across from an old house, long since condemned.

The town hall, however, is a nice building, three stories of stone and marble built in 1908 as a combined town hall and high school. The high school moved out in the fifties, but the town hall is still here. I've had some of the most stressful moments of the last school year here.

I never wanted to take on the job of union representative. For one thing, I'm pretty new to the district and teaching in general. Some said I'm too young. Or too inexperienced. Or too much an outsider. And for other reasons, I try to keep a low profile whenever possible.

We climb the three flights of stairs to the third floor and the school department.

Peggy Young is standing in the large vestibule outside the school department. She's a formidable woman. Seventy years old if she's a day, she has a sharp wit and makes plenty of self-deprecating comments mixed in with acid remarks about the *youngsters* running the school committee. She's been teaching at South Hadley High School since before I was born, and almost every member of the school committee was once one of her students.

It astonishes me she hasn't handed out detention slips to them.

"There you are," she says to me. "It's about time, the meeting begins in less than five minutes. I see you brought along your jock friend. Is he going to keep his mouth shut this time?"

"Well—" That's all I manage to sputter out before Tyler speaks.

"You old battle axe. I'll keep my mouth shut when you re-tire to the nursing home where you belong." His words are rude as hell, but he says them with a grin. Tyler and Peggy have a unique relationship. I have the feeling he antagonized her just as much when he was her student.

She whips up her cane and taps him, hard, on the shoulder. "You don't talk back to me, jocko. You might be a teacher now, but I remember when you skated by with nothing but C's."

Tyler says, "How are 'ya, Miss Young?"

"I'll be better when this contract business is over and I can get back to focusing on my teaching. How are you doing? Still chasing inappropriate girls?"

Tyler bursts into loud laughter.

Moments later, the superintendent appears, followed by two members of the school committee. Silently, we follow them into the meeting room. With any luck, we'll get a settlement before things get much worse.

The superintendent sits down at the head of the conference table. A bad sign—Michael Barrington has been a thorn in the side of the teachers of South Hadley. He took over the job a couple years ago—the third superintendent in four years—and morale in the school system has been at an all-time low. Today his lips are tight, and he says nothing as he takes his seat.

The two school committee members sit at the table across from us.

Dianne Blakely is in her fifties. She had two daughters in South Hadley Schools until last year, and has been a vocal critic of the high school faculty ever since her youngest daughter was expelled from the high school for vicious bullying. The school system still hasn't gotten its footing after a bullying-prompted suicide made international news a few years ago. Sometimes penalties are too harsh and sometimes incidents are swept un-der the rug. Blakely's daughter caught the wrong end of that extreme—a series of twitter posts including some graphic pho-toshopped images of another girl resulted in her being thrown out of high school for a year. I'm not supposed to know any details about that, but the fact is—everyone knows. There are few secrets in a town this size.

I'm grateful my secrets are my own.

The other school committee member is Susan Greeley. Su-san is younger than her counterpart, thirty or so, and she has two children at the elementary school—one of them was in my class last year. Susan is reasonable and well liked, and I suspect she's here to soften whatever blow is coming.

Blakely leans forward and says, "Let's bring this meeting to order then. Susan, can you take minutes? I'd like to record everyone who is present."

Susan nods, her face a little strained. She begins writing on a pad of paper, as Blakely speaks.

"Mister Paladino, first of all, I hope you are doing okay. Your accident yesterday, was it serious? Any injuries?"

I shrug. "My car may be totaled, but no one injured. So that's good news."

"Well, then. Let's get to business. Has the union accepted our latest proposal?"

I shake my head. "I'm afraid not. The proposal still doesn't address our primary concerns. First is the elimination of de-partment head positions and replacing them with this curricu-lum coordinator. We've addressed this several times—you're giving teachers the same workload for this position, but taking away the extra pay. That's not acceptable. It's not acceptable that you did it by fiat after the union's proposal last Spring."

Blakely shakes her head. "That's an unfair characteriza-tion. The school committee acted out of fiscal needs, not—"

"You eliminated the position after the union demanded a pay increase."

"The Department Head positions are not negotiable—"

I interrupt. "During our last union meeting, the members agreed to file suit for unfair labor practices."

The room drops into silence. Barrington, who has been silent up until this point, clears his throat. "Do you think that's wise, Matt?"

"Mister Barrington, the decision was unanimous. You changed the terms of employment for all of the department heads without consulting the union or modifying their contracts. The lawsuit was a compromise position. A significant number of the teachers are arguing for a walkout over the health insurance and retirement provisions."

Barrington looks frustrated. "There will be no walkout while I'm superintendent."

"Then I would urge you and the school committee to come up with some kind of compromise, because in the absence of an agreement, that's what is going to happen."

Peggy says in a stern voice, "Superintendent, you won't intimidate the teachers of this town like you and your football jock friends used to do when you were a kid."

Barrington flushes red. "Mrs. Young, you can't—"

"I'm seventy years old. I'd already been a teacher for decades when you were a pimply boy in my freshman English class. And I'm telling you now, if you don't concede on something then you'll have to figure out how you're going to educate the children of this town without teachers."

Blakely's mouth forms a prim line. "It seems we are at an impasse."

I sigh. "So you don't have any alternative? No new proposal?"

Blakely shakes her head. "No. This is as far as we go."

I look to my left. Tyler frowns and nods. I look to my right. Peggy looks resigned. I nod slightly, then say, "Miss Blakely, Mister Barrington. On behalf of the South Hadley Education

Association, I'm informing you that you have a one-week deadline. If the school committee is unable to consider a compromise by next Thursday at midnight, then the union will vote on a strike."

Barrington jabs a finger toward me. "You'll regret this, Matt. Don't think I won't forget it."

I swallow. Barrington likely isn't making empty threats. I've heard rumors of retaliation against teachers he doesn't like.

Blakely stands. "We're done here."

My chair scrapes against the floor as we all come to our feet. "Mister Barrington... Miss Blakely ... Miss Greeley. Thank you for your time."

I don't trust myself to say anything appropriate as I lead the others out of the office.

CHAPTER FIVE

MISS WELCH? (ZOE)

"I DON'T WANNA EAT my vegetables," Jasmine says for the four-hundredth time. Just in case I didn't hear her before. It's been a little more than a week since I came home, and her grief is starting to turn sullen.

I wave a fork in her direction. "I'm not arguing with you, Jasmine. If you want ice cream after dinner, you'll eat."

Nicole, still in her uniform after a day on patrol, leans close to me. "You're starting to sound like a mother."

That sets Jasmine off. She slams her little fist into the table, sending her plastic cup full of milk flying across the table. Milk splatters everywhere, including on me.

"You're not my mother!" She bursts into tears and runs out of the room. Moments after she runs out of the room, I hear the back door slam.

I stare after her. I know I should follow. I know I should hold her in my arms and comfort her and do all that motherly stuff. She's right. I'm not our mother, our mother is dead and we're all alone.

Nicole squeezes my shoulder. "It'll get better," she says.

"I hope so." I throw my napkin on the wet table and stand. "I'll be right back."

I don't hurry. Jasmine needs a minute to collect herself anyway. Instead, I dawdle to the back door and switch on the outside light, illuminating the space between the house and Dad's garage.

I still haven't been in there. It sits dark and hidden in the twilight behind locked doors. I have a compulsion to call a contractor and have the thing bulldozed and taken away.

Instead, I open the back door and step down the cinder-block steps to the gravel pathway behind the house. It's still warm, and the scent of turned soil, hay and manure drifts my way. South Hadley, like much of the Pioneer Valley, is a weird mix of college town and rural paradise, with working family farms across the street from eclectic bookstores and coffee shops. Mom and Dad rarely locked the doors when I was growing up.

The light is on in the stable, the building backlit by a sky washed with orange and red.

A thought nags in the back of my mind as I approach. I never expected to be taking care of my little sister. Much less my little sister and a nine acre horse farm and three horses. This morning I met with Veterans Services and the admissions department at UMASS Amherst. Veterans Services is trying to get an exception to the normal admission procedure so I can start college this semester. I don't know if it's going to happen, but either way I'll either be working full time or going to school soon. I can't afford to take care of this place, to take care of my sister and the horses and everything else. The life insurance will pay off the house, but there won't be much left after that—maybe enough for a year. A cold pit of anxiety runs through me as I approach the stable.

Jasmine sits on the top rail of Mono's stall. His gigantic head is in her lap, his tail swishing about.

"Hey," I say.

Jasmine leans closer to the horse. She has a look of intense concentration on her face. Her hands move carefully, taking long strands of hair on the back of his neck and deftly braiding them together.

"He loves you," I say.

She doesn't respond. I'm not equipped for this. I stand helplessly, overcome with a surge of grief. Why didn't Mom and Dad make any provisions for this? I'm not cut out to be somebody's mother.

"I miss them too, you know." The words come out of me, even though I know it's the wrong thing to say. "I loved them."

She looks up at me for the first time. Her face is streaked with tears. "All you did was yell at Mommy."

I wince. Her words are correct. My last leave, a two-week visit, was punctuated by half-a-dozen skirmishes between me and Mom. It was always the same thing. When was I going to stop playing soldier? When was I going to come home and go to college? Didn't I know the Army was dangerous?

That was a laugh. Didn't I know it was dangerous? Who had she thought she was talking to? I was there.

I blink, once, twice, then several times, because my vision is blurring. The last thing I'd said face to face to my mother had been ... cold. Not hateful, but angry. I'd just finished loading my duffle bag in the back of Dad's Austin Healy so we could ride to the airport. *I don't normally take it out in the snow,* he'd said. *But this time I'll make an exception.*

Mom had hugged me, but I hadn't responded well. Then she looked me in the eye and said, "You know I just want you to have a good life, Zoe."

"I do have a good life," I said. Then I got in the car.

I didn't tell my mother I loved her. Now I'll never get the chance..

What should I say to Jasmine? How could she understand? I don't even understand. I say, "That's true. Mom and I fought a lot. I still loved her."

She turns away, back to her task.

My shoulders sag. I need to talk to someone. A professional, or... or a *mother*. Because I don't know how to help her through this. I don't even know how to help me through this.

I blink back tears again and say, "I want you in by full dark, Jasmine. Okay?"

She shrugs.

"I mean it."

Jasmine lets out a sigh and says, "Okay. I'll come in when it's dark."

I stumble back toward the house.

Inside, Nicole has already cleaned up the table, except for Jasmine's plate with its cold vegetables, and she's hand washing the dishes. "Thanks," I whisper.

"Is she okay?"

I shake my head. "No. I don't know what to do." After a few silent breaths, I tell her about the visit I'd received earlier in the day.

"The court's appointed someone called a *guardian ad litem*... she came out today. Wanted to see the place, and interview me."

"For the guardianship hearing?"

"Yeah," I say.

"You don't have anything to worry about."

"I know... but... I worry anyway."

Nicole looks out the window toward the stable.

"She's braiding Mono's hair," I say.

Nicole shrugs. "Maybe that's what she needs right now. But... Zoe? Can I suggest something without you getting mad?"

I raise my eyebrows.

"I think you should consider a therapist. Not just for Jasmine. For you."

"What... I don't need—"

The house phone rings, interrupting me. I stand there, mouth open, for just a moment. The phone rings again, a harsh ringing tone. My parents have had the same phone since the 1980s, an old Slimline phone mounted on the wall with a rotary dial in the handset, heavy enough you could use it as a weapon. I walk across the kitchen and snatch the phone off the wall.

"Hello?"

"Miss Welch?"

Without pause I say, "I'm sorry, Mrs. Welch passed away last week. This is her daughter Zoe." I've already had to say those words to the cable company and a credit card company who called wondering why their payments hadn't arrived on time. This week I need to sort out Mom and Dad's personal effects and bank accounts and everything else. I've been putting that off for days and days. And I don't have a clue where to start.

Not. One. Clue.

The caller coughed, then said, "I'm sorry... I know. Miss... Zoe... this is Matt Paladino."

Matt Paladino? Who?

One second later it hits. "Oh! Mister Paladino! Hi, what can I do for you?"

"Well, I wanted to check in with you about Jasmine."

"Okay. How have the last few days been?"

He stumbles over his words a little. "She's—well—she—" He takes a deep breath, almost comical. "She's not doing well. Just... listless. She's not playing much with the other girls, and not as animated in class."

I breathe out. Then I speak at a near-whisper. "Same as at home. She's not interested in anything except her horse. I can't get her to talk or play any games or eat."

"What is she normally interested in?"

The question makes me want to lash out in frustration. *I don't know!* How am I supposed to say that to a complete stranger? How am I supposed to tell a complete stranger, her *teacher* for Christ's sake, that I don't know much of anything about my little sister?

"Miss Welch? Are you there?"

"Please," I say, grasping for time. "Don't call me that. Zoe is fine."

"Zoe... can you think of anything I can do here that might engage her?"

Nicole's face tilts in extreme concern. Because of the tears. On my face.

"I don't know," I whisper. "You don't understand... I've been away in the Army for five years. Since I graduated high school. No idea what she likes, or what she does, or what she's interested in. I don't know her favorite color or ice cream or anything except that damn monster horse."

On the other end of the line, I hear his intake of breath, his intake of *judgment.* He doesn't say what I might have expected. "Maybe that's the best place to start then. With the horses. You know she draws them all the time. Especially a big black one. Or at least she did last year. We haven't had many opportunities for art the first couple of days of school."

I nod, slowly exhaling. "Yes. You're right, of course."

"Do you ride?"

"Yeah. I'm not as much into it as she is, but our Mom trained horses and gave lessons. You can't grow up in our house and not know horses." Now Nicole looks impatient, wanting to hear whatever Mister P's side of the conversation is.

He chuckles. "I grew up around animals too. I hear you."

"Farm?"

He doesn't answer the question. "I'll talk to the Principal and the counselor tomorrow. Maybe we can change up our curriculum plans for the next few weeks. I'd like to see her more engaged. And Miss Welch... Zoe I mean..."

"Yes?"

"Don't beat yourself up. It's not your fault. You were off wherever you were—that's what happens. Just take care of her now. She's a great kid. I hate seeing her so... despondent. Can I suggest... if you aren't busy, why don't you stop in at 11:30 tomorrow and have lunch with her? The kids love it when parents—I mean family—" He sighs. "You know what I mean. I think it would help."

I blink back tears. Again. Damn it. Now Nicole's going to want to hug me when I get off the phone, and I don't think I can take that.

"Okay. I'll be there."

GRAVESTONES (MATT)

Lucas Cervone, a stout nine-year-old with bright red cheeks, looks up from the table when I speak to him.

"It's my cat, Mister P."

"Oh yeah?" I ask. It's impossible to tell. The green blob on the paper seems to have three legs—from this angle it looks like a giant booger. Lucas is either sarcastic or a terrible artist. He hasn't been in my class long enough to know which. "What's his name?"

"Mister Willikins," Lucas says.

"Well, that's just great Lucas. Keep going. I want you to write three things you love about Mister Willikins."

He grins and returns his attention to the green blob. I move on to the next student, keeping an eye on Jasmine Welch as I do so. Jasmine is sitting at the next table over with a look of deep concentration on her face. She's sketching a picture in gray and black.

The girl next to Lucas is Beth Grice. She's drawn a unicorn. Or maybe it's a rhinoceros. It's pink and sparkly, so probably a unicorn. "Beth, that looks great!"

She blushes bright red. Beth is the shyest girl in my third grade class—I don't think I've heard her speak a word yet. We're only a week into the school year, of course, so she's got some time.

I move over to the next table.

Jasmine's picture is remarkable for a third grader. It depicts a black and gray horse. She's drawn the horse's mane flowing back into the air with little ribbons tied around its braids, and a little girl is riding on the horse's back, her own pigtails trailing behind her. It's a third grader's work, of course, with nothing in the way of perspective. She's dramatically captured a feeling of motion.

"Jasmine, that's wonderful. Tell me about it."

"That's my horse," Jasmine says. "His name is Mono."

"Mono?"

She nods. "Mom says it's because he used to be sick. It's a joke, but I don't think it's funny."

Mono? Maybe not belly-laugh funny, but definitely weird funny. It's strange hearing her talk about her mother in the present tense. I met them twice, once during a parent-teacher conference and a second time during a field trip last fall. Jasmine's father was a warm man with a ready smile and a ragged gray beard. His wife seemed a lot more uptight, and I didn't get much of an impression from her. I got the feeling that they were people I might like.

A brief whine hisses from the speaker at the front of the room. The school secretary. They finally have the intercom working again. "Mister P? You have a visitor coming, a Miss Welch."

"Thanks," I say back to the disembodied voice. I straighten and walk toward my desk. Lunch is in five minutes.

"All right, boys and girls. Please start packing away your crayons, it's almost time for lunch. Make sure your name is on your picture, then put it in my box."

The kids start packing everything away, some of them scrambling to write their names on their pictures.

Jasmine doesn't move. She has her mouth scrunched over to one side, and one eye is squeezed almost shut. She's rubbing a gray crayon on a square in the corner of the picture.

I stand to get a better look, just as the door to the classroom opens.

"Zoe," I say.

She's wearing a knee length skirt today, brown and red, with matching top, and I have to look away from her very blue eyes. "Come in."

"Mister P," she says.

"Matt," I respond. "Please." I walk toward Jasmine's table. "Jasmine, if you can put your crayons away."

The bell for block 1 lunch rings. That's us.

"Almost finished," Jasmine says. That's when I see what she's drawing in the corner of the picture. Zoe seems to see it at the same time. A quick intake of breath and she takes a step forward.

Jasmine is drawing two gravestones in the corner of the picture. One says, "Mommy" and the other "Daddy."

Zoe mutters something under her breath, then I meet her eyes. I quickly look away. "That caught me by surprise," I say, quietly.

"Hey, Jasmine," Zoe says conversationally.

"All right, please line up," I say to the class. As always, it takes several minutes for the class to get it together, though it is definitely faster than the second grade classes are at the beginning of the year. I guess I'm moving up in the world.

I herd my class down the hall to the cafeteria, noting Zoe walking along next to Jasmine. Jasmine is talking, which is a good change... but I've also heard her stammer several times this week. She used to be a big talker.

My Mom's still alive—but I never did get over Dad's death. I know how she is feeling.

That breaks my heart. Whatever else happens this year, I want to help that little girl get through this ordeal.

Everything in the cafeteria is business as usual. Once my students are in line for lunch, or seated at their tables, I walk over to the lunch line.

Zoe is at the back of the line next to Jasmine, so I end up right next to her. I can't help but look at her. She's crazy beautiful. Narrow waist, generous breasts, fantastic legs. She's smart and confident. Whoever ends up with her is going to be a very lucky man.

Shut up, Matt. Whoever it is, it's not going to be me. I'm her sister's teacher, and ... that's just a bad scene.

Even so, she turns to me and in a wry tone asks, "So is this going to be as bad as Army food?"

I grin. "Maybe." Although food served on the road and on a train, night after night, probably does compare, and not favorably. Of the three dishes available, I point out the most edible one, broiled chicken. Once through the line, we part ways. Zoe goes with Jasmine, and I head to the faculty table, where I sit with Mary Jane Reese, a transplant from Alabama who sounds like sweet-cream butter spread on toast—and Rhonda

Williams, a fifty-year-old widower who lost her husband in a snowplow accident two winters ago.

Immediately, both of them ply me with questions about the union meeting tonight, the possible strike, whether or not the school committee is going to budge, and a number of other questions I can't answer. I make it clear to both of them that they'll have to wait in suspense just like the rest of us, then focus on my eating.

My eyes fall on Zoe again. Zack, the nine-year-old sitting next to Jasmine, shouts, "You were in the ARMY?" Zoe throws her head back and laughs, her teeth flashing white. It's nice to see that she is capable of smiling. But then Mary Jane speaks in an unpleasant tone to Rhonda.

"Look at her," she says. "Her Mamma's not even been dead two weeks and she's over there laughing. What's wrong with that girl?"

Rhonda mutters, "She was in my fourth grade math class. Years ago. Thought she was better than everyone else because her father taught at Mount Holyoke. Then she runs off to the Army of all things."

Mary Jane speaks again. "They should leave fighting to men. It's Obama's fault. Do you think she's a lesbian? A lot of those women in the Army are."

"All right," I say. I lean close to them. "That's enough. Her little sister is in my class, and they just lost their parents. Have some class."

Mary Jane's eyes widen and she covers her mouth with one hand in an almost comical expression. Rhonda looks indignant, her face turning the shade of a plum. I grumble and take out a paperback without saying anything else. The book hasn't been keeping my interest, but almost anything is better than listening to these two.

"Well, I never," Mary Jane mutters.

Finally, it's time for lunch to end. My class is standing, and Zoe stands with them, stretching her arms high above her after sitting on the too short seat for the last twenty minutes. The stretch arches her back, pushing her breasts out, and I have to look away.

Christ.

My class goes to music now, and I get the next fifty minutes free for my planning period. I head back to my class alone, needing to get my head clear.

It would be a bad idea to get involved with a student's parent—sister—whatever.

It would be a bad idea to get involved with someone who just lost her parents and is grieving.

She's demonstrated no interest in me at all.

I don't know anything about her.

Cool your heels, Matt.

Back in my class, I sit down at my desk and begin work on grading yesterday's math worksheets. Then I hear a knock on the door.

It's Zoe. I feel a small spasm in my chest. She looks so sad.

"Miss Welch."

"Zoe," she responds, drifting into the room as she talks. "I forgot to tell you earlier, the funeral will be this coming Tuesday. Jasmine won't be in school."

"Of course.".

She opens her mouth to speak again. Tyler walks into the room, interrupting her without realizing. "Hey, buddy, did you hear the latest about the union meeting?" He stops when he sees her, his eyes widening. "Sorry—I didn't mean to interrupt."

"It's okay," she says. "I was just leaving."

"No, you don't have to go—" I say.

"I need to," she says with finality.

I nod. "I'll send you an email later to let you know how the rest of the day went."

"Thank you," she says, turning to walk out.

Tyler's eyes follow her backside, then he turns back to me and says, "I've been asking around. Everyone's going to vote to strike."

"I had the feeling," I say. "The school committee's not budging."

Zoe freezes in the doorway. She turns back toward me and says, "Forgive me for eavesdropping but... you're not talking about the teachers going on strike are you?"

Before I can respond, Tyler says, "Yes, ma'am. School committee is screwing over the teachers, and we've been trying to negotiate since Spring. The union meets tonight to decide whether or not to strike."

Her eyes dart to mine. "What happens if—you mean, the school would close?"

Tyler, oblivious of the turmoil on her face, says, "Yep."

"You have to stop it," she says to me.

Tyler chuckles. "Stop it? Matt here's been our representative through the negotiations! He'll be right in front."

Zoe's clearly horrified. "You can't... Jasmine... your class is all she has left that she looks forward to!"

"Zoe, I don't have any control over whether or not—"

"You can't," she spits out. "Don't you understand the shape she's in? And now you're going to take away everything she has left?"

I'm frozen in place. I don't have any idea what to say.

Tyler, diplomatic as always, says, "Look, lady, hire a babysitter or something. Or get your parents to watch your kid. The strike is happening."

She gasps.

"Tyler," I say, an edge in my voice.

"What?" His tone is annoyed.

Zoe's face flushes red and her hands curl into fists. She spins around and marches out of the classroom.

LUCKY CHARMS (ZOE)

Get your parents to watch your kid.

Asshole.

I'm back at my car, without noticing how I got there. I don't know the guy who walked into Matt's classroom, but his brief appearance made it clear I was dealing with not one, but two assholes. Matt gave me no hint that there might be a strike. Instead, he reassured me he'd do everything he could for Jasmine, that he would help provide the stability she needs.

Stability I can't provide her because my own little sister barely knows me.

I growl with the effort of suppressing tears as I start the minivan and put it into gear. My mind circles back. I can't remember when I was this angry, except maybe when I was in Iraq.

Intentionally, I turn my mind away from that. I'm halfway across the notch to Amherst before I calm down a little. And when I do, I'm more than a little bit troubled.

I'm angry because Matt—no, *Mister Paladino,* Jasmine's teacher—had promised he could do something for Jasmine I couldn't. And now he can't, because of the strike, which he's apparently up to his ears in organizing. It's not just him. I'm troubled now that I'd even consider finding myself depending on some guy I don't even know to help my sister.

It shows just how far out of my element I am. Sergeant Ryan would have laughed. She used to say I was one of the most hard-nosed MPs in our unit. That I never depended on anyone. And when Sergeant Ryan said that, she didn't mean it as a compliment. She meant I wasn't a team player. My default mode has always been to try everything on my own, to depend on no one, to be self-sufficient.

You can't do that in a war zone. You have to learn to depend on other people. We depended on our drivers and machine gunners, on the men and women who delivered ammo and food, on the weather and on the people who delivered the mail.

More importantly, we depended on our squad mates. And when things got bad, they got bad quick. I'll never forget the terror when we were ambushed on the way back to Iskandiriyah. Half a dozen guys went down in the first couple minutes, and our SAW gunner, an infantryman, panicked and wouldn't get back on his gun. You couldn't blame him—it was a dangerous, bloody mess. I was on the ground, but Nicole jumped up into the truck and got on the gun and kept shooting until the barrel got so hot the machine gun jammed.

Later though, it was all bullshit. I loved Tokyo, but I was one of two women in our unit, and every time I turned around one of the jerks would be trying to play grabass. I quickly regained my reputation for being a loner.

What do I do now? Jasmine can depend on me, but it's just us. And deep inside—I don't want us to be all alone. I guess I did depend on at least two people.

My Mom and Dad. I depended on them. It never even crossed my mind that they wouldn't be there, today, tomorrow, next week, next year.

It never occurred to me that when I left last February, it would be the last time I saw them.

And what hurts ... I can't go back. I can't go back and say to my mother that I'm sorry. That I was a self-absorbed bitch, that I was inconsiderate, that I didn't consider her feelings. It's too late. It's too late to go back and repair it, it's too late to put my arms around her and beg her forgiveness.

What. The. Hell? As I approach the traffic circle near Atkins where I collided with Matt Paladino's car the other day, I struggle to get a grip on myself. Seriously? This isn't who I am. This isn't who I want to be.

I turn on the radio. I was so out of whack when I got in the car that I didn't even put on music. Now that is weird. An unfamiliar pop song begins to play. Fifteen minutes and I'm parking in the lot near the Visitors' Center at UMASS Amherst, across the street from the administration building. Nervously, I lock up the minivan and walk across Massachusetts Avenue. It's a very unfamiliar environment. The valley overall gives me this sense of space... spread out, with tree covered hills rolling high above the Connecticut River.

There were times over the last five years when I regretted joining the Army instead of going to college. I had the grades—I graduated in the top 10 students in my class. My father was a professor at Mount Holyoke College, walking distance from the house, and that fact meant I could go for free. I suppose I still could, but the Army will pay for me to go to school, and I think I'll be much more comfortable at UMASS than a smaller college, no matter that my father taught there. Especially I don't want to be in a tiny all-women college, or one where my father was so well-known.

Some people rebel by drinking, or getting arrested, or picking a different sport than their parents.

I rebelled by joining the Army.

The Veterans Services Office at UMASS is a chaotic space, crowded with posters and flyers and papers and interns. It's a storm; a whirlwind of papers and pens, and at the eye of the storm stands Craig Stills, the director of Veterans' Services.

The thing about Craig is, he operates inside his own perfect no-bullshit bubble. All you have to do is look at his prosthetic legs (both of them) and arm (one) to realize he's the real deal.

I met him a few days ago for the first time—that's when I read the Silver Star citation hanging on his wall. In 2005, somewhere along MSR Tampa just a few miles east of Iskandiriyah, he'd saved a soldier's life and sacrificed his limbs in the process.

"Zoe!" He calls out in a strong voice. It sounds like broken gravel. "Come in, sit down!"

"Hey," I say. I walk toward his desk. It's piled high with files and books. I look at the titles with interest. *Achilles in Vietnam. Soul Repair: Recovering from Moral Injury After War.*

Huh.

"You can borrow them if you want. My office is kind of a lending library."

"I'll think about it."

"You hanging in there?"

I nod. I don't want to say too much. I don't want to talk about what's going on inside. I just want to get down to business. "What have you heard?" I ask. I try to hide the trembling in my voice. I'm starting to realize—I really care about this.

He grins. "It took some doing, since you're long past the deadline. But you're in."

"I am?" As I shout—well, scream—the words, I jump to my feet, knocking half a dozen books and some papers off his desk.

As the books hit the floor, I shift to horror.

"Christ, I'm so sorry." I kneel to pick them up.

His smile just gets bigger. "Zoe, they wanted you in. Everyone knows you've gone through a brutal time. You deserve it."

I carefully don't answer as I set the books back on his desk. He senses my reticence. "Here's how this will work. It's going to take a while for your veteran's benefits to come through. Probably a couple months. We can get you a small advance for books and you'll be able to go ahead and register for classes. You need to do that as quick as you can, classes start Monday. All right?"

I nod. I'm overwhelmed.   He walks me through the first steps. I've got a long laundry list of things I'll need to do. Visit the IT office in person, because I can't wait the days it normally takes to get an account set up. Figure out how to use the online systems. Register for classes. Get my textbooks. Fill out paperwork and more paperwork for the GI Bill.

I don't care. I'll do all of it. Most of it I'll have to do tomorrow, because the elementary school gets out in forty minutes and I need to get home to meet Jasmine. Let's hope South Hadley's teachers don't go on strike, because if they do, I'll be dragging her along for all of it.

I manage to get back out to my car and on my way home in plenty of time. As I drive back to South Hadley, I remind myself that I'm going to need to work my class schedule around Jasmine's school hours.

When she gets off the school bus, I'm outside sweeping the wraparound porch. The wind blows dust across the porch, and as I sweep, a few flakes of paint, already peeling, break loose. She shuffles away from the bus and toward the house, her head bowed, eyes on the ground.

I stop sweeping and watch her. I wish I had some clue how to help her. Of course, what she needs is Mom and Dad. And there's nothing at all I can do about that.

"Hey. How was your day?"

She walks up the steps and looks at me. The boards creak under her feet. "O—O—Okay," she responds without enthusiasm and with a pronounced stammer. She walks right past me, opens the front door, and disappears inside.

Damn. I set the broom against the wall and go inside the house.

Her book bag is on the floor near the stairs, and I can hear her thumping around upstairs. That was quick. I stand there, listening. This is a very old house, and here and there loose boards make it easy to tell where people are. Jasmine is in her room. That doesn't last long. I hear her walking again, but no longer in the soft sound of sneakers.

She thumps down the stairs wearing riding boots.

"Homework?" I ask.

She seems to thud to a stop at the bottom of the stairs. "I don't have much," she says. "Can I do it after dinner? I want to ride Mono."

"I don't know, Jasmine…." My voice is hesitant. I don't like that—I rarely hesitate when making decisions. What's the right thing to do here? Her eyes begin to well up with tears.

I sigh. "Yeah. Okay ride until dinner time if you want." I need to muck out the stalls anyway. Which raises another issue. How the hell am I going to take care of three horses while I'm in school? It's nearly four in the afternoon, and the horses haven't been out of the paddock to graze today, though I fed them hay first thing this morning.

Mom pretty much spent all her time with them… feeding them, taking care of their stalls, of their food, of their every little need. I don't know how I'm going to manage, because horses need a lot of taking care of.

By the time I get to the stable, Jasmine is already on her way to the paddock with her saddle.

"Make sure you run the other two."

She nods. Jasmine is short of words lately.

I sigh when I step inside the stable. All three stables are soiled, of course. Shoveling out the stalls is a familiar task. Scrape it down to the bottom, then lay out a new bed of shavings. I dump and scrub the water buckets and refill them. The last few days I've been able to let them spend a lot of time either in the paddock or grazing, but soon enough winter will be here and they'll be in their stalls a lot longer during the day and night. And that means mucking out the stalls twice a day, because muddy or wet conditions mean infections.

Shovel in hand, I get started. The thunder of hooves outside tells me Jasmine is running Mono hard, with the other two horses on tethers. In the meantime, I shovel. I scrub. I sweat. I've been in the Army five years, and I'm in better physical condition than the vast majority of American women. By the time I'm finished, my shoulders hurt. Shoveling out stalls and scrubbing requires a different set of muscles than I'm used to using.

Maybe I should sell Nettles and Eeyore. I'd hate to see them go, but I'm not sure how I'm going to take care of them.

Selling Mono, however, isn't an option.

Finally finished.

I step outside of the stable and look down the hill.

Our land stretches nine acres, running mostly behind the line of houses along College Street. Jasmine is down there at the far end, where our land abuts Paul Armstrong's. Mono is still moving quickly, Jasmine bouncing in the saddle, the other two horses right behind. I turn to walk back to the house, stretching my arms and shoulders. It's 5:30 and I haven't even started dinner.

I look in the fridge with a frown. I've never cooked dinner much—living in the barracks in Tokyo, I didn't have to. Plus, for the last few days, we've eaten casseroles and other food dropped off by well-meaning faculty friends of my father's. That's all gone now.

When I was in Tokyo, we all ate in the mess hall or on the economy. I have Mom's old recipe book, though, and sometimes when I was teenager she made me cook with her. And options are limited—all that's left in the fridge is chicken legs.

Fried chicken it is. I wash my hands and get the meal going, noting that I'm going to have to go grocery shopping. One more thing I'm not equipped to do.

I bread the chicken, then carefully drop the pieces into the hot oil. Despite my caution, a drop of oil burns my wrist.

The phone rings.

I walk over to it and pick it off the cradle, then walk back to the stove, the cord stretching across the kitchen.

"Hello?"

"Hey, it's Nicole. What are you doing?"

"Cooking dinner." As I answer I open up a bag of frozen green beans and pour them into a pot of hot water. No potatoes. Or rice. I've got half a loaf of bread. No butter, but… best I can manage right now.

Nicole launches into a story. "Okay, so classes start on Monday, and all the kids are moving in, right? You're not gonna believe what happened."

She pauses. Waiting for me to ask, I guess. "What happened?"

"A bunch of freshman guys get into a fight in the North Residential Area at the dining hall. It's the stupidest thing I've ever heard of—one of the guys wanted sushi, and another one called him a not-so-nice name, and the first one punched him. It turned into a brawl."

"A brawl? Seriously?" The chicken is sizzling now, a satisfying sound. Smells nice too. I see Jasmine through the window… she's leading the horses back to their stalls for the night. Third grade or not, she knows how to take care of the horses. At least I don't have to worry about that.

"Yeah, seriously. We made fourteen arrests, and classes haven't even started yet."

I throw my head back with a full-throated laugh. I am so glad I didn't consider applying for a job as a cop.

"So what happened next?" I ask. I walk to the bare pantry trailing the phone cord behind me. Nicole goes on telling her story, elaborating with more and more outlandish facts.

What the hell?

I kneel. There's a hole in the baseboard of the pantry, and it looks like something's been chewing near there. Then I see the tiny black dots.

Mouse droppings. I shudder.

Then I hear Jasmine scream.

Instantly I jump to my feet, dropping the phone. The phone's on the end of a long wound-up cord, which retracts suddenly, yanking the handset across the floor until it crashes into a cabinet.

Jasmine is at the kitchen door, eyes wide, staring at the pan of frying chicken, which is now burning with foot high flames. She screams again, and I launch myself across the kitchen to the sink, searching for the fire extinguisher. It's not where it belongs. I shove cleaning fluids and various unnamed items around until I yank the extinguisher out from the very back of the cabinet. Without hesitating, I pull the pin and aim the extinguisher.

It's empty. Nothing at all. Damn it!

I search, my mind first turning to the sink, but water will just make an oil fire worse. Then my eyes fall on the five-pound bag of flour.

I tear it open wide and pour it on the flames. With a loud whomp! the flames are smothered and the kitchen is enveloped in silence and smoke.

I gasp for air and stare at Jasmine, who stares back at me. In the background, I can hear Nicole shouting into the phone. "Zoe? Zoe? Is everything okay?"

I hesitate, then lean down and reach for the phone. "Everything's okay," I rush out. "Pan caught fire, but it's out now."

"Are you shitting me?" Nicole screams.

"Nicole, I gotta go."

"Zoe, wait —"

"I gotta go." I hang the phone up.

Jasmine is still staring at me.

"What?"

She says, "I've never seen a fire in here. Mom never did that."

Mom never caught the kitchen on fire? I don't know what to say, but my chest tightens and I want to say something unkind. I can't even imagine what to say that might be appropriate. I just turn back to the pantry and look for something for dinner, because we sure aren't having fried chicken.

I stand in the pantry. Pretty slim pickings. Some staples, like flour, but I'm no baker. Pasta is all gone (we ate it), so is the spaghetti sauce, the tortillas, the rice.

I need to go grocery shopping.

High at the top of the pantry is a box of Lucky Charms. Every once in a blue moon, Dad would buy a box. He wouldn't let anyone else have them, which is why it's way up there. I step on the bottom shelf to be able to reach to the very top and pull the box down.

It's half full. "All right," I say. "Change of plans. We're eating Lucky Charms."

Her response is caustic. "We're eating what? Mom never made me eat cereal for dinner."

"Well you know what, Jasmine? I'm not Mom." I drop the box on the table, then walk to the fridge.

Ahh, damn it. There's no milk. I sigh, then say, "Okay. Okay. That's not going to work." I look back at her. "Pizza?"

She nods. Then she says, in a very low voice, "Sorry, Zoe."

I suck in a breath. Jasmine should not have to apologize to me. She's going through hell, and I need to remember that.

"It's okay, sweetie. Pizza it is. We should both go shower though. You go first."

She runs out. I sag against the counter, exhausted.

I'll call Nicole back later and apologize. Meanwhile, I'm looking at the disaster of the kitchen. Flour covering the stove. Oil splattered everywhere. Oily black soot coating the range hood and the wall above that.

That'll take some cleaning.

I turn to walk upstairs, but stop in my tracks when the phone rings again. *Who the hell is that?*

I pick the phone up off its cradle once again. I need to get a shower and change into not-horse-and-fire-smelling clothing, and go to the bank and get some cash, then we'll head to the pizza place up the street. Hopefully this will be a quick call.

"Hello?"

"Zoe? It's Matt Paladino."

My mind stops in place, and my body follows. I breathe a sigh and say, "What … what can I do for you?"

He hesitates. I'm guessing that means it is bad news. "I wanted to let you know—the teachers union met this afternoon. The vote was near unanimous to strike."

I close my eyes. "Do they even care how this is going to disrupt people's lives?"

I can almost hear his sigh. "Zoe…"

I exhale. "I know. I get that there are reasons. But … you can't just disappear, Matt. You can't. She's lost everyone she depends on. We don't have any other relatives, and she barely knows me, and you're the only adult she even knows. You can't just disappear."

There's a long silence. Then he says, "I'll do the best I can, all right?"

I guess that's the best I can expect.

CHAPTER SIX

RED (MATT)

RED JACKSON WASN'T called Red because of his hair. It was because of his temper. He'd always had a bad reputation as a scrappy little bastard, a dirty fighter, a not so smart guy with a chip on his shoulder. I encountered him for the first time when his family joined the Ringling Brothers Circus when I was twelve. Red was about two years older than me, and at that age two years makes a big difference in size. He had the frame and muscular power of someone already well into puberty, who regularly worked out on top of that. I wasn't in bad shape… after all, my parents had me up on the rigging by the time I was 10. I was still considerably smaller than he was.

We were on the northern tour that fall—New York, Washington DC, Philadelphia—when Red's father, a cat handler, joined the circus. If Red ever had a mother around, I never heard anything about her. That Saturday afternoon, I was hiding out. I'd spent the morning doing my chores, laying out the spare ropes, arranging the costumes and laundering them, and cleaning up the trailer. It was almost one in the afternoon when I finished that, and the adults were all practicing for that night's show. I made myself scarce.

No matter where we were, we always tried to arrange the trailers and equipment in the same way. It made for a much quicker and better organized set-up and teardown. Most of the time, when I wanted to hide, I picked a spot behind the funhouse—it was invariably a dead spot on the lot, surrounded by generators, trailers and ticket booths.

That particular day, I couldn't take my usual spot. I'm not sure where we were. Allentown? Pittsburgh? Somewhere in Pennsylvania anyway. The lot shape was unusual, long and narrow and curved, so we were configured very differently than normal. I found a spot not far from the ticket booths where I settled in, sorting through my Yu-gi-oh cards.

The cards were precious to me. I didn't get much of an allowance, though every once in a while Papa would give me spare change. Whenever possible, I would pick up extra work on the lot. Shoveling manure, cleaning out trailers, whatever, it didn't matter to me. I didn't get paid anywhere close to minimum wage for those jobs, but over time I'd used that occasional pocket change to amass a sizeable collection of cards, including some rare collectible ones.

Those days were gravel and dust, the heat and humidity of Indian summer, the longing I felt whenever I saw Carlina Herne, the daughter of one of the animal trainers. She was thirteen and had long flowing locks of black hair that hung well below her shoulders. Her eyes were sapphire, her lips curvaceous and inviting.

Or I suppose they were inviting to somebody. Not to me. She was a year older than I was, but she was so far out of reach she might as well have been the daughter of the President.

That didn't stop me from thinking about her constantly, watching her whenever I could, fantasizing that one day, she would realize that I wasn't just a kid… I was a flyer; one day I'd be the star of the circus just like Papa. As it was, the only words she'd ever spoken to me were, "Get out of my way, runt."

They weren't kind words, but they'd been said in her rich, lilting voice. I treasured them.

The first sign that something had gone awry that day was when a stranger appeared, towering over me. I looked up, assessed the situation, then stood. In front of me was a kid a couple years older than me, with powerful shoulders and upper arms. His expression wasn't friendly, but it wasn't hostile either. Looking back, I still think it's possible Red set out that day to make a friend.

His desire to make a friend evaporated when Carlina came around the corner of the building.

Carlina with her flowing black hair, her shapely body, her tantalizing eyes.

Red saw her, and decided… what? To impress her? He looked back at me and his eyes narrowed. "Give me those cards."

I started to back away, confused. I shook my head, and began putting the cards in the metal tin I carried them around in.

His face screwed up into an angry bunch. "I said, give me those cards."

"L–L–L– leave me alone."

I was wholly unprepared for the punch. Out of nowhere, he brought up his right fist and jabbed it at my face. He connected hard, and my vision went black instantly, and I fell down on my ass. He kicked me in the side. "I said, give me my cards!"

"Leave me alone!" He kicked me again, and I started to cry.

"Look at the little baby cry!" Then he grabbed the box of cards off the ground next to me. "Don't you ever touch my stuff again."

My last sight of him that day was when he walked over to Carlina and said casually, "Hey. I'm Red. I'm new here."

The remainder of that fall was terror, sometimes mixed with rage and frequent boredom and anxiety. Red was the perfect bully. He came out of nowhere, struck by surprise, and humiliated in the process. As the fall continued, he got bigger every day, while I stubbornly remained the same size. Small. I wasn't just physically small. He made me feel small. I didn't understand how or why this had happened to my life.

What I did understand is that within two weeks of his arrival, he and Carlina were a couple, and I was in fear of my life every day.

***

Of course, it wasn't always that bad. That winter, when we returned to Florida, I had a reprieve from Red. He and his Dad went wherever they went for the winter, and I prepared to spend four months in school in Sarasota. School was never a good experience—I was always a stranger, an oddity, a circus freak. I was there for a few months a year; always out of sync with both the curriculum and the other kids.

Something had changed. Carlina's family had joined the small community of circus families living in Sarasota—they were renting a house five doors down from mine. So during those four winter months, normally a period of bewildered shock and sadness, I was on a high.

It's not that she noticed me. After all, she was an eighth grader and I was a seventh grader. We shared no classes. I didn't care. I knew that somehow, this winter was my chance.

I had little opportunity to do anything about it in the first few weeks. Dad had made the decision that this year would be my first one actually performing in the ring. I would be doing a few simple tricks—a simple crossover and a half somersault. As always, he insisted on incessant practice to make sure we were safe. I was under strict orders to come straight home from school, park myself at the kitchen table and finish my homework no later than 3:30. Once homework was done, it was back out and to the gym.

The gym was owned by the circus, with unusually high ceilings and plenty of netting. It was here that we practiced during winter quarters—an endless procession of leaps and jumps and falls to the net. The first day that winter, I didn't fall to the net to Papa's satisfaction.

"You think this is a joke, Matty? You think you're going to screw around on the ropes?"

"No sir—it was a mistake."

"You can make your mistakes when you're chasing that girl. Not on the ropes. You understand?"

I felt the skin on my face heat up. *How did he know about Carlina?* "Yes, sir."

He nodded, his expression grim. I could tell from Tony and Messalina's faces that I was going to remember it. Both of my older siblings had been in training longer than I had. Tony just stared off into space—sometimes it was better to not get involved. Messalina stared frankly, her face curious, one eyebrow raised. Her wild curly hair, normally flowing free, was tied into a bun whenever we practiced. That didn't subtract from her essential character, which was far wilder than her hair.

"Five hundred falls. Before you cross the ropes again, you do five hundred falls. The right way."

Tony and Messalina gasped.

Five hundred? That would take forever. It was crazy harsh. I started to stammer and protest, but then stopped myself. There was no point in that—when my father said something, he meant it. I wouldn't be allowed to do anything until I fell to the nets five hundred times.

The thing about my Dad—he was a legend in the circus world. Our family was the prime act at Ringling Brothers. He was the first flyer in history to make a quadruple forward somersault, and he was the only flyer who performed it in the ring on a relatively regular basis.

My father commanded respect. When he said move, we moved. So I said, "Yes, sir," then got started.

I ran to the ladder and started climbing up. It was going to take a long time. Down below, on the floor, Mamma said something to him. His face twisted, and his lips formed a firm line. "No, it's not too harsh. He'll learn. They'll be no accidents on my watch."

I can do this, I thought. It took about ten seconds to climb the ropes, and no time at all to fall. Unfortunately, I couldn't start until practice was over—I wouldn't be performing my amateurish tricks until I finished this job. It was 8 o'clock before I began. The first ten were easy... climb up the ladder, instead of the platform, and drop-down. Each time, my father grunted in satisfaction. The next ten were almost as easy... my arms and legs were growing fatigued from climbing the ladder over and over and over again. On the fourteenth fall, I hit at a weird angle, and scraped a rash down part of my back.

"Do that one over," Papa said.

I kept my mouth shut, and swallowed. Up the ladder I went, then dropped down. This time I hit correctly, but I felt pain where the rope had scraped me.

I was on jump number thirty-four when my father said, "Keep going. When you get home tell me how many you did." Then he turned and walked out, leaving me alone in the gym.

My first thought was, does he expect me to keep going? I could just go home and tell him a number. Even as the thought ran through my head, I grabbed the ropes, planted my foot on the ladder and started climbing up.

It was midnight when I staggered home. I don't know how I got there, because I was moving in an exhausted haze. My body was incredibly stiff, and what had started out as a single rope burn had turned into ugly red welts all over my back. My biceps and thigh muscles ached, my mouth was dry as the Texas scrub country, and under the surface I felt a seething rage.

When I opened the door to the house, I immediately saw that Papa had the living room to himself. He was sitting on the threadbare couch with a copy of Variety in his lap. The magazine was unopened; the television was tuned to the Tonight Show.

We met each other's eyes.

"Hundred and fourteen."

He nodded. His face stretched into the same grin he always had when crossing the empty space in the ring. Then he nodded.

"Good job."

Papa was a stern man, and not one to hand out compliments. At his words, I felt a wave of emotion... Pride, mixed with an extraordinarily powerful love.

It took me twelve days to make those 500 falls. For virtually all of them, I was alone—nobody stayed at the gym to count or make sure I was doing what I was supposed to be doing. They didn't have to. Something inside me drove me to completing that monstrous task. When it was all over, on the last day, my father wrapped his arms around me, and said in a rough voice, "Matty. I'm proud of you."

I DON'T LIKE YOU THAT WAY (MATT)

During the two weeks when I was learning to fall, dropping into the net over and over and over again, I was exhausted.

Every day at 7 o'clock, I was on the school bus, no matter how I felt. Papa insisted I learn to fall. Mamma insisted I keep up on my school work. Between the two, there was little time to sleep. As a result, every morning I fell asleep during that thirty-five minute school bus ride. It didn't matter how loud the kids were around me.

It was on a Wednesday of the second week when I woke up suddenly, my heart pounding as I bounced on the seat on the bus. I gaped in shock.

Carlina was sitting in the seat next to me, a concerned look on her face.

"Are you okay?" she asked. Up until that point in our lives, I don't think she had ever spoken more than a dozen words to me. Winter quarters was always a little different than being on the road. Here, we were amongst strangers. We were surrounded by hundreds of kids at the school who looked down on us, harassed and bullied us, and treated us as if we were aliens. Even though Carlina and I had little or no contact when the circus was on tour, here we shared a common bond none of the other students had.

I nodded. "Yeah. I'm just tired."

"And stiff. I saw the way you walked out of the house. You look like somebody beat you up."

I tried to hide my reaction. After all, it was only a few months before that Red beat me up in front of her. "My dad is putting me in the ring next season. Training." I shrugged.

Her eyes widened a little. "You're going to fly?"

I noded. I was trying to keep my cool, stay collected, and look a little blasé about it. Inside, my heart was beating so hard I could feel the pulse in my ears. "It's not a big deal."

"You can say that, your parents are the stars of the show. It looks like a pretty big deal to me."

I was reminded then that Carlina's father had once been one of the stars himself—an experienced trick rider who performed dramatic stunts on horseback in the ring. I didn't know when it happened, but he'd lost his right leg in some kind of an accident. At least I assumed it was an accident. He no longer rode, but he did help take care of the horses and train many of the riders.

"It's—it's—it's just a job. Everybody makes a big deal about flying. Nobody even asked me if I want to fly."

"Do you?" She tilted her head and studied me after she asked the question.

My breath caught in my throat, and I felt like I was going to fall into the pool of her dark brown, almost black eyes. I shrug. "I don't know."

The bus came to a stop. I felt a pinch in my chest at the knowledge that we were going inside and she would never sit with me again.

That afternoon, when she climbed on the bus, her eyes met mine and she smiled. Then she sat down next to me.

###

I never asked her about Red. Were they... Boyfriend and girlfriend? He was a lot older than me, and they had spent much of the fall around each other. I didn't want to know—because part of me couldn't forget my humiliation when I met Red—knowing that she had seen what happened, and went off with him anyway.

It's hard for me to describe the depth of the crush I had for Carlina. For three years, I'd watched her as we toured with the circus all over the country. She was the most graceful thing I had ever seen… Always clean and perfectly dressed, even as the rest of us stank of sweat and unwashed clothes. She was a crowd favorite—riding into the ring on her white horse with her hair flowing back fast as the wind. I knew she'd never have anything to do with me—she was a year older after all. At that age a year makes a big difference. Plus, she was incredibly beautiful—luscious hair, big cornflower eyes, perfect skin.

We didn't have any classes together that winter, but we did have the same lunch. The circus kids tended to be left on their own—we weren't in school for the entire year, and the other kids called us—at the most charitable—freaks. So Carlina and I fell into the habit of eating together every day. I always brought a bag lunch – leftovers of whatever Mamma had made the night before. Sometimes it would be lasagna or spaghetti in a thermos. Sometimes it would be sandwiches or leftover stew. Carlina got the school lunch every day. It usually looked awful, and I never understood why she did it, until our third week eating together, when I realized that she was on the free lunch program.

Tactful as always, I had said, "let me see that." I was pointing at her lunch card.

She flushed red, and stuffed it away in her pocket. "No."

"What's wrong?"

"It's just a lunch card."

I shrugged. It didn't matter to me, except to wonder why the circus was paying her father so little that she could be on the free lunch program. Her father had been with the circus for many years. It didn't seem fair that he should be struggling so much financially just because there had been an accident.

###

One week after that word spread around the school: at the beginning of December there would be a winter formal dance. I'd never paid attention to such things before, although I did remember there were some the prior year. I didn't attend. Nor did anyone I knew.

This year, however, the formal presented me with a quandary. Carlina and I weren't dating. Were we? I honestly didn't know. We'd spent a lot of time around each other over the last few weeks, but that was at school. Every day I fell a little deeper under her spell. Every day I put myself in greater danger of being broken.

As the date of the dance approached, whenever it came up in discussion I would get stomach cramps, sweaty palms, tension in my chest. How could I possibly ask her to a dance? She was in eighth grade. I was in the seventh.

She was thirteen. I was twelve.

She was beautiful. I was nothing.

On the Thursday one week before the dance I got myself into trouble. It was 8 p.m., homework was done and we had all eaten a light dinner then headed to the gym. It didn't matter whether or not final exams or anything else were approaching. My father insisted we practice three nights a week and on Sunday afternoons. I was standing on the platform when he shouted, "Matty! Get down from there!"

I jerked in position, and started to open my mouth and ask, "What?"

Before I could get the word out my father screamed, "Silence!"

I knew better than to make him angry at this point. I dropped in a ball to the net, scrambled to the edge and dropped to my feet in front of him. "Yes, sir."

I almost trembled as he approached so close that our noses were touching. "Why aren't you paying attention? I called your name twice! Do you think you are immune to the laws of physics? Or the laws of our home? Have you lost your mind?" I took a breath, but didn't even attempt to answer the onslaught of questions. First, because my involuntary inhalation flooded my senses with the smell and taste of his cologne. Second because even I knew they were rhetorical questions and that he didn't expect me to actually answer them. Not when he was screaming.

"Twenty laps." He was stern as he pronounced the sentence. "Then I want you to explain to me what you were thinking about."

As I began what was going to be a very long run—one time around the gym was about a third of a mile—I started to give serious thought to what I needed to say to my father. He would expect a real answer from me, but I could hardly tell them that I was thinking about Carlina's breasts. But that's what I had been thinking about. I tried to avoid such thoughts when practicing or in the ring—because it's all too obvious when wearing tights—but I had fallen victim to my own scattered brain.

At the point he first screamed my name—for the third time apparently—I had just pictured her lips slightly parted as I cupped my hand on her right breast.

Of course, I had never done any such thing. I was twelve. And Catholic. Mamma would have had a heart attack if she had been able to see into my brain. Perhaps the running was what I needed to tire me out.

I was on my third lap when the answer came to me. I would need to tell at least part of the truth—that the winter formal was approaching and I didn't know if I should ask Carlina to the dance. It presented a number of problems over and above the question of which you say yes. I had no clothes to wear to a dance. Did guys wear suits to dances? Tuxedos? Or were khakis and a shirt okay? Should I buy her flowers? I didn't have the money for flowers. I didn't have the money to pay admission to the dance. None of this was good news.

By my fourth lap around the building, I was sweating profusely despite the fact that it was late November. And not just because of the running.

Practice was nearly over by the time I finished running. I joined my brother and sister for the last few drills, then as a family we walked back toward home. For the walk home Mamma led the way. Papa tapped me on the shoulder, and we trailed behind the group.

"Are you going to tell me what that was all about?"

I tried to gather myself for a second, then spoke. "Papa, it's—it's the winter dance."

He raised an eyebrow. "A dance, I see. What is it about this dance?"

I snuck a couple of glances at him when he was speaking. It was the strangest thing. Underneath his giant eyebrows and mustache, he had a glint in his eyes, and he was grinning.

Did he find this amusing? I felt my face flush.

"Papa... I want to ask Carlina to the dance. I don't know if I should. And I can't afford it anyway." I pause for another breath. "Are there some extra chores or work I can do to earn some money?"

"You never asked to do extra work before."

That wasn't true. I always tried to be helpful to Mamma around the house. I let it go. "Please, Papa?"

He nodded once. "Of course," he said. "You should ask young Carlina, and I'll make sure you have the money."

"Thank you!" I cried.

"Don't think you won't work for it, Matty. You'll earn that money."

Dad was as good as his word. He made me work hard to earn that money.

***

I don't remember anything that happened that Friday morning. I must've woken up, eaten breakfast, gotten ready for school. I must have ridden the bus to school... but I don't remember it. I do know that I forgot to take my lunch that day, but only because of later events. The first three periods of the day—gone.

What I do remember is walking toward the lunch room. My throat was closed and it was hard to swallow. My hands were damp with sweat, and I felt a peculiar twisting in my stomach, like a wash rag being coiled and twisted to wring all the water out.

It was loud that day in the halls. No—the hall was the same as always. It was me that was different. The shouts and laughs and talk of the other students as they changed classes and went to lunch grated on my nerves. I felt as if I were making my way into a dark tunnel, a torch held high in front of me to light the way. Strange how strongly emotional experiences create such a vivid impression. I can still hear the sound of the other students talking. I can remember the quality of the light streaming in through the windows. I remember the smell of frying potatoes drifting out of the cafeteria.

That smell still sometimes makes me break out into a sweat.

When I got to the table, she was already there. She wore a dark blue dress that complemented the color of her eyes. She smiled when she saw me and I felt a sense of relief. It was if she was reassuring me that I had nothing to be afraid of.

I knew if I didn't do it right off, I might never. So I sat down across from her at the table.

She looked at me, her expression quizzical. I hadn't put a lunch bag on the table, because, of course, I'd run out and forgotten my lunch.

"Aren't you going to eat lunch? Are you buying today?"

"I will in a minute. First... I need to ask you a question, Carlina."

My use of her name when speaking directly to her like that appeared to catch her attention. She sat up a little straighter and asked, "What is it?"

This was it. This was the moment. My stomach cramp suddenly became worse, and my throat dried up robbing me of the ability to speak.

Ask her dammit. Don't be an idiot. Just ask her.

"Carlina... I...Uh will you... Go to the winter formal with me?"

I had pictured this moment a thousand times. She would flush red and put her hand on her chest and say, "I'd love to, Matt." She would faint and I would rush around the table and catch her before she fell to the floor. She would burst into joyous tears. Or, in my simplest of daydreams, she would simply say "yes, I'd like that."

That wasn't what happened. Instead, I barely got the words "will you" out of my mouth before I saw her face fall. Into... what? Disappointment? Sadness? Embarrassment? Whatever it was, I wasn't enjoying it. By the time I finished my question, her eyes had grown wet. She shook her head. "Matty... I can't... Red already asked me."

"I don't understand. Red isn't even here."

"They just moved here for the rest of the winter. He... His dad... There was some trouble. I don't know what."

That's because he and his father are both criminals.

She screwed up her face into an almost angry expression, and says, "Anyway... I don't like you that way Matty. You know that."

I tried to play off her last statement. I tried to hide the devastating blow I just received. My throat seized as I said, "I… I… I meant as a friend. If you didn't have another date."

Red and his dad had moved here? This was a disaster.

I don't think I was very convincing. Carlina's eyes drop to the table. "I'm gonna get my lunch." I got up and left the table before she could say another word. I stood in line, and got my lunch. It was an unidentifiable meat with cheese and tomato sauce on it, tater tots, and a cup full of mixed fruit drenched in syrup. I stood there in indecision after I paid for my lunch. How could I go back over there and sit and talk like everything was normal?

I couldn't. I had to try, or she would know how badly I'd been hurt.

Walking back to the table wasn't like walking through a tunnel carrying a torch. Instead, it was like walking through death row to the execution chamber, and when I arrived the executioner was there. Red, a year too old for the eighth grade, sat next to Carlina. He had a smarmy grin on his face. Carlina's cheeks were flushed red. The color of his name.

They didn't see me.

Wasn't that's the way it always was?

***

I was too ashamed to tell Papa. He had been so absurdly pleased that I was asking Carlina to the dance. I spent the next two weeks doing extra chores around the house, earning the money for a nonexistent date.

As the night approached, Papa asked, "Do we need to pick her up?"

"Her father's bringing her."

I've always been a terrible liar, but that night I succeeded. He didn't question it. The night of the dance he dropped me off in front of the school, and insisted I call before midnight to be picked up. The dance ended at 10, so I would be calling long before midnight. I waited until he was gone, checked to make sure there were no teachers or chaperones in sight, then ran away from the school. I spent the next hour and a half in a filthy diner down the street.

The next two months were agonizing. I was a ghost, wandering the halls of Williams Middle School, invisible, untouchable. I ate lunch alone and rode the school bus alone for the remainder of my three months in Tampa. I can tell my parents were concerned—I'd stop going out after school or asking to stay late. I'd stopped actively participating in life. When we weren't at practice, either in the gym or at the fairground, I sat in my room reading. It was with massive relief that March arrived and it became time to pack and begin touring again.

CHAPTER SEVEN

Donuts (Matt)

Strike or not, my alarm goes off at six in the morning.

I fumble for the alarm, hand flailing against the bedside table several times. I almost give up, but then my hand slaps into the alarm clock with a loud *crack* and I feel a sharp pain in my hand.

Damn it! I sit up, suddenly wide awake. Light floods through the windows, and I remind myself that there will only be a few more weeks of decent weather. Winters here are ugly. Cold and wet. When I was growing up I spent the winters in Central Florida. Cold has an entirely different definition there.

My morning routine is all over by six forty-five. I have no idea what to do with myself. Normally I'd finish my coffee, put it in the sink and walk outside to head to work.

Not today, though. A small number of teachers will symbolically picket each school, but it's not expected. The strike won't last long—teacher's strikes are illegal in Massachusetts—but with luck the closing of South Hadley's four public schools will get the attention of the town's residents. The union has been distributing flyers and talking with the parent teacher organization for almost two years, and negotiating with the school committee just as long. No one was interested.

I bet they'll be interested now.

I open my laptop and browse to *Masslive.com*. Right at the top of the page is the headline, **South Hadley Teachers Stage Walkout.** The subtitle says, **Parents scramble for childcare as strike begins.**

I read through the article. All in all, it's mostly correct. Mostly. Dianne Blakely is quoted, of course, noting that the teachers of South Hadley actually sprout horns and eat children at night. Or something like that. I browse away from there to the entertainment pages. Maybe there's a decent play or something coming up.

I freeze.

At the top of the page: **Binder and Mills Circus to Perform Six Nights in Pioneer Valley.**

Oh, that's just fantastic. If I'm not back at work by then, I'll go join the circus. I scan the article. They're performing in Albany, Boston, and Worcester first, and will be here just before Thanksgiving.

I stand up, out of sorts, as if I were going somewhere. Anywhere.

But … Christ. I grab my phone and dial Tony. The phone rings without answer. I disconnect, wait thirty seconds, then try again.

He answers on the first ring.

"You gotta be kidding me. Six months I don't hear from you, and you gotta call me at six in the morning?"

"It's seven," I say.

"Not in Madison."

"Oh, bummer."

"What do you need, Matty?"

I shrug, then realize he can't see it. "Just wanted to check in. See how you were."

"Bullshit," he replies. "You saw the schedule."

"What schedule?" I say. He knows I'm lying.

"Whatever. You should come join us. It would do you a world of good."

I shudder, thinking of the helpless terror of Papa's hands slipping out of mine. "No, thanks, Tony."

"Will we get to see you at least? Dinner? Anything? Mom's all broken up she never sees you anymore. You didn't even come home for Christmas. What's that about?"

"Tony, I didn't have the money. Elementary school teachers don't get paid all that much."

Tony mutters something under his breath. Then silence. Silence that drags on, because it's heavy.

I finally break the silence. "Yeah. We'll have dinner."

"That's real generous, Matty. Real generous. Yeah. We'll talk later."

He hangs up the phone, leaving me with silence and guilt. I can deal with one, but not the other. It's time to head out.

I lock up the apartment and walk down the wooden stairwell to the parking lot. I live in a one-bedroom apartment next to South Hadley Common, just above a restaurant. It's a good location, plus the rent is cheap. Hard to beat. My commute is usually less than five minutes.

As I unlock the car I think, once again, about buying a bike. I've been going to the Gold's Gym on memorial drive pretty regularly—okay maybe regularly is an exaggeration— but every once in a while anyway. And I run a lot in the mornings. I'm nowhere near the shape I was once in, when I had to perform five nights a week.

The car is new to me, but not new. I took the insurance money from my old car and bought a 6-year-old Honda Civic. It had 45,000 miles on it and is paid for. I'm happy.

I drive to Dunkin' Donuts and go through the drive through, ordering an assorted dozen and two large cups of coffee. I take a guess and get cream and sugar for both, then head back up College Street until the white colonial is in view. Paint, once white, is peeling all over the house, and the front steps are crooked and bare. The house needs a lot of work.

Zoe's minivan is in the driveway.

I pull in, my tires crunching in the gravel. Is it weird that I just show up here? Will she think it's weird? No, she asked me to not disappear, to be here for Jasmine. That's what I'm doing.

Okay, maybe it's weird.

Anyway, I open the door and grab the donuts and the two cups in their cardboard carrier. I carry my load to the front door, cups in one hand and donuts in the other. I don't make it to the porch before the front door opens.

Zoe is there. She's wearing a gray Army sweatshirt and blue sweatpants, and her hair is disheveled, not long enough to tie back easily. Loose nearly-white hair hangs in front of her left eye. Her expression is... not exactly hostile. She tilts her head to the left slightly and purses her lips and her eyebrows squish together.

"What are you doing here?"

"You said I can't just disappear. I'm not. I get it. Here's some coffee and donuts, if I don't drop them."

Her eyes widen slightly and she reaches out to takes the coffee tray from my left hand. "Come on in."

Her voice betrays no enthusiasm.

It's dim in the front room as we enter, shades drawn. She sets the coffee down and starts opening the shades. "I wasn't expecting company. Come on in the kitchen. I don't think Jasmine's awake yet."

She walks on past the long living room into a doorway capped with a wide, shallow arch. I follow through the dining room (dominated by a large scarred farm table) and into the kitchen. A small table sits in here and the room smells heavily of smoke. An old Apple laptop is open on the table next to a mug of coffee. It has characters in Chinese or Japanese or some other Asian language, along with a bright pink heart:

私は東京を♥

It might be an I Love New York mug. Except the silhouette of Godzilla, however, leads me to believe the letters identify Tokyo or another Japanese city.

"Have a seat," she says. "I've got to admit, the donuts—that was a good move. We're out of food, I've got to go grocery shopping today."

"How is she doing?"

"Jasmine?"

I nod. Zoe's face is pensive and she looks away from me slightly. In a low voice, she says, "Same stuff we talked about yesterday. When I told her there wasn't any school today, she just went back upstairs without a word."

"You didn't make her come down for breakfast?"

Zoe shakes her head. "I don't want to push her."

That makes sense. Zoe takes a cup out of the holder and I grab the other.

"I took a risk you'd prefer cream and sugar."

"That's fine," she says. "Thank you. I wasn't very gracious when you showed up."

"You're not required to be gracious."

She raises an eyebrow. "Seriously though, shouldn't you be picketing or something?"

I smile. "There will be some people doing that. I'm actually sitting on my phone waiting to see if the school committee calls. I'm one of the union representatives—if they decide to negotiate, I'll get the call."

"You think they will?"

I nod. "Yeah. Everything else aside, people are seriously inconvenienced when school is closed."

Her expression doesn't change. "It's true. I'm supposed to start classes on Monday."

"So you are in college."

"I got accepted under some pretty dodgy circumstances thanks to family friends and the Veterans Services department."

"How do you mean?" I ask.

She shrugs. "My dad was a professor at Mount Holyoke. So—sometimes people stick together. I didn't get into UMASS on my own power."

"I'm sure you would have been accepted if you had gone through the normal process. Right?"

She smiles. "Now, how would you know that?"

"I don't. You seem pretty smart. I bet you did well in school."

She nods. "I did. Top of my class."

The words slip out of my mouth without thought. "But you joined the Army."

She gives a minute shake of her head. "That's a bit of stereotyping, don't you think? There are plenty of smart people in the Army, even if they aren't academics."

"True. Forgive me."

"Of course," she replies. "I've spent the last five years fighting stereotypes. Outside the Army they think we're all idiots. Inside the Army, the idiots think women can't be soldiers. Outside the Army too. I spent my whole tour in Iraq patrolling near

Baghdad, often on foot. My first time coming home, the guy next to me on the plane asks me how I like nursing."

She spent a year in Iraq? On patrol? On foot? I don't let my surprise show on my face. A moment later I hear loud steps thumping down the hall above us, then almost a gallop coming down the stairs.

"Jasmine," Zoe says in a still voice. "Sounds like she's already dressed to ride."

Less than a second later, Jasmine clomps in wearing riding boots. She stops in the doorway of the kitchen. "Mister P?"

"Hey, Jasmine."

Jasmine looks confused. A deep line creases her forehead as her eyebrows draw together. "What—what—what—why are you here?"

As she stumbles over the words, her face screws up in frustration.

"Well, school's closed, but I wanted to stop in and make sure you were okay. Also, I had these extra donuts, and I didn't know what to do with them, so I brought them to my favorite third grader."

Jasmine flushes a deep red. "I'm—I'm—your favorite third grader?"

I press my index finger to my lip and blow. "Shhhhh... don't tell anyone. Just come get a donut."

TRICK-RIDER (ZOE)

I'm not sure I know what to make of Matt just showing up here. My first reaction when I saw him out the window was to not answer the door. I'm a mess, my hair's a mess. I felt a moment of sheer panic, and that bothers me, because who cares what he thinks?

Apparently I do.

After eating four donuts and washing it down with a large glass of water, Jasmine announces she's going out to the stable to see to the horses. Hopefully she won't vomit the donuts onto Mono. Then she turns to Matt. "Want to meet my horse?"

"Sure, I'd love to," he says with a big lopsided smile that forms a dimple in his right cheek. The smile does stupid and undignified things inside my chest. Things I don't want, because the last thing I need right now is to get involved with my sister's teacher.

No. Just no.

"I'll go get a shower and catch up with you two in a few minutes."

Jasmine runs for the door. Matt stands awkwardly and takes another swig of his coffee. "Off to see the horses, I guess."

I smile. "Don't be nervous when you see her on Mono. She's an expert on that horse, even though he's the size of an elephant. She's safe."

He raises his eyebrows. "Okay."

I don't wait for him to leave the kitchen. I get up and walk out. I cannot believe I said what I did about the Army and being on patrol on foot. Really, Zoe? It sounded like I was bragging. And maybe I was a little bit. I'm proud of the year I served in Iraq. I'm proud of my Combat Action Badge. Still, my face feels flushed and I'm off balance as I head upstairs. I'm halfway upstairs when I hear the kitchen door bang shut.

In the shower—I always take long, luxurious showers, because you never know when you'll get another one like that—I stay for a long time, my mind turning over the conversation. What the hell is wrong with me? I'm not some silly ditz. But it would be a lie to say I wasn't attracted to Matt. A lot. He's in shape, that's clear enough, but not the over-muscular bulkiness of most of the guys I knew in the Army—guys who bench pressed at the gym every day and directly equated their muscle size to dick size. They didn't care about brain size.

Matt's built like a dancer or gymnast—muscular, with powerful shoulders, arms and calves. And he seems smart.

He's Jasmine's teacher. *Come on, Zoe.*

Does that matter?

It matters if we date, and it doesn't work out. She needs some stability in her life. She needs someone she knows, an adult she knows. She doesn't know me. I'm sad to say, but Matt's spent far more time around Jasmine than I ever have.

She was born a few weeks before the beginning of my junior year in high school. I was busy in those days—cheerleading practice ran two hours every night, plus football games, plus planning for college (my Dad insisted) while I secretly thought of a way to go my own way. I was accepted at Boston College and Dartmouth (a real long shot), along with Mount Holyoke, but I dithered over making a decision until the very last minute. Which drove my parents insane, of course. Mom fussed and yelled, and Dad did too. In April of my senior year—three weeks before deposits were due at whatever school I chose—I skipped school and met with an Army recruiter at their office next to Friendly's.

My parents were livid. Especially Mom. *You're throwing your life away. Dad is so disappointed.*

Thinking of it now, I find myself scrubbing my hair too roughly.

We never repaired that rift. They came to some peace with it—especially after I came home from Iraq alive. Dad openly wept when I got off the plane and met my parents at Bradley Airport halfway through my Iraq tour.

Mom begged me not to go back. She didn't get it. You can't just walk away. Aside from the legal complications—which of course are serious for deserters—Nicole was still over there. You don't leave your friends behind.

I squeeze my eyes shut. I don't want to think about Iraq.

I don't want to think about my Dad being disappointed in me.

Wow. My mind is everywhere this morning. I take a long shuddering breath and turn off the water, then towel myself dry.

As I brush my hair, I can't shut out their voices.

Zoe, we're just frightened for you. Don't you know there's a war going on?

Your Dad is so sad, Zoe. You're wasting your potential. You're so smart—you need to be in college.

That was all before Iraq. But later on—it was about reenlisting. How could I do that to him? I wasn't seriously considering staying in as a career, was I?

I wish I'd had a chance to talk with him about it when I was home last. He didn't understand why I'd reenlisted. Mom yelled at me about it—a lot. Dad was quiet. He was warm, and hugged me, and told me how much he loved me. I knew that, behind that, he was sad.

I struggle to shake off the past. I walk down the hall to my room—I've not even considered moving into the master bedroom, I haven't even entered the room. I change into tough jeans and a flannel shirt and riding boots I've worn once or twice in the last five years. They were a Christmas present my senior year. Because my mom always wanted my priorities to be her priorities, or at least Dad's. She loved horses and he loved academia and neither left room for me.

I tell myself to forget about it. I thump down the stairs and head toward the stable.

There I stop short.

The first thing I see is Mono, with tiny little Jasmine perched on his back. That's not so unusual a sight.

The unusual sight is Matt Paladino, third grade teacher, who apparently has unforeseen talents. He's riding Nettles around the paddock sitting *backwards* in his saddle while Jasmine laughs and giggles. Matt has a mock terrified expression on his face. Then I gasp in an almost scream when he falls off the back end of the horse. But in some miracle of bizarre tricks, he does a somersault and lands on his feet.

Jasmine claps. Nettles comes back around the circle, and I see the tension in Matt's legs as he bends them slightly, then runs alongside the galloping horse and jumps back into the saddle.

It's one of the most expert displays of horsemanship I've ever seen. And I grew up around horses and horse shows.

I walk up to the fence and lean against it, resting one foot on the middle rail. Matt sees me and reins Nettles in. The horse rears up with a loud whinny, then comes back down to all fours. Matt flushes.

"I didn't realize you were a trick-rider," I say.

He shakes his head. "I grew up around horses, that's all."

Liar. He did a lot more than grow up around them.

"Where was that?" I ask.

"Oh, Central Florida."

Whatever. Jasmine is captivated, though now I'm worried she'll try some hare-brained jump like that off of Mono. It's obvious, watching her in the saddle, that this is where she belongs. On the ground she's despondent. Melancholy. Eyes on the ground. Hair in her face.

In the saddle her eyes are bright, she's active and looking around. She's in love with that horse.

"You want to ride with us, Zoe?"

Jasmine's question instantly melts my concerns about Matt. "I'd love to."

Five minutes later I'm riding on Nettles, an Andalusian gray—my horse since my seventeenth birthday. You can tell he's older—his hair is almost entirely white now. He's still a strong, athletic horse, a little over fifteen hands. Nettles broke a leg during a race at Rockingham Park, and would have been put down, but Mom bought him for next to nothing from his owner and nursed him back to health. It was a miracle—instead of shattering, the leg broke cleanly, a greenstick fracture. A horse recovering from a fractured leg is very unusual, but it's become more common in the last few years. Mom drilled me on all of that knowledge, of course. I spent many nights and weekends with Nettles when he was recovering. He doesn't race any more, but he's still a beautiful horse.

The three of us head across the property with Mono and Jasmine setting the pace. The horses are happy and the weather is beautiful. We ride south down the pasture at a gallop, clods of dirt and grass being thrown up by the hooves of the horses.

Almost at the south end of the property, Jasmine pulls Mono to a slow canter parallel with the fence. I fall in on her left, closer to the fence, with Matt on the other side.

"Whoo," Matt says. "It's been a long time since I've ridden like that."

"How long? Where? When did you learn to ride like that?" My questions are pretty intrusive, I realize.

He shrugs. "I told you, I grew up around horses. A lot."

In an excited voice, Jasmine says, "Zoe, did you see him? Riding backwards? And that somersault! Wow! Will you teach me how to ride backward? Will you? Please? Please?"

"I don't know—"

Matt meets my eyes when I say the words. He doesn't say anything.

"Maybe sometime," I finally say. "I want to make sure you're safe."

At the sound of hooves and a shout, I look up. Paul Armstrong is riding toward us from his property on the other side of the fence.

CAN I? CAN I? (MATT)

The guy riding toward us is almost a stereotype of a cowboy. Possibly thirty five years old, he looks like he was born in his saddle. He wears loose clothing and well-worn boots. Muscular, with strong arms and a square jaw. His face is red, as if he's been out in the sun and wind for his entire life. Or maybe he has high-blood pressure.

Whoever he is, Zoe brightens instantly when she sees him. Before, she was a little guarded, asking me probing questions about my past. Questions I don't want to answer. This guy— her eyes widen and her mouth shifts to a very genuine smile, showing bright white teeth. Her expression is captivating. And directed at horse guy.

I hate him.

"Matt, this is my neighbor, Paul Armstrong. Paul, Matt Paladino. He's Jasmine's third grade teacher."

Paul maneuvers his horse right up to the fence and reaches across to shake my hand. I take it—he has a firm grip. "I recognize the name—you're one of the negotiators for the teachers' union, right?"

"Yeah," I say, a little puzzled. I realize he's wearing a wedding band. "Do you have kids in the school system?"

Paul chuckles. "No, but I had a rash of parents calling me to see if they could schedule all-day sessions while school is out."

Zoe says, helpfully, "Paul owns the Armstrong Training Center—they do horse camps and lessons, and compete all over the East Coast."

"Oh, I see," I say. I don't know much about the horse-show circuit, other than the fact that it exists.

"When I saw you three I wanted to come over, Zoe, and offer some help. If you need to take care of things while the strike is on, you're always welcome to send Jasmine over. We can slide her right into one of the classes with the other girls."

This irritates me. Why? Maybe it's because Zoe looks so happy and grateful, when she was just suspicious of me. Maybe it's because Paul Armstrong is a great big lunk of a guy, the kind of carefully cultivated five-o'clock shadow guy that women seem to chase.

Jasmine seems excited. "Can I? Can I?"

Zoe raises an eyebrow. "Are you sure?"

He leans closer to the three of us. "It's what neighbors are for. And friends. I'd love to have her over. I know you've got a lot to take care of."

"I do start classes on Monday. And there's so much to do. I'd be grateful."

Paul says, "Forgive me for asking, but—do you have plans for a—a—you know —"

"Funeral?" Zoe asks. Her voice is somber, and her eyes dart to Jasmine. In a calm tone, she says, "Both of them were cremated. There's going to be a memorial service next Tuesday at Abbey Chapel, at Mount Holyoke."

Paul nods. "I'll be there, then. I'm gonna miss your Mom. She was one hell of a horsewoman."

"Thanks," Zoe says in a subdued voice.

"Sorry," he says. "Anyway, Jasmine, we'd love to have you over, any time."

Jasmine grins. "Thank you!"

Paul says his goodbyes, then Jasmine and Mono take off at a gallop, and I'm left alone with Zoe. Her smile fades a little, her blue eyes following Jasmine.

"I've enjoyed this, Matt," Zoe says. "Thanks for coming over."

"I meant what I said, Zoe. This strike won't last long, but I'll come by pretty much every day to see Jasmine. Okay?"

All kinds of warm feelings wash over me when Zoe smiles. Then they're dashed when she says, "So seriously, anyway, where did you learn to ride like that? No one just *grows up around horses* and learns those kinds of tricks."

I shake my head and try to laugh it off. "You weren't supposed to see that," I say.

She just arches an eyebrow.

I chuckle. "I practiced. For a long long time. I used to think I might end up in a circus, before I went to college."

That's as much as I was willing to say.

CHAPTER EIGHT

THANKS FOR THE NEWS (ZOE)

A S IF MONDAYS weren't normally bad enough, this one I start classes on the biggest campus in Massachusetts. I'm already feeling overwhelmed.

The campus is as big as an Army base, with as many people on it. More than thirty thousand students and faculty members. The first problem I run into is just getting parking. I circle the lot next to the Visitors' Center once, twice, three times, before I finally find a space in the back row a mile away from everything.

It's okay. I left early, so I'd have time to get to my first class. But even though I've been here, I didn't appreciate the scale of the place. My first class is at Bartlett Hall, which is—somewhere on campus near the library. At least the library, a 24 story building, is visible enough I can use it to orient myself.

I find the building with ten minutes to spare. It's crowded, with kids everywhere. When I step inside, I feel like I've been plunged into a tunnel—it's dim, with halls lined with dark brick and flickering fluorescent lighting. Fantastic. I push my way through the kids and find my way to class.

My eyes widen when I finally find the class. Lecture hall. It's packed with maybe two hundred students. I'm nearly the last to arrive. The hall filled up from the back, so I easily slip into a desk in the front row.

Written on the whiteboard at the front of the class, in large bold letters, is: English 115 American Experience. I have a stack of textbooks. *Narrative of the Life of Fredrick Douglass. The Oxford Book of American Poetry. The Cornel West Reader.* I'm not sure I know who Cornel West is, or was, and I've never read much poetry. I did well in high school, but as I sit in this room full of 18 year olds just starting college, I feel inadequately equipped for this. Like I'm in the wrong place.

The rest of the day won't be any easier. I have calculus and chemistry classes later in the day. Chemistry was my worst subject in high school. Who am I kidding? What am I doing here?

I stuff my doubts, arrange my materials and wait.

Finally, the teacher—a PhD candidate in the English department—appears and begins the class. Overall, it isn't that different from sitting through a training session in the Army—something I've done plenty of. The audience is a lot more varied, but when I look around carefully, I can see that even here, there is a uniform. Three quarters of the guys wear too-baggy knee length khaki shorts and either t-shirts or polo shirts. The girls have a variety of different tops, but almost all wear black leggings or too-short denim shorts. It's weird.

I tug my attention away from my surroundings and begin taking notes. It quickly becomes apparent that there will be little margin for error in this class. Two exams and a final paper will determine the entire grade. Blow one and I could blow the entire class.

That's fine. I don't intend to blow anything. I spend the next hour and fifteen minutes taking detailed notes and reviewing the syllabus. There's going to be a lot of reading in this class, but it's not more than I can handle. Depending on what job I get. Because I have to get a job. GI Bill benefits will help, but they won't pay for everything. I've got money from Mom and Dad's life insurance, but it won't last all the way through college.

I reign in my out of control thoughts. I don't need to worry about everything in the world right now. Just this class. Just right now.

Finally, class gets out. As I stand, a boy approaches me. A student. Probably eighteen or nineteen. I fling my bag over my shoulder and retreat before he can say anything. I'm not in the mood right now.

My second class—calculus—goes much the same, except that I realize that in the last five years I've forgotten all the math I ever knew. I'll need to get back up to speed. Maybe there's some online practice I could do, or I'm sure I can get *Calculus for Dummies* or something similar. I can't be the only clueless person.

After class, I meet Nicole at the campus center for lunch. The dining hall is packed, but students give her a wide berth, a development I find amusing as I follow her through the line. Within two minutes of sitting down with our food, the tables on either side of us are clear, despite the overall crowding.

"Do they always give you this much space?"

Her lips curl up into a fierce grin. "You know how it is."

I do. It was a similar reaction to the one I got when guys in the Army found out I was military police. Either they became intentionally provocative—as if daring me to interfere—or they made themselves scarce.

"How's your first day of class?"

I fill her in the first two classes, including my doubts about my ability.

"Don't be silly," she responds. "You're smarter than most of these kids, and you were accepted to better schools than this out of high school. There's no reason you can't do well."

I sigh. "I've been away from academics for a long time."

"Have you given much thought to what you want to do? What you're going to major in?"

I shake my head. "I'm not sure. I wish I had the kind of certainty about life that you do."

Nicole shrugs. "I always wanted to be a cop. But that was more Dad than anything."

"How does it stack up to being an MP?"

She laughs. "About the same. You remember what it was like patrolling barracks sometimes. It's not so different here, except that these kids have far less accountability. Let me tell you about a call we had last year."

She smirks, then says, "Okay, so these days they've got a fairly good handle on the frat parties. But every once in a while things start to fall apart. So one Friday night last year I get a call—all available units to respond to one of the frat houses just off campus. We get there, and the situation was out of control. It seems they had a low key party going on, but some-one spiked the drinks with PMA."

"Oh, no," I say. PMA—paramethoxyamphetamine—is a powerful hallucinogen, and has some nasty side effects. We'd had more than one encounter with the stuff as MPs.

Oh, the lovely things you learn in the Military Police.

"Yeah... we get there, and it's immediate urgent triage. One guy's standing on the ledge on the second floor yelling that he's going to jump. We had two passed out, a couple hallucinating, and several of them puking their guts out. So two of the guys start to get out of control, and I'm getting them cuffed, when a student comes running out of the building butt-ass-naked."

"Christ," I mutter.

"Yeah. He's screaming and hallucinating, and get this… someone had sprayed his dick with pepper spray."

"Ouch," I say.

She chuckles. "You aren't kidding. Poor guy was howling in pain, kept yelling that he was being tortured by monsters."

I sigh. "You know what, Nicole?"

"What's that?"

"I'm glad I didn't apply for a job on the force."

She throws her head back and laughs, then hiccups. "Fair enough. You always did hate dealing with drunks."

"I'm guessing you get your share of them here."

She smiles. Then she says, "Oh, so what ended up happening with Jasmine's teacher? And where is she now?"

I finish chewing my burger, then say, "She's over at Armstrong Farm. Paul slid her into one of his classes."

"You said her teacher came by the house?"

I nod. "He seems—very considerate."

Nicole's eyes narrow. "Considerate? What the hell is that?"

"I just—I don't know—"

"Holy crap," she says. "You've got a thing for him. What's going on?"

"Nothing's going on!"

"There is. Zoe, I've known you your entire life. Something is going on."

"Nicole, stop—"

Her smile grows. "You're blushing."

"Shut up."

"Zoe, seriously—"

"No, you listen," I respond. "Think about it a minute. What if I get involved with this guy and it turns out to be crap? Jasmine needs him. We don't have any relatives around, you know. It's just me, and she doesn't know me worth a damn."

Nicole sighs. Then she says, "That's pretty defeatist."

I shrug. "It is what it is."

"I think you should have him over for dinner. Tell him to bring a friend, that you want to set me up with someone." Her words come out sounding like an order.

"You're crazy."

"I want to meet this guy. Where is he from?"

"Central Florida. He didn't get more specific than that. But I'll tell you this—he's spent his life around horses. He rides tricks—he's good enough to be performing."

"Woah," she says. "But he's a teacher."

"Thanks for the news, Nicole."

Nicole grins. "You set up dinner."

I sigh. She's right. I do need to know more about him. I close my eyes, then say, "Fine. I'll call him."

"Excellent. I'll wait."

"What? Right now?" I hate that my voice squeaks.

"When is better?" She raises one eyebrow. That's because she sees right through me.

"Fine," I mutter. I take out my phone and find Matt's number, then dial.

It rings. Three time. Four times. Five times. I'm about to disconnect when it goes to voicemail.

"Hey, this is Matt Paladino. Leave a message. Please make sure you leave your number and when is a good time to call back."

I take a deep breath, then another one, suddenly uncomfortable. The phone beeps.

"Hey, uh... uh... Matt ... this is Zoe. Zoe Welch. Listen, um... I'm having a friend over for dinner Friday. This is going to sound weird but… maybe you could come? Bring a friend. Um… call me."

The whole time I talk, Nicole stares at me, a bemused look on her face. When I disconnect, she says, "Well, that was smooth."

I almost choke with embarrassed laughter. Then I almost just choke. Did I just ask Matt out to dinner?

THE PROFESSOR (ZOE)

Jefferson Welch—my dad—was a great big bear of a man. Just a little over 6 feet tall, he had the broad shoulders of a football player. He was a gentle giant—he wore square, plastic framed glasses long before they became retro-stylish. His gray hair—gray for as long as I can remember—was always a little bit too long, a little bit too disorganized. Even on special occasions, when he would wear his tuxedo and mom would wear a dress, his hair was still a chaotic mess.

His beard grew and shrank with the years. When I was in elementary school, the beard had the wild unkempt appearance of an isolated hermit living in the mountains. One of my earliest memories was tugging on his beard. He would let out a great big laugh and tickle me until I screamed. In the last few years, probably from around the time mom got pregnant with Jasmine, he'd taken to keeping it trimmed short and neat. I think it was even though the hair on his head had been gray for years, he felt sensitive about the beard, because it was the last to go.

Those early memories of my father are all short flashes and images. Dad sitting in his office in the back of the house upstairs. He had always planned to build in bookshelves, but never got around to it, so for most of my childhood there were stacks of books against two walls in his office, many of them taller than I was. His desk was an antique, but not a valuable one. I think he and mom bought it at a tag sale when they were still in graduate school, and he just wasn't concerned with upgrading to anything fancier.

Dad kept his desk turned toward the window which overlooked the pasture behind our house—from his seat while he worked, he could see mom riding. My father never talked much about his work life. He taught English literature at Mount Holyoke and was a highly respected member of the faculty. Eventually he became the department head, and I have to assume he had a lot of academic publications. I've never read any of them. I still haven't been in his office either, and I should go in there soon, if only to make sure there isn't an old coffee or tea cup on his desk growing mold.

I was seven when dad took me to work with him on "Take Your Daughter to Work Day." I had to sit through a couple of classes, but boredom wasn't as big problem as you would expect for a child that age in a college classroom. The girls in the classes instantly adopted me. I still remember one of them— her name was Samantha—let me sit in her lap during class, and drew flowers with me. She made me laugh, and I cried when I realized I wasn't going to be able to come back every day.

It's not that I didn't love Mom. I did. It's just that she seemed to always fill up whatever space she was in, and not always in a good way. She loved to laugh, to tell funny jokes and stories, and she loved her horses. If I was outside and she saw me, I was automatically drafted into whatever it was she was doing. It's not that I didn't love working with the horses, but I also loved other things. I like to sit under the trees and read books, and when I was younger than that to play with my dolls. That was all a little too much for her—so by the time I was nine or 10, I was well-versed with all of the necessary chores around the stables and grounds. I spent Saturday mornings alongside mom while she gave lessons—just as Jasmine ended up doing.

That's why sometimes my dad's garage was a refuge. I'd never been allowed in there by myself—Dad was incredibly disorganized, but had eidetic memory. He would set his tools down randomly, and know   where he could pick them up the next day, week, or year. If someone else came in and moved a tool, it could mess him up for days. When I think of the garage, I think of stacked automotive manuals, Dad's secret vice. A wall and workbench laden with tools, many of them mysterious to me when I was younger, but more and more familiar as I grew older. On Saturday afternoons for most of my life, Dad disappeared into the garage where he tinkered with and tweaked the Austin Healey.

Along the wall on one side were pictures of the evolution of the car. When he bought the car it had no discernible color—it was mostly rust. Both headlights were missing, the three remaining tires were dry rotted and flat, and the fourth wheel rested loose on the tow truck that brought it to the house. The soft top wasn't just down, it was missing. Significant rust holes marred the body, and a spider web of cracks interrupted the tiny windshield.

I was too young, but I can imagine the conversation that must've ensued when the wreck of a vehicle appeared in our yard. Mom was nothing if not a practical woman, and even her hobbies were related in some way or another to her professional life. She never understood how Dad—a literature professor after all—could spend his weekends covered in grease and dirt as he lay on his back underneath that tiny car.

I understood completely. Not that I'm particularly interested in cars, although I know a lot about them thanks to the time I spent in the garage. No... I understand because the garage was quiet. Mother and her horses never intruded. Mom and Dad loved each other deeply, but they were very different in personality—sometimes Dad just needed a break. Over the course of my childhood and into my teenage years, I watched in silence, and sometimes helped, as Dad rebuilt the vehicle from scratch.

The transformation of the car did not proceed the way anyone would expect. Dad's lack of organization carried into his rebuilding efforts—he tended to jump around from one thing to another depending on what had caught his interest. Not just that, but finding parts for a more than 50-year-old car was sometimes a challenge. He participated in online discussion boards, periodically visited junkyards, and found deals where he could. He learned to do his own body work, and I remember many months sitting in the corner with a book watching him as he welded and shaped sheet metal into new body parts, replacing large swaths of rust and holes.

I was almost 12 when he took the engine out with a chain hoist and began to rebuild it. For the next year, the body of the car stayed in the driveway, carefully secured underneath a protective tarp. In a more organized fashion than I had ever seen, dad meticulously took apart every single piece of the engine, labeling and organizing them across the floor of the garage. There were hundreds of parts in varying degrees of decay. Almost lovingly, he rebuilt it, cylinder by cylinder, valve by valve, as I watched and sometimes helped.

His instructions were usually terse. "Get me the Phillips screwdriver," he would say. "Come hold this while I retighten the bolts." Such instructions were normal in the garage, but unlike the Jefferson Welch everyone else knew. Outside the garage, he was talkative, exuberant. Inside the garage, I saw a different man—one who was tightly focused, deeply absorbed in what he was doing. I often imagined this was what he looked like at work when he wasn't teaching classes. I wondered sometimes if anyone else saw my father the way I did.

That knowledge made me feel privileged to see him in ways that were mine alone. Not even Mom was around him when he worked like this.

I was a freshman in high school before I was allowed in the garage alone.

It had been a particularly tough week...well...that's not true. It had been a particularly tough few months. In August, Mom had rescued two horses from the feedlots, something that wasn't supposed to even exist anymore in the United States. Feedlots were large auction houses that would gather hundreds of horses, many of them in varying degrees of health. They would auction them off to the highest bidder—and those they couldn't sell would be sold in bulk to truckers who ship them to slaughterhouses in Mexico. A large informal network of activists and horse lovers work to try to buy the horses before they are sent to slaughter. Sometimes they're successful—and sometimes they aren't.

As always, buying a feedlot horse was a chancy thing, and this time was even more so than usual. Both of the horses were extremely sick, and one died within a week of their arrival. They had to be quarantined from the rest of the horses, and the surviving one required almost 24-hour attention for several weeks. Then that horse died too. Mom was heartbroken—it truly was horrible for her. During that period, I'd had no time to myself at all. I fell behind on homework, and found myself sometimes dozing off in class. Mom never asked me if I wanted to spend 12 hours a day assisting her with taking care of the horses. She just assumed I would. I would get home from school and go straight to the stable.

Two months of this took me to the breaking point, and when my midterm exams arrived I was failing two classes. Up until that point I'd been a straight A and B student—and I went home that day with my report card dreading the outcome.

I knew that Dad would be disappointed, and mom angry. I never expected the reaction I got.

"I cannot believe that you're failing classes," she shouted. "Jefferson, I insist that she drop her extracurricular activities until she brings her grades back up. If she can't pass her classes, she doesn't need to be in cheerleading and sports." I stared at her in disbelief. How could she possibly say that? I had already dropped out of cheerleading, because she hadn't allowed me to go to the required four night a week practices. My response was instinctive, and came out without thought or preparation.

"It's your fault! I already dropped out of cheerleading! I'd be passing my classes if I didn't spend all my time taking care of your damn horses!"

She looked as if I had kicked her in the face. I had, really. Her horses were everything. It wasn't that she was intentionally forcing me to do anything—it was just that she couldn't see anything else but her own need to rescue those animals. Her response was instantaneous, outraged denial. "That's not true. You need to take responsibility for your—"

"Lucy." Dad's voice was quiet, but firm.

"What?" She said, giving him an irritated look.

"She's right. She spends every free second helping you with the horses. You need to let her go. She needs to spend some time on school. And on her own life. She hasn't even been out with Nicole in weeks."

Mom's mouth had closed. Then she sagged and said, "I didn't realize." She thought for a moment... then a moment more... then looked at me and whispered, "I'm sorry."

Without a moment's thought, I rushed forward and wrapped my arms around her. She was my mom. A hero in her world of horses. And no matter how old I was, the love of having her arms around me never left.

That night, my Dad knocked on my door as I was getting ready for bed.

"Come in," I said.

He opened the door and leaned in. "Hey, Zoe. Listen ... I was thinking earlier, about the whole thing with your Mom. I know sometimes she gets ... involved, and kind of pulls you in too. If you ever need to just get some space, feel free to go hang out in the garage."

I blinked in shock. I'd never been allowed in there alone. "Really?"

He nodded. "Yeah. I know you'll leave my things alone. And ... just so you know ... I'm proud of you. You did good tonight."

"Thanks, Daddy," I had whispered.

With that he had ducked out and closed the door.

NO RIGHT (ZOE)

I lean over the vanity as I finish my mascara. Waterproof. I don't usually bother with much in the way of makeup, but today is different. *Today is my parents' funeral.*

Today is my parents' funeral. I have to close my eyes at the thought. I tell myself to get it together. I don't have time for this, and Jasmine needs me to be stable.

I take a steadying breath and open my eyes.

In the black dress I'm wearing, I look like a zombie. I've never had much color in my hair or skin—the most colorful part of my body is my eyes.

It doesn't matter, really. I walk down the hall to Jasmine's room.

She's sitting on the bed, staring into space. She wears a black dress too.

Children her age should never wear black dresses.

I have a hundred things I want to say to her. But I can't. Instead, I walk into the room and sit on the bed beside her.

She immediately sniffles. "Do you think they're in heaven?"

I wince. Because she would start out with a question I don't know about, don't understand, don't believe. I don't know what I believe. I start to just say yes, of course they are. Jasmine has a finely-tuned bullshit detector, and I'm not a very good liar.

After a good minute, I say, "I don't know much about heaven and hell and … all that stuff."

"Do you believe in God?"

I nod. "I do. I don't know if anyone knows what happens… you know… after we die. But I think they're in a good place. I think they're still watching out for us."

She sniffles. Then she says, "I miss them. I miss them."

"I do too."

She whispers, "I'm scared to go to the funeral."

"Oh… how come?"

"They'll be in a box right?"

"An urn," I say. "They were cremated together, and they're sharing an urn."

"That's good," she whispered. "They loved each other."

"Yeah. Yeah, they did."

I stand and take a breath, then I hold out my hand. She takes it, and we walk downstairs where Nicole is waiting for us. The three of us step out of the house together. It's a little chilly this afternoon, and a couple of the trees in the yard have begun to transform into a bright yellow color. I shiver. "Are you cold?"

Jasmine nods.

I duck back inside and search in the front closet, retrieving two of Mom's wraps—one green, the other black.

Jasmine smiles gratefully when I wrap the cloth around her. "Let's go," I say.

The wrap smells like Mom's perfume.

None of us speak as we get into Nicole's patrol car. I'm not up to driving today. Jasmine rides in her booster seat, which Nicole already moved over. Once again I'm reminded how much I wish Mom were alive. She'd want to see Jasmine grow.

Nicole turns around in our driveway, then pulls out onto College Street. In less than a minute, we're passing the campus at Mount Holyoke College. We park across the street from the chapel.

Men and women I don't recognize are streaming across in singles, couples and small groups.

"Are you ready?" I ask.

"Yes," Jasmine says.

I don't think she is, but there's nothing we can do. I look over at Nicole. She's gripping the steering wheel hard. This is tough for her too—my parents often acted as a second set of parents for her.

The three of us walk across College Street, Jasmine holding my hand. People gather in knots in front of the chapel. Most of them go quiet as they see us approaching. We pass by the groups silently, and ascend steps of the chapel.

Like most of the rest of the Mount Holyoke campus, Abbey Chapel is a large building constructed of brownish-red stone. When I was in high school I would sometimes wander around the campus, and occasionally spent time at the library, a Collegiate Gothic building next to the chapel. It's a beautiful campus... large gothic buildings spaced around wide green spaces.

Inside, the chapel is huge, with towering rows of columns rising sixty feet to pointed arches. Rows of stained glass windows flank both sides, and at the far end a giant blue and purple flower in stained glass. The chapel seats hundreds, and while it isn't completely packed, it's far from empty. Most of the attendees are students—current as well as past. I also see a smattering of my mother's friends from the horse-show circuit. There's no way my parents knew all of these people. Then I realize—my parents were killed in a bizarre freak accident. A flying commercial oven? It was in the news for days. I bet some of these people are just freaks. Curious freaks, who want to see what's left after a violent and nonsensical death.

I can hear the sounds of a hymn being played, very faintly. *How lovely is thy dwelling place.*

We finally reach the front, and immediately a woman approaches. I'd guess sixty-five, she's a tiny woman with short cropped gray hair. She wears the somber garb of a priest.

"Zoe? I'm Anne Davies."

Ahhh… I recognize the name immediately. An Episcopalian priest, she's the Dean of Religious and Spiritual Life at Mount Holyoke, and was a friend of my parents. We've spoken on the phone several times this week as she took care of organizing the memorial.

"I want to express my condolences again. Your parents were well loved and very respected. And your father's loss is a severe blow to the college."

I'm at a loss for words, but it doesn't matter because she starts talking again. Details. How long the service will last. When I go up to speak. I haven't prepared any remarks. I don't know what I'm supposed to say. I agreed to speak. Finally, she steps back, and I see it.

At the front of chapel, where you might normally find the altar or coffins or whatever it is that normally stays at the front of a chapel, there is a table covered in a white cloth, and above that the urn. *The Aristocrat Adult Blue Cremation Urn*, cost $385, discounted to $350. I know that because I had to make that decision, along with many others. A pall covers the urn.

I owe Anne Davies… she'd organized most of this—with Nicole's help—and I hadn't even thanked her.

I turn to her and say, "Please forgive me. I haven't even thanked you for making all this possible. I was lost."

Her face softens and she moves closer and puts her hand on my shoulder. "You've got a lot to shoulder now, Zoe. I'm happy to help—your parents were friends. And if you need to talk to someone at any point, let me know. Please."

"Thank you," I whisper. I don't understand why her words make my eyes water.

Jasmine and I walk to the front of the chapel together while Nicole hangs back. I don't know what to do, but Jasmine seems to, dropping to her knees on the kneeler that faces the urn. I kneel next to her, the green cushion feeling odd against my knees.

She has her hands steepled with elbows propped on the rail, and her eyes are closed. She starts to talk, and I almost fall off the kneeler.

"God," she says. She speaks the words in a low, urgent tone, spitting them out like machine gun bullets. She knows what she wants to say. "I don't know you, but Mom said she did. So if you're there, please watch out for my Mom and Dad and make sure they're in heaven and happy, and watch out for Zoe. Amen."

I'm staggered by her words. I don't get a chance to say anything, because she gets up and walks to the pew in the front and sits down.

I don't feel nearly as equipped to pray as my little sister. I decide to try. I close my eyes. I'm not praying out loud. In my head I try to form some coherent words. But all I can get out is, *Mom, please forgive me.* Then I'm horrified because tears start spilling out of my eyes. I squeeze them shut, trying to force the tears back. I don't—I can't—

Once I get control of myself, I reach in my purse and take out several tissues, then wipe my eyes and blow my nose. Finally

I get up from the kneeler and start walking toward the very empty pew. The one reserved for family.

Huh.

Matt is kneeling in the aisle, saying something to Jasmine, who sits next to Nicole in that long empty pew.

I approach, and when he senses my presence, Matt stands up. "Zoe…"

I'm already emotionally exhausted and this thing hasn't even started yet. But I do see Jasmine grab for his hand.

"Why don't you sit with us," I say. "I think Jasmine would appreciate it."

He nods. It's an awkward moment… he's standing to Jasmine's side closest to the aisle. I'm on her other side. Nicole is sitting next to Jasmine. It would be weird to have him next to the aisle. He starts to step over, and I do at the same time, and we nearly bump into each other. So he backs away, gesturing with his hand for me to sit. I do, and he walks around and sits on the other side of Nicole.

The ceremony begins as the music quiets and Anne Davies takes her place at the altar. She calls out the words in a loud clear voice, "I am the resurrection and the life, saith the Lord; he that believeth in me, though he were dead, yet shall he live; and whosoever liveth and believeth in me shall never die." From there she continues reading from the Book of Common Prayer. It seems strange to me. I know these customs from one or two weddings and funerals I've attended in my life, relatives of my father. None of it is familiar. For the next thirty minutes Davies and an assistant continue to offer prayers and ceremony.

Finally, she says, "And now Zoe Welch, the daughter of Jefferson and Lucinda, will say a few words."

With a lump in my throat, I walk to the lectern in the front of the church.

Tears form in my eyes as I turn around and look out at the ... mourners? ... in the chapel. There must be three or four hundred people here, maybe more. I recognize a bare fraction of them. And I feel a mounting anger at the large number of young women in here, young women who weep uncontrollably, demonstrating for everybody how shocked and wounded they are by their professor's death.

They didn't know him. They have no right.

I don't understand why it makes me angry. Why does it disturb me? I want to tell them all to shut up, quit their crying and go home.

I'm lying. I do know why it makes me angry. It's because, so far, I haven't been able to cry, except a pitiful few tears.

So I open my mouth and begin to speak.

"My name is Zoe Welch." At the words, the very few people in the audience who were otherwise occupied fall silent. In this cathedral sized building, full with hundreds of strangers and family friends, I can't hear a sound. No whispers, no coughing, just the steady swoosh swoosh of my own heartbeat in my ears.

The silence extends. Maddeningly, I can't seem to come up with any words. I should have prepared. I should have written a speech. Or some notes. Or something. My breath is shallow and rapid. I close my eyes, trying to force myself to calm down. I can see people becoming uncomfortable in the audience. Barbara Mean, the Dean of Students—a fussy woman who my parents occasionally had over for parties—looks like she's going to have a stroke. The nervousness in the audience increases my own anxiety, a negative feedback loop that could only end in my own utter humiliation.

Then my eyes drop to the front row.

Jasmine. She's sitting there in the front row, holding her teacher's hand. She looks lost and alone and sad. Just like that, I calm. I know what I have to say.

I clear my throat and close my eyes for just a moment. I remember my words to Jasmine this morning. Do you believe in God? I do, though that's as defined as it gets. I go ahead and whisper a silent prayer anyway. Please let me say the right thing to help her heal.

"Most of you knew Jefferson and Lucinda Welch professionally. You knew my father as a professor—I know he was popular, but that's about it. He ran the English department here, right?"

At my question, the room breaks out in quiet chuckles. I continue. "Those of you who were friends or colleagues of my mom knew her as a dedicated horse trainer and teacher, and before that, as the director of the equestrian center at Mount Holyoke. Both of them were well known in the community. Both of them were highly respected. But I don't know them that way. My sister Jasmine doesn't know them that way."

I meet Jasmine's eyes, and I say, "What I know is that Mom put every little picture me and Jasmine drew in school up on the wall in our hallway. The silly drawings of cows and unicorns I made as a first grader, and the awful sculptures I made as a high school student—all of them graced our life, because she valued her daughters."

I take a deep breath. I'm struggling, because my eyes are watering. "What I know is summer Saturdays spent in the garage with my dad when he tinkered with his Austin-Healy. That car was his hobby, and I was privileged to be able to spend most of my adolescence working with him."

I say, "Mom nursed our draft horse Mono back to health after rescuing him, then gave him to Jasmine to learn to take care of and ride. That giant horse kind of scares me, but he is the bond between Jasmine and my mother. And though people and horses will come and go in our lives, that bond with Mom and Dad will never die, no matter what happens."

Jasmine is sobbing now, and I hope I've done the right thing here. I keep talking. "When I finished eighth grade, my Dad said, Zoe, I'm proud of you. And it was the proudest moment of my life." I slam the door on the bitter thought that he didn't say it when I finished high school and joined the Army. Instead, I take another deep breath and say, "I remember how shocked I was when I was a high school sophomore and I found out my mother was pregnant again. Like any teenager, I was horrified by the idea that my parents did anything that might cause pregnancy." More laughs from the audience.

"But then, along comes the biggest gift any of us could have had—Jasmine, my little sister." Shit. I struggle to keep from breaking down. Instead I say, in words that barely come out in a staggering whisper, "Mom, I don't know if you can hear me. I promise I'll take care of your little girl."

I can't talk any more. I break down, sobbing, and next thing I know Ann is leading me away from the podium. She whispers, "Zoe, that was beautiful." And she's crying too. I sit down next to Jasmine, and she falls against me, both of us crying now. I was the last speaker, I think. Ann is up there doing whatever it is that priests do... I don't pay a whole lot of attention to the words. Instead, I focus on holding on to Jasmine, because she needs me right now.

And I'm determined not to fail her.

CHAPTER NINE

4-F (ZOE)

I T'S FOUR DAYS after the funeral. The table is set. Five dinner plates. Candles. I've mixed a salad, opened a glass of Cayuga White from the Pioneer Valley Vineyard, and everything would be perfect for dinner except that smoke is pouring out of the oven. When I realize it, I rush over and open it up—bad idea. I catch a face full of smoke directly in the face. I begin to cough and grab for the oven mitts.

The good news is, as I pull the platter out of the oven—it didn't catch fire. The meal, a roasted salmon, looks decidedly charred.

Why the hell can't I manage to cook a meal?

I'm so incredibly frustrated. It doesn't help when Jasmine sticks her head in the room. "Did dinner catch fire again?"

"No!" I cry out. "It's fine." It's not fine. I have three dinner guests who will be here any minute, and no dinner to serve. Because this won't fly. I let the platter drop onto the top of the stove with a loud bang and open the window and turn on the ceiling fan.

The smoke is now circulating around the room instead of staying decently at the ceiling. Fantastic.

I hear the doorbell ring and I suppress a growl.

"I'll get it!" Jasmine shouts. She doesn't need to shout. I have no intention of getting the door. I don't care if they ever come in. I stare at the ruined dinner. I didn't have a backup plan. Where the hell is Nicole? This was her idea. The least she could do is show up on time and help rescue me from my own misery and embarrassment.

No such luck. Nicole has been in and out of this house since we were five. She wouldn't bother ringing the bell. That has to be Matt or his friend Tyler.

I lean close to the pan, trying to look without my eyes tearing up from the smoke. Is it salvageable?

I turn up my nose. If I was homeless? I still wouldn't eat this.

Seconds later, long before I get a chance to sink into the floorboards and disappear, Jasmine comes back with Matt.

Matt looks around and says, "Having some trouble?"

I give him a thin smile. "No, no trouble. How are you?" Then I blow the smoke away from the pan.

I can't serve this. I pick it up and walk toward the garbage can, then flip it over and let the ruined food spill into the can.

Matt smiles.

"So," I say. "What time is your friend coming? I was planning to order Chinese."

"Tyler?" He asks. "He's checking out the books in the living room."

"Oh," I say. A moment later, Matt's friend appears.

He's taller than Matt and more muscular. Not in a better shape kind of way—more of a bodybuilder type of way. He has a completely fake, sculpted look I've learned to associate with a hundred different guys in the Army who had little in common with each other except their consistent need to sexually harass any women who crossed their paths.

He approaches, holding out a hand. His eyes drop to my chest furtively. "Hey," he says. "I'm Tyler. We met in Matt's classroom, right?"

"Yes," I say. Does he even remember the circumstances?

"Hey, Zoe. Matt's told me a little about you... you were in the Army? Nurse?"

Asshole. To a significant number of chauvinists, any woman in the Army must either be a nurse, a clerk or a whore.

"I was Military Police," I reply. Now watch what happens. With roughly two-thirds of the guys I meet, saying that results in them trying to show they've got a bigger dick than I do.

"Oh yeah?" He says. "I was never in. Though I used to think about it a lot. I coach football, I used to play for UMASS. The Army wouldn't let me in—4-F. Broken foot."

I don't know what 4-F is. Unless it means full of shit. But I'm used to this conversation. A lot of guys are threatened by women who have been to war. I dealt with a hundred guys like him in the Army. Guys who talked all about the brotherhood of arms but saw no problem with grabbing a fellow soldier's ass or breasts—if that fellow soldier was female. Guys who exposed themselves. Guys who called you a slut if you touched someone and a cold bitch if you didn't. Guys who labeled some girls as *Sand Queens* because of the attention they got in the desert from lonely guys.

Fuck them. I just turn back to the kitchen and say, "So Chinese or pizza? Which is it?"

Matt raises his eyebrows, as if to ask, "Is everything okay?" I don't bother responding.

Jasmine is the only one who responds. "Can we do Chinese? We had pizza the other night."

"Yeah, sweety. We can do that."

You can't bullshit a horse (Matt)

When I arrive at her house a few days after the funeral, Zoe is clearly off balance and confused. Not to mention irritated with Tyler. I don't blame her. For one thing, Tyler can be a monumental prick—best friend or not. He also seems to be an expert at picking at people's sore spots. It would have taken an idiot to miss the flash of anger when he asked if she'd been a nurse. I'd bet a million dollars she's heard that question more than once. Which makes no sense at all in this day and age.

Tyler seems to sense that too. He backs off a little, just in time to hear the front door open. "Hey!" calls a female voice.

"Nicole!" Jasmine shouts unnecessarily. Maybe she is as uncomfortable as I am.

I decide to try to get in-between the shots being fired by Zoe and Tyler. "You said you were stationed in Japan last?"

Zoe flashes me a look of gratitude. I like that. "Yes… I was in Tokyo for three years at Hardy Barracks."

"I didn't know we still had many troops in Japan."

"Tens of thousands," she says, a faint smile on her face. "And a lot of them go hang out and get into trouble in Tokyo. My job was mostly to deal with those guys."

"That doesn't sound like fun," I say.

She shakes her head. "No, not that much. But I loved living in Tokyo."

"Tell me about it."

Tyler interrupts. "How about we order dinner first?"

Jesus, he has no manners at all.

At that point a woman walks into the room. About Zoe's age, brown hair, brown eyes. Easily as fit as Zoe. She looks at Zoe and says, "I thought you were cooking?"

Blank faced, Zoe looks at her and says, "I was." Then she sniffs. The other woman grins.

Zoe laughs. "Matt, this is my best friend Nicole."

My cue. "This is Tyler."

We discuss what we're getting—chicken and broccoli, Mongolian beef, General Tso's chicken—then Tyler volunteers to go pick it up. A few minutes later he's gone, leaving me and Zoe talking with Nicole and Jasmine.

"So," I say again. "You were talking about Tokyo?"

She nods, and says, "First, can I get you a drink? White wine? Or beer? I have Guinness and Sam Adams."

"Sam Adams," I reply. "Thanks."

"Wine," Nicole replies.

Zoe starts talking as she opens the refrigerator. "Let's see—what I liked about Tokyo. From where I lived, everything you could ever want was within walking distance. Theaters, music, clubs, restaurants. Everything's super convenient. Nightlife was fantastic—me and some friends used to go out and grab drinks, you could stay out all night. The flip side to that was so many soldiers stayed out drunk all night, and we had to police them up in the morning."

Nicole snorts.

"Let's see... fashion. Always interesting and beautiful clothes. I loved the food. I didn't love taking the train. In fact the first time I rode, I got jammed in between a bunch of guys and was groped. I couldn't even tell who it was, or move because it was so packed. After that I took women-only trains."

"Women-only trains?"

She nods. "Because of the pervs."

I shudder.

"Anyway," she says. "Aside from that, I loved it."

Nicole says, "Unlike Zoe here, I didn't re-enlist after Iraq. I'd had enough of that ... I always wanted to be a cop, and now I get to do that."

Jasmine leans against one of the counters and says, "I didn't know that."

"Didn't know what?" Zoe asks.

"That you re-en-listed." She pronounces the word carefully. "What does that mean exactly?"

"It means I asked to stay in the Army after my first tour was up. I liked being in the Army."

"Do you wish you were still there?" Jasmine's face is guarded as she asks the question.

Zoe says, "I'm where I want to be, Jasmine. With you."

Jasmine flushes. Then she says, "What if Mom and Dad were still alive?"

Zoe shrugs. "That's ... not what it is. I don't know the answer to that. The moment I learned you were all alone, I came, Jasmine. And I'd do it all over again, every time. Okay? You're my sister. I'll take care of you no matter what."

Jasmine looks at her and whispers, "Thanks."

I swallow and look away, caught for a moment in the grip of uncomfortable emotions. Zoe's declaration was powerful.

My eyes catch Nicole's, and she gives me a strange look. Suspicious, really.

"Well, let's go sit on the porch while we're waiting. We won't have many more nights this warm." Zoe doesn't wait for an answer—she takes her glass of wine and walks to the side door and lets herself out. Jasmine's right behind her, leaving me behind with Nicole.

I start for the door, but come to a stop when Nicole says, "Matt?"

"Yeah?"

"I gotta ask you a question… I saw the way you were looking at Zoe. What are your plans?"

I shake my head. "I don't have any plans."

She walks a little closer—close enough I can see a very faint scar on her forehead covered with makeup. She says, "They've been through a lot, Matt. Zoe's been through a lot."

I nod. "I'm aware. For what it's worth, I lost my father suddenly too. I know how hard that is."

"Not just that, though I'm—I'm not glad to hear it, but I'm glad you understand. She's been through a lot even before that. She doesn't talk about it, but Iraq was no cakewalk."

"I can't imagine it was," I say.

"Just be careful."

I stare at her and say firmly, "I don't have any plans. If you must know, yes, I'm attracted to Zoe. A lot. And I care about both of them. The end. All right?"

She nods. Fine, that's done. I turn away from her and walk out the side door.

Zoe and Jasmine sit together on the porch swing. I take a seat on a wicker chair nearby. As I do, Zoe says, "So, Matt. You said you were from central Florida?"

"Not far from Tampa and Sarasota."

She shakes her head. "This must be a big climate change."

"Culture change too," Nicole said. "I thought Florida was full of rednecks."

I chuckle. "That and snowbirds."

"Snowbirds?" Nicole asks.

"A snowbird is a relocated Yankee."

Zoe bursts into laughter. I honestly don't want to talk about where I grew up, or how I grew up, or where I spent most of my time as a child. Not the trailer parks, or the sand spurs scratching at my heels, not the crowds or the constant moving around. I don't want to talk about any of it. I say, "What about you, Nicole? Are you from around here?"

Just as I say the words, Zoe says, "Matt hasn't told me any details, but he grew up riding. Really riding."

Nicole asks, "Did you do horse shows?"

I shake my head. "No, I don't know anything about the horse show circuit. What about you?"

Nicole laughs. "My dad's a cop in Springfield. But Zoe's mom did the show circuit sometimes. But not the high-end stuff."

I raise an eyebrow. "High-end stuff?"

Zoe says, "It's kind of a class thing. Some of the shows, they've got the thirty or fifty thousand dollar horses. They're not even allowed to be horses… they don't get to roll in the mud or race because they might get hurt or mess up their appearance. It's like the more prized they are as a commodity, the less they're prized as … as animals… as companions. Mom wasn't about all that. She didn't show horses, she had a relationship with them."

The sudden passion in her voice captures my attention. Zoe says she isn't a horse person like her mom was, but the way she's talking makes me think otherwise. She keeps talking.

"The thing is… when you're upset… when you're not in the right frame of mind… a horse knows. You can't bullshit a horse. You can't lie to them or put on a happy face. The horses know. They can see right through you, and reflect the truth right back."

Nicole leans back and stares at Zoe as if she's hearing this kind of talk for the first time. And maybe she is. Because Zoe stops suddenly.

"That's intense," I say. I decide to let the smallest part of my past out, even if it's missing some details. "And true. My um … Uncle Nick used to say the same thing. He taught me to ride, over the objections of my parents."

"Why didn't your parents want you to learn?" Zoe's question is quick.

Because they wanted me to follow them. I shrug and grin. "Why do parents do anything? I don't expect them to make sense." I don't say that my parents looked down their noses at everyone who didn't do what they did. I don't say that Nick wasn't actually an uncle, nor how my parents responded when they found out I was learning to ride. I don't talk about Papa's sudden death and how it changed everything.

SELF-CONTAINED (ZOE)

Matt grins when he asks his question—*why do parents do anything?*—but the grin looks fake. Whatever happened with his parents, it's clear he's still very bitter about it. He clams up a little, and even though I'm intensely curious about his background, I think it's time to change the subject. He's not going to suddenly open up just because I keep probing.

So I ask Nicole something about the UMASS Police Department, knowing that will generate a long story. I keep an eye on him. He's quiet. Broody almost. Every once in a while his eyes shift to me, and once he catches my eyes, an electric shiver runs all the way to my toes.

Luckily, once I asked the question Nicole is off. I missed the beginning of the story—which seems to concern a riot that broke out after the basketball team won last winter. Or lost. I'm not clear which it was. Apparently several hundred students went on a rampage, breaking windows and carousing drunk in downtown Amherst.

"Would you believe more than two hundred arrests? It's crazy. South Hadley has two dozen cops. We have sixty-one on the force at UMASS. All because of the drunks!"

The sun is going down as she speaks. To the west, you can see the hills on the other side of the Connecticut River leading up to Mount Tom, all of it silhouetted by flaming orange and red light.

Jasmine says, "Why do they do that?"

"Oh trust me, when you get to that age your brain will melt too."

"Won't," Jasmine responds.

"Will too," Nicole says. "Trust me. You can't help it. It happened to me too, and your sister."

I shake my head. "It might have happened to you, but not me."

Nicole shakes her head and waves a hand dismissively. "I'm not going to throw Zoe under the bus. Trust me. It happens to everyone."

Jasmine gets a gleeful look on her face. "Tell me! What did she do?"

Nicole shakes her head. "It's not fit for little ears. Ask me again when you're ten."

"That's *forever!*"

Nicole shrugs. "That's the breaks, kid."

Headlights turn into the driveway. Tyler is back. I bring the porch swing to a stop and stand. "You guys want to eat out here? It's so nice out."

"Yeah," Matt says. "Let's do it. I miss warm weather sometimes."

"Come help me then. We'll set up at the picnic table over there. Need to grab plates and everything."

Matt stands and follows me back into the house. I rummage in the kitchen, pulling together plates and silverware and paper towels, and pass them to Matt. Once he has those in hand, I gather the wine bottle and a cold six-pack.

"Hey!" Tyler shouts as we come out of the house. "I was beginning to wonder if you two were ever coming out! I thought maybe you'd decided to go ahead and—"

His words are cut off by a sudden slap on the shoulder from Nicole. "You behave," she demands.

"Jesus," he mutters, his voice mock offended. "Yes, officer."

Matt snorts at Tyler's response. As Matt puts out the plates and I pass out more drinks, Nicole says, "Tell me the truth, Matt. You're such a mild mannered guy. Where did you dredge up this Neanderthal?"

"Neanderthal?" Tyler says. "I'm a perfect specimen of modern day manhood."

Nicole chuckles. "All brawn and no brain?"

Jasmine giggles.

"Well," Matt says. "Male elementary school teachers are few and far between, at least in the early grades. We band together for self-protection."

Tyler comments, "Plus, it's a fact that you can't go out without a wingman."

"You mean," Nicole says, "someone to console you after you get shot down?"

He grins, but doesn't answer.

The banter continues, but I don't pay as close attention as I normally might. I'm uncomfortably aware of Matt, sitting directly across from me. After scooping his food onto his plate, he opens a package of chopsticks and begins to eat with them. I've never noticed before how dark his eyebrows are, or how thick his lips are. He smiles at a joke Nicole makes, his lips curling up to reveal closely spaced white teeth that stand out against his slightly olive skin and the slight shading of beard on his face.

Tyler finishes an improbable story about his college roommate, which Nicole tries to top with another story.

"Okay, so you know the two of us enlisted together, right? After we finished training both of us were assigned to the 23rd MP Company at Fort Drum, which is too hundred and twelve miles from the middle of nowhere. As new privates, our job was basically to stand around most of the time on guard duty. We'd occasionally go out on patrol, but always subordinate to some sergeant or corporal, right? Anyway, there was one gate on the post we'd pull guard duty every couple of weeks. The Commanding General would drive in and out that gate."

I groan. Of course she'd pick this one. She grins at my groan. "Anyway, when the General came through, we were supposed to get out of the guard post and stand at attention and salute. Almost always we'd get a call ahead of time that the General was on the move, so we had time. This one night we're both there, and it's cold and raining and threatening snow. And of course, no one calls us to tell us the General was out. So we see the car coming, and it's dark, and we don't know who it is, but I step outside and the car is maybe fifty feet away when I realize it's the General. So I call back, and out comes Zoe. She's in a hurry, and somehow gets a bootlace wrapped up around the chair she was sitting on. She moves, the chair moves, it gets caught in the doorway and she falls face first, right into the mud. And I'm standing there, saluting, and she's laying prone on the ground covered in mud just as the General comes to a stop right in front of us. You should have heard the splat when she hit the mud."

Oh, God. Hearing it is almost as bad as experiencing it was. I can feel heat rising to my face.

Tyler is grinning and Matt has his eyebrows raised. "So what happened?"

I pout. "I finally get up and instead of finding him long gone, the General is there, and he has his window rolled down. He asks if I'm all right, and I tell him yes, just my pride was hurt.

And he says, 'Good, because that's the funniest damn thing I've seen in years.' Then he drives off. The next day I got a special order from the General's office giving me a two-day pass."

"At least that worked out well in the end," Matt says.

I snort. "I suppose. What sucked was I couldn't go back to the barracks and change. So I was stuck out there for almost nine more hours. Muddy. Cold. Wet."

"You've seen worse," Nicole says. I give her a cool look. That may be true, but it doesn't mean I want to talk about it.

Tyler said, "So what's your story? You got a boyfriend back in Tokyo?"

I shake my head. "I dated a guy there for a while. It wasn't a good fit."

It wasn't a good fit is code for *the asshole cheated on me.* Some things Matt and Tyler don't need to know. Nicole catches it and just takes a drink of her wine. She was on her way out of the Army by the time I went to Tokyo, so she never met Chase. She heard about him, because even after she got out, we still talked all the time. FaceTime carried me through a lot of ugly and sad times. In those days, mostly sad. Chase screwed me up pretty good. He cancelled on me at the last minute one night when we had a date. And that would have been the end of it, except that I decided I still needed to get out of the barracks, and went on my own to the theater in Roppongi Hills, which showed first run American films.

And of course that's where I ran into Chase, his arm wrapped around a tiny little Japanese girl with big tits and an attitude of self-importance.

He saw me and I saw him and I left in a big hurry. Not long after, my phone started ringing, over and over again. I didn't answer.

Chase was a mistake in the first place. He wasn't a soldier—a college dropout who had wandered on his own into

Asia, eventually settling in Japan, where he found a job teaching English at a private school in Tokyo. It was a nice job if you could get it, I suppose. He didn't get paid too much, but he was able to live in Tokyo rent free. He was good looking, with an easy going attitude. He was a prick.

"What do you think, Zoe?"

Crap. I snap back to the present when Matt's voice cuts through. Nicole is looking at me with an eyebrow arched. I don't know if the guys noticed my exit from reality, but she sure did.

I don't even bother to try to cover it. "I'm sorry. I was away for a moment. What were we talking about?"

Tyler bursts out laughing. Of course he would. I smile a practiced, fake smile. A smile they won't see through. Because I'm off balance now. I join in the banter for a few minutes. Nicole goes off on another story about being a cop at UMASS. She has no end of interesting stories, and some of them might even be true.

More than once as we eat, I find myself looking at Matt. Something about him seems different. I'm not sure what it is about him. He's more—I'm not sure what word I'm look-ing for—he's more self-contained than most men I've known. It's not that he's emotionally distant—many guys are, but he doesn't come across that way at all. He does come across as a very private person. Self-contained. He described Tyler as his best friend. The two of them don't seem all that close. Guys who have been friends a long time share a lot of in-jokes. They insult each other and laugh and have a certain easy air about them which is unmistakable. If I had to guess, I'd say Tyler doesn't know Matt at all.

I decide then and there, I'm going to find out a lot more about Matt Paladino.

CHAPTER TEN

Who are you again? (Zoe)

WHEN THE ALARM goes off the next morning, I groan a little. My head hurts from one too many glasses of wine.

Nothing to be done for it. The horses don't care if I'm hung over. I have to get moving.

I'm out of bed and having a cup of coffee by 6:45, and Jasmine joins me a few minutes later. Then we walk together, wordlessly, to the barn.

It's not cold enough yet that the horses can't pasture on the grass, but it will be soon. And hay costs money that I don't have. So out into the pasture they go. I check the stalls. All three need to be mucked out this morning.

"You're okay leading them out?" I ask.

Jasmine doesn't sneer, but gets pretty close. I fit the halters on each of the horses, then I pass Mono's lead to Jasmine. I follow behind her with Nettles and Eeyore.

Mono looks eager to go, prancing a little bit. I was twelve at least before I was handling horses the way she is. She's a natural, and she loves it. When Mono stops to eat the lawn instead of going on to the pasture, she pulls him up like a pro.

Once we get to the gate, Mono raises his head and tail high and blows a loud snort, then paws at the ground. He's ready to go. I steer the other two horses into the enclosure, but I keep a close eye on Jasmine as I release Nettles and Eeyore. Mine are much more docile than Mono.

She reaches up and unhooks the lead and steps back. He wheels around, knickers at the other horses, and takes off at a gallop. Eeyore and Nettles follow, whinnying behind him.

It's crazy—I never wanted to be like Mom, living my life around and for horses. In fact, sometimes I resented the hell out of her horses, because it seemed that they got far more of her love than I did. But—something about them—I've missed them. I've missed this. And I never would have guessed that was even possible.

We head back together and wordlessly begin work in the stable. She cleans the water buckets while I muck out the stalls. I'm so intently wrapped up that I don't hear a car outside. I nearly jump when someone coughs behind me. I spin around in shock, my heart thumping.

Oh. It's a woman—forty-five maybe, wearing an expensive coat and pants and shoes which don't look suitable for the inside of a stable. Beside her is a pensive looking ten year old girl.

"Oh—hello...."

She begins speaking in a quick, businesslike tone. "Hi. Is Lucinda around? What time should I come pick up Mary? No one was here last week when I got here—"

"I'm Zoe Welch. Who are you again?"

The woman stops talking but looks impatient. "I have to be going. Can you just let me know where Lucinda is—"

I cut my eyes to the girl—Mary?—and say, "She's not—"

Jasmine cuts me off. In a factual voice, she says, "She's dead."

The woman's eyes widen in shock. "What? Oh my God! What happened?"

"Car accident," I say. "And you're here for?"

"Mary's lesson, of course." The mother looks nearly offended that my mother is dead. I want to punch her in the throat. Mary, meanwhile, looks like she's going to burst into tears.

Jasmine says to me, "Mom has a small group of girls on Saturday mornings." Then she says to Mary, "Come on, Mary. Walk with me down to see Mono?"

The little girl nods and takes Jasmine's hand. Both girls run off.

I take a breath, trying to focus myself on not committing any violent acts this early in the morning.

"I don't know what your arrangement was with my Mom."

"Your Mom? I'm so sorry." She actually looks genuinely sorry. She seems to sink into herself, as if whatever hot hair she had inside propping her up had been released through a slow valve. She says, "I used to bring Mary here Saturday mornings. But I guess—"

"You still can, for now," I say. "I don't know if I'm going to take on all of her work, but I can for the next couple of weeks until things are sorted out."

"Are you qualified?" She looks skeptical.

"I've been riding since I was younger than they are. And I assisted my mom for years before I went off in the Army. You can leave her."

The woman looks inappropriately grateful. I think she has somewhere to be, and looks at this as a babysitting engagement. Fine. Something about the girl just made my heart sad.

The woman makes her escape. It makes me wonder how many other students there are, and where they were last week? Where was I? It's all fuzzy. Did they knock on the door and we just slept through? I can't remember. What I do know is that I need to clear the fog out of my brain and get moving.

I walk out of the barn and scan the yard. Jasmine has a bail of hay on the back end of the garden wagon, a four-wheeled cart made out of a steel. She's showing Mary how to stuff the feeding nets with hay for the night. I approach the two of them.

Mary is still sniffling. "Hey, you guys," I say in a low voice. "So—is the normal drill same as it used to be?" I look at Jasmine with the question.

She says, "Chores, stalls, everything, then lessons. Usually there's three or four girls."

I nod. "Okay. Well, we're almost done in the barn. I'll go sweep up while you finish bagging?"

"I got it, Zoe." Jasmine's voice has an edge to it as she says the words. I expect her to roll her eyes next.

I shrug. She does have it. So I walk back toward the stable and begin to sweep. I find myself doing with aggression. I'm gritting my teeth. Mary's mother—she never even introduced herself—immediately raised my hackles. Her perfect suit and perfect shoes, her self-centered initial reaction to my mother not being there, all conspire to fill me with rage. I sweep harder and harder, grinding my teeth and trying to contain the red hot emotion that surges inside of me. I feel as if my face is contorted, my forehead hurts and I'm struggling to keep my chin from trembling and I'm horrified to realize that I'm crying. Crying. I don't want to cry, I don't need to cry, I need to stay strong for Jasmine and how the hell am I going to do that if I can't even keep it together?

I drop the broom and walk toward the back of the stable, staring up at the corrugated metal ceiling with its streaks of rust along the edges and—

"Zoe? Are you okay?"

I spin around in horror.

Matt Paladino stands in the door of the barn, his face a mix of concern and … what? I don't get his expression. His eyes are wide and brown and focused on me like laser beams. He moves toward me and says, "Are you all right?"

"Of course I'm all right," I say, but the tears running down my face—still running down my face—reveal the lie. I don't want him to see me like this. I don't want anyone to see me like this. I step back into the darkness of the stable, but he steps forward.

"Zoe? You're crying."

Gritting my teeth, I say, "My parents just died."

He walks closer. "I know. And I know how much that hurts."

My shoulders sink and I turn away from him. "Go away, Matt."

He doesn't go away. Instead he approaches even closer. Then he puts a hand on my shoulder. That's all it takes. I let out a sob, then another, then he pulls me to him. I manage to keep my arms up in between us, my palms flat against his chest, but he wraps his arms all the way around me. And I cry.

He whispers in my ear. "It's going to be okay. It's going to be okay." I know he's lying. I just cry harder.

"I've got to pull myself together," I cry. "My mom's students are coming. I think." I sniff and hiccup. I hate this.

He says in a low tone, "You go in and clean up. I've got this for now."

Relief and embarrassment flood me at the same time. I back away and run into the house and scrub my face.

NOW KICK (MATT)

When Zoe runs inside, I do the only thing I can. I keep one eye on the girls outside and begin shoveling the stall which she'd been working on. I was never a stablehand or anything like that, but I know horses and what needs to be done with them. Growing up like I did, that sort of knowledge is ingrained.

Carlina's dad—who had insisted I call him Uncle Nick—once said to me, *It's all about your relationship with the horses, Matty. They'll break anything. They'll get into anything. But they also love you if you love them. Which means you gotta take care of 'em.*

I gave up that life a long time ago, but this I can handle.

Jasmine and her friend come back into the stable and Jasmine lets out a little cry. "Mister P!" She runs over and hugs me.

I smile. "Hey, Jasmine. Who is this?"

Jasmine says, "This is Mary. She takes riding lessons."

"I see. And what have you two been up to?"

"Stuffing hay bags," Jasmine says in a tired voice. I half expect her to roll her eyes. I'm familiar with it. Horses are grazing animals—designed to eat slowly and steadily. Throw a bale of hay in front of them and they'll eat it too quickly. Instead, most stables stuff hay inside bags, where the horses have to chew it a little at a time as they pull the hay through the mesh bag. Back when I was learning to ride, Carlina's father Nick used to make his hay bags from discarded netting once used by the big-top acts.

I move into the next stall over, carrying the muckrake. "You shovel and I'll sort."

"Okay," Jasmine says.

We get to work clearing the stalls of refuse. A moment later Zoe returns, looking composed. She raises an eyebrow when she sees the two girls shoveling, then shrugs and begins working on the third and final stall. "Soon as we're done in here we'll get going on the horses, okay?"

Jasmine grins.

"Mary," Zoe says. "Who have you been riding?"

Mary doesn't answer right away. In fact, she looks like she might crawl underneath the wheelbarrow.

"She mostly rides Eeyore," Jasmine says. "Mary's still new."

"That's fine," Zoe says. "Everyone starts somewhere."

A few minutes later we've finished with the stalls and the floor of the barn. Everything is swept clean and dry and the barn smells of fresh sawdust.

"All right," Zoe says. "Let's head out to the paddock."

Both girls take off running. I walk at Zoe's side, but don't say anything, preferring to absorb the warmth. But as we get about halfway to the paddock, where I can see Zoe's three horses grazing, she asks me, "So, what brings you back here today?"

I cut my eyes over to her face. She looks good—fresh, her hair loose, no makeup on. I don't have a very good excuse.

"Come on," she says.

I shrug. "Honestly, it's because I wanted to see you. Last night wasn't enough."

She snorts. "So you come and find me falling apart. That's fantastic."

"Everybody is entitled to fall apart sometimes. And you've got plenty of reason."

She opens the gate and says, "Slip in there quick, sometimes Mono tries to nose his way out."

I follow her instructions, knowing that no matter how strong I might be, I would never be able to stop a thousand pound horse if it was determined to go somewhere.

She slips in beside me. It takes a few minutes, but we get the horses together and saddled up. Zoe double checks behind me—as I would were our positions reversed—but she finds no fault with how I saddled Nettles.

"You going to tell me now where you learned so much about horses?"

I shrug. "I grew up with the circus," I say.

She snorts and shakes her head. There's nothing quite like the truth to misdirect people. With an exasperated tone, she turns her attention to Jasmine.

"All right, kiddo, let's get you saddled up."

Zoe leads Mono to a position next to a three-foot step ladder and Jasmine climbs up, then into the saddle. She doesn't give the slightest hesitation, no matter that the horse is huge for her.

"Take him out slow," Zoe says. Jasmine listens, riding Mono out at a slow trot.

As Zoe gets Eeyore positioned next to the steps, she says, "You love to keep some mystery around you. Why is that?"

"I'm just a very private person," I say. Zoe helps Mary into the saddle as we talk. "Besides, I'm a public school teacher. You kinda have to stay private."

"Heels down," she instructs Mary. "Now kick."

Mary kicks, but it's such a slight kick I'm not sure Eeyore even noticed.

"Kick harder," she says. "You won't hurt him. But you've got to tell him what you want."

Mary does it again, kicking harder, and Eeyore begins to walk.

Zoe walks sideways, keeping an eye on the girl.

"Eyes on where you're going," Zoe says. "Hands at your side. I want you to ride to the barrel, then circle it and come back. Okay?"

Unlike Jasmine, Mary perches on the animal, back rigid, arms tense by her side and clutching the reins as if she might fall off any second. She nods at Zoe's words, a short jerk of her head.

"Mary, I want you to relax just a little. Eeyore can tell you're nervous. He won't hurt you, he's a very gentle horse. When you get to the barrel, turn with your whole body, all right? Eyes back on me! Eyes back on me! Lead him with your whole body!"

As she calls out the words in a confident tone, I keep an eye on Zoe. She's a natural teacher, though I don't know if she realizes it. She watches both girls and their horses as they circle the training ring, her feet shoulder width apart, shoulders loose, her attention focused and intense.

I take a deep breath as I watch her. It's an unfamiliar feeling. I'm attracted to her of course—that's a given, she's a beautiful woman. But this is different. She's gentle. Smart. She passionately loves her sister, and by the looks of it, her horses. Her life.

It's been a long time since I've wanted to be with someone like this. Not since high school and Carlina. But as I watch her here in the sunlight of the morning, calling out instructions to the two girls on horseback, I realize I want her more than anything I've wanted in my life. High school infatuation was just that—infatuation. This desire... it's something new, and far more powerful.

I DO THAT SOMETIMES (ZOE)

A little after noon, Mary's mother picks her up. The horses are grazing happily, and it's long past time to get some lunch. As Mary is driven away, Matt says out of the blue, "Do you guys want to grab some lunch? Maybe up at the common?"

The words come out forced. Then again, most of the morning, he seemed a little off. I caught him looking at me oddly several times, and I'm not comfortable with the feeling I get when I look at him. A little like I haven't eaten and my thoughts are unfocused and confused. Plus, I spent way too much time today looking at him.

Which makes me lightheaded.

"Okay." I don't know who answered him, because I sure wasn't ready to. Despite my reluctance, I find myself driving in the van, Jasmine at my side, following Matt up to the Village Common.

The Village Common is a mixed residential and shopping area across the street from Mount Holyoke. A bookstore, several restaurants, shops, offices. Dad used to spend a lot of time at The Thirsty Mind, a coffee shop lined with shelves filled with one dollar books. In fact, that was one of the few things we did regularly together when I was in high school. At least once a week, after school, I'd go up to the coffee shop and spend the afternoon with my dad there. We didn't do anything—I studied and he graded papers. The thought of walking into the Thirsty Mind right now fills me with fear. Almost as much fear as I have when I think about going into the garage.

I still haven't gone in there since I got home.

Matt parallel parks his car and I pull in behind him. I don't get him. Doesn't he have anything to do? I know the teachers are on strike, but ... what does he normally do on Saturday mornings? I'm sure he doesn't spend them shoveling horse shit. I guess I'm still a little gun shy after Chase, because I don't want to open up even a little.

I don't know the first thing about Matt Paladino.

Except that my heart beats a little faster when he's near me.

He steps out of the car in front of us, and for a second I just sit there looking at him as he unfolds from the seat in his blue jeans and shirt.

He's too good to be true. And I've been down that road before. I've never felt so conflicted in my life.

"Zoe? Zoe?" Jasmine's voice is high pitched and irritating.

"Yeah?" I say, shaking my head.

"Are we gonna go?" Her eyebrows are raised up in the air, and I realize I've been sitting here, lost in thought.

Here's the thing. I try to stay pretty put together. Every dick in America thinks that women shouldn't be in the military, and especially that they shouldn't be in combat. Sometimes I feel like I have a responsibility to represent my gender, to show that I can be just as tough as the guys. I have to pretend that I don't have nightmares, that I don't get scared, that I don't sometimes think about the things that happened and get sick and afraid for my soul. When I think about it, part of the problem with Chase wasn't him at all. It was me. He'd ask me what was wrong and I wouldn't say. How could I?

I can't even admit it all to myself.

I sluggishly get out of the car, suddenly feeling defeated.

Matt gives me a quizzical look, raising an eyebrow. "You okay?"

I fix a smile on my face. "Of course."

Jasmine jumps up and down and says, "So what are we having for lunch? What are we having? What are we having?"

"Sushi?" I ask. "I've been wanting to try Iya."

He gives me a sheepish look, even as Jasmine shouts "No!" in horror.

"I've never had sushi."

"Oh, well, then you have to try it. Trust me."

So I lead the way into the Japanese restaurant. My Japanese is very rough—I lived there for a year, but my language skills are pretty sparse. It turns out to not matter—our waitress is blonde haired and blue eyed and clearly not from Japan.

I dispense with Jasmine's objections by ordering chicken teriyaki for her, but Matt and I spend ten minutes discussing the menu. He settles on the flying tiger roll—shrimp tempura, salmon, avocado, spicy mayo.

Soon enough, our food arrives. After the waitress steps away, Matt leans close and grins. "Hey... they forgot to cook my fish."

I laugh. "Trust me."

"Are you sure you aren't trying to kill me?"

I nod. "I'll prove it," I say. I grab my chopsticks and snatch a piece of his roll and take a bite. Oh, my. This place is good. I close my eyes, savoring the flavors. "Go on," I say. "Try it."

Reluctantly—and with considerable difficulty—he picks up a piece and puts it in his mouth.

I'm immediately rewarded with wide eyes. He chews as Jasmine says, "You'll never get me to eat that. Eww. Dead fish."

"Better than live fish," Matt says. Then he smiles. "A lot better. That was delicious."

"Actually... in Tokyo you can order live sashimi."

His eyes widen. "Are you serious?"

I nod. "It's delicious, but ... I couldn't eat it." Internally I wince. I actually had nightmares after the night Chase and I ate *ikizukuri*—fish prepared alive. It sounds crazy, but—I saw people torn apart, I've seen people I knew, people I was friends with, screaming their lungs out in pain and horror after roadside bombs. People. The thought of even a fish suffering like that—I couldn't deal with it.

Don't judge. I'm well aware that a hamburger comes from an animal, as does the bacon I love to eat. At least some attempt is made to kill them humanely. I can't stand seeing anyone suffer. Involuntarily, my mind goes to Iraq.

You know, when those idiots in Congress talk about women not serving in combat? They don't know what the hell they're talking about. Sure, I wasn't infantry. But most of my tour in Iraq, I was detailed to an infantry platoon. Who else was going to search women during midnight raids? You can't imagine what it was like. Night after night sometimes. Break down the doors of suspected insurgents. Wailing of women and children in the background, the men laying face down, wrists ziptied behind them. I'd search the women as the men were searched by my infantry compatriots. I can't count the number of children I saw crying as their fathers were carried away.

I went through every danger the men did. I went through the firefights, the mortar attacks, the roadside bombs, the ambushes. I still had to put up with the harassment, the occasional grab at my ass, the stupid comments and names. The jerks who figure if you're a female in the military you must be a nurse or a whore.

I take a deep, cleansing breath. Be present.

Both Jasmine and Matt are staring at me.

"Sorry," I say. I feel heat on my cheeks. Awkwardly, I take a drink.

"You went away there," Matt says.

"I do that sometimes."

He looks me in the eye with an expression that seems to say I understand. But I know he doesn't. That's the kind of lie that can lead to heartbreak. I'm not interested.

I need to steer my state of mind anywhere else. This is crazy. What the hell is wrong with me that suddenly all I can think of is Iraq?

"What's the latest on the strike?" I ask. Inside, I'm pleading with Matt to take the bait and shift the conversation to safer ground.

He takes it. "I think the school committee is going to cave. The downside is that the union is going to end up getting fined, for sure."

"Why? What kind of fine?"

"Well, it isn't legal for us to strike. Last time it happened in Massachusetts, the local teachers union got slapped with a hundred thousand dollar fine. But they won. I think we will too."

Jasmine says, "I want to go back to school. The strike is stupid."

"I want to go back too, Jasmine."

"Will you still come see us when school starts again?"

I swear to God my heart stops beating. I don't breathe, and I don't think he does either for a second. Then he nods, eyes on me. "Yeah, if that's okay with you and Zoe."

CHAPTER ELEVEN

You're safe (Zoe)

A HEAVY FOG SITS on South Hadley, the kind of thick white fog that hits when a foot of snow rests on the ground and the air gets warm. The kind of fog that keeps you from seeing more than twenty feet ahead of you. The kind of fog that suffocates.

I'm outside in the fog in my nightgown, the one I haven't worn since high school, and it is cold. Something is wrong. I don't know what it is. I hear somebody crying. Whimpering really. It's a forlorn sound, sad and lonely and full of so much grief it's like touching a live wire.

My feet are bare, and I'm walking down the middle of College Street. Abbey Chapel is to my left, its brown, Gothic stone rearing up high in the fog and darkness like a raging horse, oppressively dark. I walk a little faster, but my feet are blocks of ice, and I can actually feel pain shooting up my ankles and calves from the cold. I need to get home and I don't know why my father hasn't picked me up from the Village Common. I need to get home now.

Something is behind me.

Or someone.

I begin to run. My feet slide a little on the ice, the road hasn't been plowed very well, and the fog is getting thicker and whoever is out there is getting closer and closer. The college is now behind me, and I'm running down the hill, my feet slipping out from under me and on either side I can see prisoners, cowering beside the road in their rags, hands tied with zip ties, the stink of horse and sweat and fear overwhelming even in the cold and fear shoots through me.

I have to get home.

Ahead, I can see it. The house, on the right side of the road, and the house is dark, no lights on except one in the garage, in Dad's workshop.

I run for it. I can hear the grumbling from the prisoners, the shuffling of feet behind me, and I want to cry out in fear. Dad will be in his workshop, he'll be in the garage tinkering on a puzzle and we'll be warm and safe in there and I get to the garage and the door is locked. I can hear them behind me, whoever it is, and I start to scream.

I bang on the door, hard, with the flat of my palm. The crying and whimpering is louder than ever. I curl my hands into a fist and bang on the glass. I can see the light inside, and there is Dad's silhouette. The door is open and I cry out and run inside, wrapping my arms around him.

Oh, dear God, I'm safe. He shuts the door behind me and curls his arms around me, and I can feel something wet running down my face as I push my face against his sweater, something wet and warm and I pull back and look.

"You're safe, Zoe," he whispers, his voice sibilant. His face is split, lips and left cheek and cheekbone flayed open, eyeball half exposed, crazily rolling around in its socket, and a bubble of mixed spit and blood forms in the gap between his teeth.

I shriek in terror and push away.

***

It's dark and I'm in my room. Sitting up, my heart is pounding and I wipe sweat off my neck. The whoosh of the blood pumping in the vessels of my ears barely drowns out my breathing.

Dear God.

I gasp for air. I'm in my room. It was a dream. It was a nightmare. I'm at home.

Then I hear crying and for a second terror strikes through me again. It's a high pitched moan, a mix of terror and incredible grief. I reach over and switch on my light.

I can still hear the crying.

Jasmine.

I stumble out of bed, the blankets falling to the floor. I'm still disoriented, the terror of the nightmare thick in my throat. I open the door and walk down the hall, my feet causing the boards in the center to creak like crazy. Then I open Jasmine's door.

She's laying face down, knees pulled up under her, and she's sobbing and moaning.

"Hey," I whisper. I move toward her, dropping to my knees beside the bed. I reach out a hand and run it down her back. She cries harder.

"Jasmine? Was it a dream? Are you okay?"

She just wails louder. I reach out and lift her off the bed and she wraps her arms and legs around me, crying even louder than before, great gasps of air followed by loud wails.

"What is it, baby?" I whisper. "It's okay. It's okay." I pat her back as I say the words, knowing they aren't even true.

"It was Mom," she sobs. "She was dead."

"Oh, Jasmine," I say. Her, too. "I'm so sorry."

"Why don't you come lie down with me," I whisper.

She nods urgently. "Can I?"

"Yeah, come on."

I carry her into my room, laying her gently on the bed. I crawl in beside her and pull her to me. She cries for a little while longer, but slowly drifts off to sleep, her face nestled against my shoulder.

Once she's asleep I lay with my face toward the window. The red oak outside is waving a little in the wind, the shadow of the branch against the window like a hand. The colors will be changing soon. Dad's workshop is still out there in the garage, untouched since he died.

It takes me a long time to get back to sleep.

SURE, I'LL COME IN (MATT)

The banging on my door goes on for an unreasonable amount of time.

My eye cracks open, and I see it's four-thirty in the morning. I must be dreaming. I close my eyes and burrow under the covers, only to hear the thumping on the door again.

What the hell?

I sit up in bed, blinking my eyes. Then I hear the voice outside.

"Matty! Wake up!"

Shit. It's Messalina. I stand up, stumble a moment, then I grab a pair of sweats and a t-shirt and put them on. She starts thumping on the door again, and I shout, "Hold on, damn it."

The thumping stops. I lurch to the apartment door and yank it open.

My door opens to a wooden landing at the top of a long flight of stairs above the restaurant. My sister Messalina stands on the landing. Her hair, purple and pink, flows down her back, and her makeup almost hides the acne scars. She's wearing a black leather jacket and black jeans and looks appallingly wide awake for this time of morning.

"Don't you know what time it is?" I demand.

"Sure, I'll come in. Thanks for asking." She pushes her way past me, and the smell of her perfume instantly trips my consciousness right back in time to South Florida, melting blacktop, chalk and the creaking of the ropes. The feeling of falling, over and over again. The road and sweat.

The smell of resentment is repulsive.

I close the door and warily re-enter my apartment.

She looks around, one eyebrow arched. "So this is your place."

I swallow. Having a family member here… it forces me to see things through her eyes. And I don't like what I see. A pizza box sits half open on the coffee table next to an empty beer bottle. The walls are bare except one item, a copy of the cover of Life Magazine from March 1996. My parents grace the cover, side by side as they soar through the air to their catchers, smiles on their faces. I was just a kid, but I can still remember the excitement of that cover. A few books are scattered on the shelves, and a stack of worksheets sits on the small kitchen table I bought at Ikea.

It doesn't look like anyone lives here—more like a temporary bachelor pad.

"Haven't finished moving in yet?"

So she's going to be a bitch. Fine. "No. This is it. Welcome to my home. What are you doing here?"

She walks into what passes for a kitchen and begins to fill the coffee pot with water. "Where's your coffee? It's late."

"No kidding." I walk to the cabinet and open it up. She reaches past me and grabs the bag of coffee beans from Rao's. It's one of my few luxuries. I grab it back, and pour some into the grinder.

"Seriously, Messalina. What's going on? It's great to see you and all, but it is four in the morning."

"You know, you could not be an ass for a change."

I grind the beans, the sound shattering the quiet, then pour them into the filter and start the coffee pot. "I could. But why? Besides, you're the ass for showing up this early in the morning."

She lifts herself up onto the counter, then reaches into her pocket, an exercise in frustration because her jeans are so tight. She has to almost contort her body to get her hands in there. Finally, her hand reemerges, clutching a silvery piece of foil wrapped around a stick of gum. She peels it, pops the gum into her mouth, then balls up the wrapper and throws it at the trash can.

The wrapper bounces off the edge and lands on my floor.

I don't take the bait. We stare at each other in silence for a few minutes, then she says, "Mamma's hurt you know. She doesn't say it—she'd never do that. But I can see it. She's hurt."

I open my mouth to say something, but no words come out. Then I close it. I don't actually have to say anything. Even so, I try again. I mumble the words, "I talked with her last week."

"And when was the last time you saw her? When was the last time you saw any of us, Matty? You go away to college and just leave your whole family behind?"

I flinch. "I've been busy. You know I represent the union here? I've got kids to teach. A lot going on."

"Bullshit. You get summers off. Hell, you could come fly with us."

I snort. "Right, Lina. That's never going to happen."

"Come on, Matt. You know it wasn't your fault. Everyone knows that."

I flinch.

Hands slipping from mine. Eyes wide, screams from the stands.
"Fuck off."

She sighs and shakes her head. "We miss you, little brother."

The coffee pot's only halfway done, but I pull a mug down and pour, letting the mug catch the coffee coming from the filter as I try to hide the shaking in my hands. I hand her the cup and pour myself one.

"So what brings you to town so early, anyway? The circus won't be through until November."

She shrugs. "We're in Albany this weekend. You should come out. It's not far, and Mom would love to see you."

"You guys are going to be busy if you've got shows."

"Come *on*, Matt."

Christ. Her eyes are watering. I take a breath. "All right. We'll get together. If not in Albany, then when you're in Boston or Springfield."

She seems to sag a little. "Fine. What's so damned important that you can't do it this weekend?"

I grimace. Her gaze is a little too intense for my comfort. "It's complicated."

She chuckles. "What's complicated?"

"I don't have plans for Saturday... yet. But there's this woman...."

"Oh?" she says, raising her eyebrows.

I nod. "Yeah. Yeah. And ... anyway... um..."

"Are you always this articulate?"

Smartass. "Yeah. I'm planning to ask her to dinner and drinks Saturday. All right? It's the right time, and I don't want to screw this up."

She grins. "Well, you go, brother."

CHAPTER TWELVE

SPIT IT OUT (MATT)

AFTER MESSALINA LEAVES, I go back to sleep. She had been driving from Albany to Boston, so coming here was merely a twenty-minute detour. Unfortunately, I'm jarred by her visit, coming as it did early in the morning and unexpected.

I toss and turn for two hours, finally getting up and crawling out of bed. I shower and shave, make a pot of coffee, then open up my laptop to read the New York Times, then move on to my email. I pace. Finally I get out of the apartment, walking over to the coffee shop to get some breakfast. I can't call before ten.

The time ticks by excruciatingly slowly. It's not fair.

After breakfast, I stop in the bookstore, scanning for something decent to read. Something decent and easy to read, because my attention span is lacking this morning. I settle on a science fiction novel, pay cash for it, then wander outside and sit on one of the benches on the common.

I check my watch. It's 45 minutes before I can call.

I start reading the book. I'm a page in before I realize that I haven't understood a single word.

Not. One. Word.

Uggh.

I settle in on the bench and look up at the sky.

At precisely ten am, I dial Zoe's number.

It rings… once… twice… three times.

When she answers, "Hello?" I sit up straighter, though she can't see me.

"Hey, Zoe. It's Matt."

"What's up, Matt?"

"Listen um… I know I've been coming by to keep Jasmine company and all, and I've enjoyed that."

"Uh huh…" Her tone sounds wary.

"What I'm calling about … is … um… what I mean to say is…"

"Spit it out, Matt."

I close my eyes. I suck in a deep breath. Then I speak. "Zoe, would you like to have dinner with me? Saturday night maybe? Or drinks?"

Her response is matter-of-fact, and I can't tell if she's intentionally misunderstanding. "Saturday.. yeah… we'd have to do it early though, I've been trying to get Jasmine to bed by eight, but we'd love to."

I swallow. I'm sweating. "No, I think you misunderstood. You would need maybe a babysitter. I'm asking you to dinner."

"I don't understand."

"A date."

I can hear her breathing at the other end of the line, a thousand miles away. Or four blocks. Whatever. A long thirty seconds pass. I close my eyes and brace myself.

"I've got the number for a girl at Mount Holyoke who offers babysitting. I'll call her."

Did she just say yes?

"You'll come?"

"Yes, I'd like that."

I exhale. Then I smile broadly, my cheeks stretching. I probably look like an idiot, but I don't care. "All right then."

"You're still coming by to ride with Jasmine?"

"This afternoon, just like we planned."

"I'll see you then."

Maybe it's just in my head, but her voice sounds lighter as she says goodbye.

I THINK I LIKE YOU (ZOE)

"I don't understand why I have to stay home." Jasmine's voice is plaintive. She's propped up against the doorjamb of the bathroom. I'm leaning forward, looking in the mirror carefully as I apply mascara.

"I told you, it's a date."

"With Mister P?" Her face screws up with a funny expression. "That's weird."

My makeup is all wrong. So is my hair. I brush it again. I'm wearing a sleeveless dress, light blue, almost the exact shade of my eyes. I start to fuss with my makeup again—no. Time to give it a rest.

I walk downstairs, Jasmine trailing behind me. "I c—c—can get pizza?"

"Yep," I say. Her stuttering worries me and frustrates her.

The doorbell rings.

I walk toward it, my heels clicking on the wood floors as I walk. I rarely wear heels of any kind, but I couldn't resist. I open the door. It's a young woman. Round faced, wide smile. "Hi, I'm Megan," she says.

"Come on in," I reply. I step back and let her in the house. We spoke on the phone at some length the day before yesterday, after Matt invited me to dinner. For a date. I found Megan through an ad she had posted at the Village Common. An early childhood education major at Mount Holyoke, she seems to be sane and responsible, so that's all good news.

"Jasmine… meet Megan."

"Hi, Jasmine," Megan says in a sweet tone.

Jasmine rolls her eyes. That's a great start.

"Megan, here's twenty dollars if you want to order pizza. There's ice cream in the freezer, but I told Jasmine she had to eat dinner first. Bedtime at eight."

"I kn—kn—know all that, Zoe." Jasmine looks severely annoyed.

I smile at her. "Yes, but Megan doesn't. While I'm gone, she's in charge. Make sure you listen."

"I don't listen to you."

I sigh.

The sound of a car rolling on gravel catches my attention. I bend forward and kiss Jasmine on the forehead. "Behave while I'm gone."

Jasmine crosses her eyes and purses her lips. Then she waggles her fingers at me for good measure.

"I can tell we're going to get along," Megan says to Jasmine, laughing.

A knock on the door grabs my attention. I open it.

Oh.

Usually I see Matt dressed in jeans and polo or button down shirts. Tonight he's wearing black pants, with a black shirt that emphasizes his shoulders and upper arms. He smells good. Cologne? It's there, but I can't quite tell what it is.

His eyes widen as he sees me, and they drop, scanning me all the way down to my shoes and back up. It's quick—like he doesn't want me to see it. But unmistakable.

"You look stunning, Zoe."

My face and neck grow hot.

"Thank you," I say, suddenly awkward.

He says, "I'm ready if you are. I'd like to say hi to Jasmine, though."

I turn and look. Jasmine is standing in the doorway to the dining room, a sour expression on her face. Matt walks over to her and crouches down so they are eye to eye.

"Jasmine," he says. "I owe you an apology."

What?

Jasmine looks startled out of her cynicism for the first time all afternoon. "What? Why?"

"Well, you see, I wanted to take Zoe out on a date. I didn't ask you, and maybe I should have."

"Do y-y-you … like her?"

He smiles. Then he nods. "I like you too, Jasmine, but in a different way. You can count on me, I'll be your teacher and friend, okay?"

Jasmine suddenly hugs him. He's crouching and sways a little, but doesn't lose his balance. I can hear her say, "You can go out with Zoe. I don't mind."

***

"Sometimes I don't understand you." Matt's tone is frank as he says the words, almost an hour after he picked me up. Concerned, not angry.

"What do you mean?" I ask. I try to keep my poker face on, but I've never been very good at that.

He grins a little as he stabs another bite of calamari with his fork. "I mean, you're very tightly wound. You don't talk at all about the last few years of your life. All I know is you've been in the Army ... and in Tokyo. That's it."

I look away. I feel like I'm losing my appetite, and my stomach twists with an unreasonable level of anxiety.

Talk.

I don't want to.

Talk.

I let out my breath with a long, slow exhalation. I'm fidgeting, my hands playing with the silverware. Me. No. I stop fidgeting and look at Matt, then I say the first words that come out of my mouth. "It's hard for me to trust."

He nods. "Yeah. Me too."

I shake my head. "No... you don't understand. I don't ... I mean... " Shit. I try to compose myself.

He takes my hand. "No need to get so flustered."

His tone is unreasonably reasonable. It makes me want to punch him. Or kiss him. Instead of doing those things, I ask, "Have you ever seen anyone die?"

He blinks, and for a second I think I see pain flash in his eyes. He tries to hide it, but the pressure of his hand on mine lessens too. I've disturbed him somehow. He leans back.

Maybe Matt has his own secrets hidden away.

"Tell me," I say.

His eyes don't quite meet mine when he says, "My father. He died in an accident. A few years back. I was ... there. Why do you ask?"

His father. How have I known this guy for weeks and not known that his father was died in an accident? Why haven't I asked him about his parents? Or did his evasiveness about growing up frustrate me enough on some level that I just stopped asking? Suddenly I'm second guessing myself—and wanting to trust even less.

And his question. Why do you ask? I pull back just a little. It's enough that he releases my hand. I reach for my Cosmo in an effort to hide my discomfort. I haven't had much to drink— just a few sips. This time I take a long one, the sweet liquor flooding my taste buds.

He waits for an answer. Finally I say, "I don't talk about the last few years much because in some ways they were just... I can't explain it to anyone who wasn't there."

"Wasn't where?"

"Iraq," I say. "I thought I could. I talked about it some with Chase."

He gives me a quizzical look.

"Chase... my ex-boyfriend. We dated for several months in Japan. Then he ditched me."

Matt winces. "Was he there? In Iraq?"

"No... and honestly, after a while, it seemed like he didn't want to hear about it anymore."

"Why, was it too... I don't get it. I'd listen to you always."

It's like a punch in the gut. We haven't made those kinds of declarations, and I'm not ready to. "Don't be an idiot, Matt. There's nothing there to talk about."

He raises a hand as if he were surrendering.

"It's okay," he says. "I didn't mean to make you uncomfortable."

Damn it. I look away, suddenly feeling tears in my eyes. The thing is, I do trust him. Jasmine does too. I know it's our first date, but I feel a crazy sort of happiness with him. "You didn't," I whisper. "I make myself uncomfortable."

Huh. My Cosmo is all gone. I didn't notice drinking it. He notices though, and waves down our waitress.

"Another cocktail?" she asks.

"Yes, please."

"Me too," Matt says. He's drinking beer, some local brew I haven't tried. Our dinner should be here soon, and I hope it's sooner than soon, because there's an uncomfortable silence after what I just said.

I sigh. "I enlisted in the Army right out of high school."

"Along with Nicole?" he asks.

"Yeah."

"Why?"

I stare at him with a blank face. Why? That was the million-dollar question. My mother asked me that, my father, my teachers. I remember Mom crying as she nearly begged me to go to college instead. I had a free ride at Mount Holyoke. I was accepted to Brown and Boston College and Carnegie Mellon. Why would I give all that up and join the Army instead? I finally say, "I didn't feel like I was ready for college. And … you know, my parents were academics. Or my Mom was before she started with the horses. That was her thing. He was a professor. They both wanted me to be them. But I didn't know what I wanted. It seemed like a chance to find out."

"Did you?"

"Did I what?"

He smiles. "Did you figure out what you wanted?"

I swallow. Then I slowly shake my head. "No. I still don't know any better than I did five years ago."

"What was the Army like?"

Our waitress arrives with another Cosmo.

Just in time, too.

I pause to take a drink, both because it buys me some time and because I'm getting a warm feeling throughout my upper body. I don't want to talk about this. I don't want to talk about it at all. I find myself blurting out words I hadn't intended to say. "Some of it was great. I loved living in Japan. But I also spent a year in Iraq. That was … awful."

"You said you were Military Police?"

I nod. "Yeah. But most of my tour in Iraq I was TDY."

He looks confused. His expression reminds me in an unfortunate way of Chase, who used to get annoyed whenever I used too much military terminology. Matt doesn't look annoyed, just confused. "TDY is temporary duty. I was assigned to 23rd Infantry Regiment. See, it's all men in the Infantry, but we were assigned to an area where we regularly had to kick in doors looking for insurgents and contraband. They needed women along on the patrols to search the female Iraqis."

"That must have been scary," he says.

I shake my head, which is pretty much the opposite of how I feel. "Sure. Scary sometimes. Dangerous. And … dehumanizing. In Tokyo, my job mostly involved controlling access to the barracks and periodically retrieving drunken soldiers from the local bars. In Iraq… you know, you can't imagine it. Kick in the doors of a house, you've got the adult men being tied up and searched, the women screaming, the children crying. And it goes on for a long time, and you're just hoping the whole time that you don't get attacked from the outside while you're in there. One time that happened… we're inside, shaking down this family, and insurgents opened fire on the place. Two of the kids were killed."

I close my eyes. His hand touches mine, a touch that is almost excruciating in its closeness. I don't want to feel vulnerable. I open my eyes and look in his.

"You don't have to talk about it if you don't want to," he says, looking me in the eyes. "If you need to, I'm here, and I'll listen."

I feel myself slurring my words as I say, "What makes you think I want to talk about it." I don't pull my hand back though, and that's strange.

He smirks, one side of his mouth rising higher than the other. "I don't know that you want to. But it's clear you need to. You're bottled up tighter than a drum."

"What about you?" I ask. "How is it I'm just finding out tonight that your father passed away?"

A flash of pain crosses his eyes, and I feel ashamed. I lost my own parents just a few weeks ago. Why poke at someone else's wounds?

He says, "I just don't like to talk about it."

"Fair enough," I say. "I don't much like talking about this stuff either. But there's one thing you need to know."

He raises both eyebrows in question.

"I don't put up with any bullshit. Ever. My last boyfriend cheated on me. You understand what I'm saying?"

"I understand he must have been a complete idiot."

I smile. "I think I like you, Matt."

He chuckles. "So what's next for you, anyway?"

I'm starting to hate that question. Really I am. I don't feel like I'm even beginning to be ready to formulate an answer beyond the next week or two. I intentionally restrict my answer to the immediate.

"Well, I've got Jasmine's guardianship hearing on Monday. Which I'm told is just a formality."

"Guardianship hearing?" he asks, cocking his head.

I nod. "When my parents were—when the accident happened—Jasmine was at summer day camp. No one came to
pick her up. They called my parents and couldn't get through,
of course. It took about 48 hours before word finally got to me
in Japan, and almost 48 more before I was home. Jasmine was
in an emergency shelter in the meantime. My parents' wills
didn't make any provision for custody, so the court has to ap-
prove me becoming her legal guardian."

He shook his head. "I had no idea. They couldn't … they
wouldn't take her from you, would they?"

"My attorney says there's no reason that should happen. And the guardian ad litem… that's a court appointee
who came out to ask me questions… she says she'll recommend
Jasmine stay with me."

I say all these words and mean them. I don't feel as confident as I sound. Beth Martin, the attorney Nicole recommend-
ed I get in touch with, has assured me there's absolutely no
reason for me to lose guardianship of Jasmine. All the same,
every time I think about it, I get an unfamiliar tight feeling in
my stomach. I never expected to be raising my sister, but now I
can't imagine doing anything else.

Love her smile (Matt)

"Come with me," Zoe demands as she stands to walk into
the courtroom. Jasmine, looking anxious, stands next to her.

"Of course," I say.

She grabs my hand, and the three of us walk into the court,
accompanied by Beth, her attorney. Beth is forty-five or so,
with a shock of short cropped, gray and white hair. She wears a
pale gray suit, and the whole effect would be drab except that
her eyes are the deepest blue I think I've ever seen. She prob-

ably weighs ninety pounds—at least she does when carrying her suitcase. Tiny, aggressive—she gives the impression of a ferret.

Zoe walks with her back perfectly straight, and her left hand is bunched into a fist. Her cheeks have a spot of color on them, and when we enter the room her eyes fix on the judge. I've never seen her this nervous.

Once the room is clear, the judge, a stern looking man with graying hair, says in a very casual tone, "Okay, let's get a look here. This is in the case of the petition for guardianship of one Jasmine Welch by her sister, Zoe Welch. Ms. Welch, are you represented by counsel?"

Beth Martin stands. "Beth Martin, your honor. I'm representing Miss Welch."

"Is the guardian ad litem present?"

A woman I haven't met before stands. She's tall, remarkably tall, and lanky, with dark brown skin. "Melanie Lamott, your honor. Department of Children and Family Services."

"Everyone have a seat please," the judge says. I star to take a seat at the back of the room, but Zoe grabs my hand and pushes me into the seat next to her.

The judge looks at Jasmine. "Jasmine… you've had a rough time. Do you understand why you are here?"

Jasmine nods.

"Can you explain it to me?" the judge asks patiently.

"You-you-you…" Her face screws up in frustration. Then a flood of words bursts past the block. "You're decided whether I can stay with my sister."

The judge nods. "That's right. Can you tell me how you feel about living with your sister?"

Jasmine squeezes Zoe's hand tighter. The squeezes her eyes shut and says, "Puh… puh… please let me stay? *Please?*"

The judge smiles at her, a kind expression on his face.

"Miss Lamott, I have the written report you've submitted. Do you have any comments to add to it?"

The woman shakes her head. "Only that I've met with Miss Welch, and I believe she'll be a fine guardian for her sister. It would be an injustice to separate the two of them."

Beside me, Zoe's left hand flies to her mouth and her eyes water, even as her right hand squeezes mine. I find myself letting out a breath. I hadn't realized I'd been holding it, just like Zoe. There was never any doubt. All the same... you never know with bureaucracy, right?

The judge responds to the guardian, saying, "Then you recommend an immediate custody order?"

"Yes, your honor."

The judge looks at Zoe. "You're young to suddenly become de-facto mother to an eight year old, but your service record is exemplary. I think you'll make a fine guardian, Miss Welch. I'm ordering that your sister continues to be in your care, and your application for guardianship is granted. Good luck."

I both pull Zoe and Jasmine to me in a tight hug. Zoe goes silent for a moment, then she bursts into tears.

"I don't know why I'm crying," she laughs.

Beth smiles and says, "Congratulations, Zoe."

Zoe's hold on me loosens, and we stand as we break apart from our hug. Suddenly Zoe looks sheepish, her eyes everywhere but on me. The hug was too close. I've never met a woman more nervous than her. I reach out and take her hand, and say, "Why don't we go have some lunch and celebrate."

Despite whatever reservations are still eating at her, she flashes me a delighted smile.

I love her smile.

We walk out of the courthouse hand in hand.

WHAT ABOUT SPIDERS? (ZOE)

We hurry out of the court. Even though everything went the way we wanted, the anxiety and stress has been tougher than I expected. Jasmine is swaying on her feet, and it's time to get her home. I'm grateful again that Matt came along and sat with us in the court. Especially now, because he lifts Jasmine up, and carries her out of the courthouse. She wraps her arms around his shoulders, and looks almost as if she might fall asleep.

"What do you say we go to lunch, Jasmine?" I try to keep the anxiety out of my voice as I asked the question. I thought I was calm before the hearing, but now I'm feeling incredibly shaky.

"What are we having?" She peeps up from Matt's shoulder.

"I was thinking about Antonio's."

Jasmine grins. The courthouse is in Northampton, not far from Amherst. We get in the car, across the river, and head to go get lunch.

We get stuck in traffic halfway across the bridge. It won't take long—traffic in the Pioneer Valley means a five-minute de-lay, not the hours it might take to drive somewhere in Tokyo. As we're sitting on the bridge waiting to move, I look up in the rearview mirror. Jasmine is sitting in her booster seat, and tears are streaming down her face.

"Jasmine?" As I say her name, she begins to sob. Matt wrenches around in his seat, his eyes widening.

"What's wrong?" His question comes out at the same time as mine. "Sweetie, what is it?"

"I—I—I —th—th—th… thought they were going to make me go back to the shelter. I was scared." Her crying becomes more forceful as she says the words. I feel a twist in my stomach. It never even crossed my mind that she was afraid that might happen.

How could I be so stupid? Of course she was afraid. Even I was afraid of that. I had lawyers and common sense and at least some knowledge of the law telling me that they weren't going to take her away from me. Even so I was afraid. Jasmine had none of that knowledge, she had nothing to reassure her.

What kind of a guardian am I going to be? When I can't even think of the most obvious problem?

Matt, twisted around in his seat, reaches back and takes her hand. "Kiddo, we would never let them take you away," he says. "Not even if dinosaurs were chasing us down and chomping on our feet."

It seems this is just the right thing to say, because she smirks. Then she asks, "what about spiders?"

"Not even spiders."

Now she has one eye closed, and a furrow appearing between her eyebrows. "What about... rats?"

"Rats don't bother me." He looks serene as he says the words.

"Snakes?"

"I eat snakes for dinner."

She giggles. "Beatles?"

Matt twists his mouth, and pauses, then gets a sly grin on his face. He shrugs. "Beatles, you're on your own."

Jasmine laughs.

In a more serious voice, but still warm, he asks, "You didn't like that shelter, did you?"

"I hated it. It's stupid."

Matt nods soberly. "I think so too. They should have let you sleep in the barn."

Traffic is moving now, so I have to look at the road. I can almost hear her eyes roll. She says, "That would have been fine. I could have slept with Mono."

He smiles and says, "You are a smart girl, Jasmine."

CHAPTER THIRTEEN

Come with Me. (Matt)

BY THE TIME I was in high school I'd filled out—I was no longer the scrawny runt who had jumped 500 times into the net as punishment for my father. The summer before my junior year, after a year of intense upper body training supervised by Papa, I'd begun catching. Well, in practice—I wouldn't start catching in the show until my senior year.

I should explain some things about being a catcher. It's not like being a catcher in baseball, where if you fail to catch the ball then you grab it and toss it back to the pitcher. If the catcher in a trapeze act misses, there's a good chance somebody's going to get hurt or killed.

The catcher is the base of the team… The person who everyone depends on for their very lives. The catcher has to be absolutely trustworthy. Not someone who screws around, or drinks, or goofs off on the ropes. Some of the most intense parts

of my training to become a catcher weren't in the ropes at all—
they were sitting at the kitchen table while Papa paced back
and forth lecturing. His hair was growing gray in those days,
but his teeth remained the same gleaming white exposed by his
grin whenever he jumped. During his night lectures, he had
an intense energy about him—it was impossible to look away.

"Your brother might have been a catcher, if he wasn't so
scrawny. And if he didn't screw around so much. Not you—
you, Matty—you will be the catcher of the family."

And so, the spring and summer before my junior year in
high school we toured. For the first time I had an actual role in
the family's act. Papa had put me in a real role, a role of intense
responsibility. We practiced every morning for hours, breaking
in the early afternoon to rest up before we went in the ring.
Then I performed with the family. If I continued to do well in
the ring, and in practice, then I would begin catching during
the show the year after.

I hadn't spoken with Carlina since that awful day in Middle School—not until three days before my 16th birthday.

It was August and we were somewhere in Tennessee. Jackson I think. I'm not ashamed to say I was hiding out—that
morning I'd received an intense tongue-lashing from my father
for some offense or other, and I'd taken my Nintendo DS—
I'd won it in a raffle—to go sit in the very top of the stands,
alone. I slumped down into the seat and stayed out of sight.

I might have missed the sound if I hadn't lost my earbuds
a few days earlier. As it was, I just kept the volume down low
so no one would notice me up there. In the center ring, Frank
and Marina Kurtz were practicing the partner adagio. Along
with the Flying Paladinos, they were one of the star acts, and
the audience always hushed in awe at the beautiful dance.

During practice it wasn't so beautiful. With no music playing, and the sound of their coach simultaneously counting and

clapping his hands in rhythm, it was clear that this was a grueling, difficult act. I'd seen it hundreds of times, but even I paused the game to watch as they began their final round of practice.

That's when I heard the sound of someone crying. Muffled, but clear enough to identify.

I sat up in my seat and looked around. I couldn't see anyone nearby. So I stood, stretching up on my toes. Then I saw her.

It was unmistakably Carlina, even though she was curled up in a seat, face to her knees, not many rows below and one section over from me. She must have come up here—like I had—to be alone, and almost certainly hadn't seen me.

For almost two minutes I stood there frozen.

Normally my instinct if I saw any girl crying would be to offer help and assistance. But even though several years had passed, I still remembered the sting of being dumped for Red. I still remembered the misery of sitting at the diner during the dance. Carlina had been... cruel. Looking back, there's no way she didn't know how infatuated I had been with her. Why did she string me along for so long? Maybe if Red hadn't shown up, it might have happened. No way to answer those questions. I didn't know Carlina at all.

I wanted to believe that I was over her, but Carlina was the sun I revolved around through my adolescence.

I slipped through the stands until I came to a crouch next to the weeping girl. This was the closest I had been to her since middle school... Now she was seventeen and astonishingly beautiful. Without thinking I put my left hand on her knee and said, "Hey. What's wrong?"

She jerked at the touch, raising her face up and staring at me wildly. "How did you know I was here? Were you spying on me?"

The question didn't make any sense. Why would anyone be spying on her? I shrugged it off. "I was up here myself. Sometimes I need some quiet and to get away from my family."

"Leave me alone," she said. Tears were still streaming down her face.

Was I always going to let her stab me in the heart? "All right, if that's what you want. I was just checking to see if you were alright." I stood up, intending to walk away and never look back. I made it four steps.

"Matt. Please... I'm sorry. Don't go."

I didn't turn around right away, because I didn't dare let Carlina see my face. Because the rush of emotions that went through me was a storm of confusion, joy, vindication and hope. I took two seconds to compose myself and turned around.

I didn't know what to make of her expression. Grief stricken? I took a step back toward her. "Tell me what's wrong, Carlina."

Her eyes started to water again. "Red... He..."

I tried to suppress the immediate feeling of anger and disgust.

"I broke up with him."

I knelt back down, facing her next to the row of seats. "If you broke up with him, why are you crying?"

She shrugged, her face a picture of misery. "He's an ass. I should have dumped him two years ago."

I wasn't going to argue with that. What did I know? I'd never had a girlfriend. I'd never kissed a girl. I'd never even been out on a date. This freakish life limited my circle of acquaintances to less than half a dozen girls even remotely near my age. None of them had ever interested me... except her. None of them meant anything. So I didn't know anything about relationships, or why a girl might break up with a guy and cry about it the same day. I did know that I wasn't going to let myself get sucked into her orbit again, only to flame out and crash. I'd be her friend if that's what she needed, but nothing more.

So I did something that seemed the right thing to do. I reached out and took her hands, placing them between mine. Then I permanently put myself in the friend zone. "It's okay. You can talk about it with me."

With that, Carlina began to unravel a tale of white trash soap opera bullshit. She'd thrown herself at a bad boy, and he turned around and acted just like what he was. He'd slept around behind her back, and when she confronted him about it, he shoved her and walked away.

"I was such an idiot. I chased after him. I told him I forgave him. I made him promise to never do it again, but I knew in my heart that that's who he is. He did it again, and I went back anyway."

I shook my head. "I don't understand. Why would you go back to somebody who treated you badly?"

She looked hopelessly confused at the question. She moaned the answer, "I don't know." Then she started to cry again.

I'm physically not capable of ignoring when a girl cries. My mother taught me to take care of women like they were more precious than diamonds. So I did the only thing I could. I put my arms around her and let her cry.

And that's how my junior year of high school began. I promised myself I wouldn't fall for Carlina again. All the same, I began to spend most of my non-working hours with her. I would meet her in the afternoons after practice, and we would sit near the paddock watching the trick riders practice under her father's tutelage. For a while, Red kept his distance. I knew better than to think that problems with him were over. Three or four times over those few weeks, I saw him hanging around the lot glaring at Carlina and sometimes me. In mid-September we had a week long hiatus. At the time, we weren't far from Louisville, Kentucky, though I can't remember the name of the town. Being stopped in camp didn't stop our normal practice hours, of course. However, it did mean we weren't spending time setting up or breaking down camp, moving, or doing shows in the evenings. I found myself with an unusually large amount of free time.

I spent all of the time that I could with Carlina. I was stunned the first time I saw her jumping from one side of the horse, bouncing on the saddle, then down to the other side as the horse galloped at full speed. It looked terrifying.

That day she rode back up to the fence, reined her horse in and said, "You want to learn how?"

And that's how I learned to ride. As the remainder of the fall continued, I spent afternoons learning how to saddle the horses, how to groom them, how to canter, trot and gallop.

It was a fantastic time. Carlina's father Nick, who trained the trick riders, said I was a natural. He was helpful and seemed pleased by Red's absence. "Call me Nick," he said, clapping me on the shoulder on the third day I was around.

The next few weeks, every waking moment when I wasn't practicing was spent with Carlina and Nick. I learned to ride, pleased by Nick's encouragement and comments that I was a natural rider. By the end of the third week, he began to teach me some basic tricks—how to ride facing backward, how to drop to the ground while the horse was moving, then regain the saddle. It was exhilarating.

I'd been in the rigging all my life, and I'd been doing increasingly complicated stunts in the last year or two. But catching—it was … boring. Not like Papa, who was famous for being the first aerialist to ever perform a quadruple. He did it in 1982, and the feat had made headlines all over the world. And no one would ever let me forget that he'd done it when he was seventeen—the same age I was now. Papa had never suggested I even try such things. It was Tony and Messalina he taught the acrobatics—I was to be a catcher. No one ever asked if that's what I wanted to do. He simply pronounced it one day, the way he pronounced everything as word from on high, not to be argued with or trifled with.

My whole childhood I'd dreamed of being like my father. And he wouldn't even let me try.

So learning to ride was—fun. It was exciting. And, probably more than anything else, it wasn't under Papa's watchful eyes, it was free, it was something I was doing.

And there was Carlina.

I loved watching her. When she rode, the curve of her hips and butt, the arch of her back, her hair flying out behind her. I loved seeing her teeth shine when she smiled and looked over her shoulder at me. I loved when we laughed together. I loved every moment we spent together, so much so that I ignored all the warning signs.

I was as happy as I'd ever been. But it wasn't to last.

It came to an end on a Sunday evening close to the end of the season.

The circus was nearly packed up, everything on the truck beds and ready to go first thing in the morning. Our last show had been at 5 p.m. that afternoon and we would be departing before sunrise.

That night, I had eaten dinner with Carlina and Nick. It was very different from dinner in our trailer. For one thing, Carlina and her dad had an entire trailer to themselves. It wasn't as large as ours, but even so it was far less crowded. Carlina actually had her own bedroom.   She cooked the dinner, a meaty lasagna. As we sat down to eat, her father had his first drink of the night—a straight up shot of gin. It wouldn't be his last.

I found the drinking to be a little scandalous. Because timing and coordination were so important on the trapeze, no one in my family ever drank except on Christmas or other major holidays when there was no practice. Horror stories abounded of aerialists families who had suffered major tragedies because of a single drink.

Of course there was no reason for Nick not to drink… He was the trainer for the trick riders, but he would never get in the saddle again. I tried to imagine how I would feel if I could never get on the trapeze again… I couldn't imagine. Plus, except for his daughter, he was alone—I never got the whole story of where Carlina's mother was, because they didn't know.

Maybe I would drink too much too, if I were in his shoes.

After dinner, we'd gone back out to the paddock. I didn't have practice that night, so there was no reason I had to go right away. We rode for a solid hour, practicing dismounting and mounting while at a canter.

I was sweaty, exhausted and happy when we returned to the gate.

My father stood there, a storm on his face. The second I saw him, my stomach lurched.

"Matty. Come with me." I felt queasy. I didn't know what was wrong. The anger in his tone made me afraid.

I slid out of the saddle and to the ground. A small cloud of dust raised to the air when my feet touched down. "I need to help put the horses —"

"You'll come now." His tone brooked no argument.

Carlina looked troubled. "I can take care of the horses, Matt."

I swallowed, fearing the worst. I followed my father as he stomped away.

DON'T YOU KNOW THAT'S DANGEROUS?

(MATT)

You'll come with me.

Those words marked the beginning of the war between me and my father.

I know that it's a little bit of a cliché. Young man, extending his boundaries; conflict with father who wants to keep him under control. It's the subject of a thousand plays and novels, it's the core of every good coming of age story (well, the ones about boys anyway). All of that is because there's a certain core truth to it. We read it in stories and believe because it reflects and is shaped by the reality we see every day.

In my case, Carlina was secondary to the conflict. It was all about the rigging and the spotlight, it was all about Papa being the star of the circus and wanting his children to continue that, it was all about his expectation and his pride.

As we walked back to the trailer that day, Papa didn't say a word. I could tell how angry he was, because I had trouble keeping up with him. His back was rigid in an unnatural way and occasionally the side of his neck twitched. I followed along, just to his right and one step behind, waiting for the moment he exploded. He turned on me just as we reached our trailer.

"Matty. You've been learning trick riding." The words shot out one at a time, equally emphasized, each of them angry in its own way.

I swallowed. "In my free time. I've been doing my practice and chores and school."

"You'll stop today." He phrased it is a simple statement of fact. But I was done being pushed around. I was done having Papa tell me what to do, when to do it, and how to do it.

"I'm not quitting."

"You defy me? While you live under my roof, you do as I say!" Papa punctuated each word with a finger pointing at my chest. The last four words this finger made contact, pushing me back a few inches.

"Papa, I'm at practice every day. I'm never sick. I never tell you I'm too tired. Every day I work hard for the family. Why won't you let me have something for me?"

His nostrils flare, and he shouts, "And what will I do when you break your stupid neck jumping off of a horse? Don't you know that's dangerous?"

He couldn't possibly be serious. The first person to ever do a quadruple somersault in the air, setting an extremely dangerous world record when he was 17 years old, was telling me that riding an old horse was too dangerous?

"And flying through the air isn't? Do you think I'm immune to getting hurt up there?"

His face flushed. "At least I can control safety up there. Nobody defies me up there. I won't lose another family member. Not on my watch, young man."

Bitterly, I spit out my response. "Your caution didn't save Uncle Mario from being crippled." I turn away from him and began walking away. He grabbed my shoulder.

"You think I don't know that? Don't you think maybe I see my brother falling to the ground every night when I try to sleep? You've never lost a family member right there in front of your eyes, Matty. You don't know what you're talking about."

I shrug away from him and step back. I know better than to bring that up. In August 1996, just a few months after the Flying Paladinos were covered in Life Magazine, the family suffered a horrible tragedy. During a performance in Nashville, Dad's brother and his wife hit the wrong way and went careening to the ground. Ordinarily the worst they would have suffered might have been some bruises and rope burns, but the safety net failed; she was killed and Mario crippled. I barely remember the accident and the aftermath—I was still very young when the family was in its heyday.

I veered away from that subject and just responded quietly, "I'm not quitting Papa."

He takes a deep breath, as if trying to calm himself. "It's that girl isn't it? The one who dumped you right before the dance."

I wouldn't have been more staggered if he had thrown a bucket of ice water on me. He knew that she'd blown me off? He knew that I hadn't gone to the dance? All that time ago? I didn't understand. I didn't understand him at all. For the first time in this discussion— for the first time in a couple of years— I felt myself wanting to cry. "You knew? Why didn't you say anything?"

Papa's shoulders sagged, a deflated balloon, all the anger flowing out of him in a rush of air. "Matty," he said in a low tone. "We could see how bad you were hurt. I didn't want to make it worse for you."

I didn't understand him. All the anger was gone out of me too, replaced with a roiling sea of confusion. "Papa, please. Please don't make me quit."

He sighed, looked up at the sky, and muttered, "Jesus, Joseph, and Mary." He looked back at me. "Fine. Keep risking your neck. But don't let it interfere with school or your practice. You're shaping up to be the best catcher this family ever had, Matty. That may not matter to you, but it does to me. It does to your grandfather and great-grandfather, looking down on you from heaven."

Aggravated all over again, I sighed. He's got to bring in the ancestors, he's got to lay on the guilt. Whatever. I had gotten what I was asking for. "I won't, Papa. I promise."

I kept my promise. There were two weeks left of the touring season before we returned to Florida, and during that time every day after practice I walked to Carlina's and we rode together. I kept up with my chores, with my school work, and almost every night performed with the family. Then I would collapse into a deep dreamless sleep.

***

The last day of our tour for the season was a few weeks before Thanksgiving in Tuscaloosa Alabama. It was late afternoon when Carlina and I had finished riding, grooming the horses and led them to their cars. As we walked out of the second car, she touched my sleeve.

"Matt. Wait…"

I stopped. I was intensely conscious of her proximity, just inches away in the cramped space. Her fingertips touched my sleeve, and the space between us seemed to shrink even more. "I just wanted to say thank you… For spending so much time looking out for me."

As I looked into her seemingly huge eyes, I wanted nothing more at that moment than to kiss her. "I've loved every second we spent together."

"Me too," she whispered.

I leaned forward in what seemed like slow motion. My lips brushed against hers. I'd never kissed a girl before. The sensation was an epiphany. Her lips were supple and warm, and as the moment extended I instinctively put my hands on her waist. Her lips parted, just barely, and her eyes closed. The moment was magic… And fleeting.

She pulled away from me. "I've got to go." Her voice was rough.

I opened my mouth to respond, but she turned away and half ran to her father's trailer.

I stood there for a long time listening to the crickets and bullfrogs with their ringing song. All of my attention was focused on the memory of that kiss, the shock of the sudden separation and her running away. I was buffeted by confusion.

Eventually I turned and began walking across the lot, back to my parent's trailer.

***

Tom Neighbors, the general manager for the circus, had a zero tolerance policy for fighting. People had been ruined by fighting on the lot—sometimes docked half a month's pay, others suspended or even fired. So I had been fairly confident as I went about my day-to-day business that I wouldn't have to worry about Red coming after me.

I was as wrong as I could be.

The attack that night came out of nowhere. I was halfway across the lot when a crushing blow hit the back of my head and my vision went black. I staggered to my knees as my vision came back, just in time for Red to kick me in the stomach. I fell backward, the pain excruciating, and before I could recover he aimed another kick. I screamed and curled into a fetal position. I was in good shape from years of swinging on the rigging, and practicing as a catcher had forced me to develop a lot of upper body strength. Red attacked me by surprise and put me down before I had a chance to do anything.

He kicked me -- once, twice, a third time, before I could roll away, scrambling to get on my feet. Just as I got up, I heard someone shout.

"Hey! Who's fighting?"

Someone was approaching in the darkness. Red gave me a vicious look, then turned and ran. I sagged, falling to a crouch and letting my elbows rest on my knees. I felt nauseous. Rory Nelson, one of the circus handlers, approached. When he saw me, he leaned close and said, "Matt? Are you okay?"

I nodded slowly. "Yeah." My voice came out as not much more than a growl.

"Who was that? You know they don't tolerate fighting on the lot."

I shook my head. Instinctively, I kept my mouth shut. "He hit me from behind. I don't know who it was."

Why didn't I identify Red on the spot? I didn't owe him anything. I think maybe I had an idea I would be the one to dish out punishment to him. Whatever it was, instinct, natural cussedness, I don't know. But I came to regret it.

"You sure you're not hurt?"

"Yeah, I'm fine." I wasn't, but I didn't want any trouble. I stood up, carefully hiding the pain in my ribs.

"If you're sure," he said.

"I am." Then I turned to walk to my family's trailer.

***

I didn't see Red again that year. I don't know where he and his father went for the winter, and I didn't care. I was glad he wasn't in Florida.

It was Carlina's senior year in high school and my junior year. As it often was, the first two weeks back were a scramble to catch up so we had some idea of what was going on. We were in different grades, but we ended up taking two classes together, economics and drama. I was thrilled... We were the only circus kids in either class, so it was natural for us to spend time studying together.

Papa and I were at a stalemate. I continued to ride whenever I could with Carlina, but practiced with the family every night. It was grueling, but I knew if I slacked even in the slightest, Papa would forbid me to see her. Late fall faded into a frigid winter, with temperatures plunging into the twenties, the frost killing off large swatch of orange groves. Dad grumbled for days about having to buy winter coats for all of us—he grumbled, but of course he did it. When March came, we were back on the road.

Carlina and I continued to spend time with each other, but by July, it was clear something was wrong. I showed up one day to ride and she wasn't there—and no one could tell me where she was.

The next day, same story.

On the third day I found her as she walked across the lot toward the main ticket booths.

She was walking with Red.

I approached, feeling my body and lips go stiff. Her eyes widened. Red crossed his arms over his chest.

"Carlina..." I couldn't continue the sentence. I didn't know what to say.

"Go away." Red's words were pugnacious.

"No... this is between me and her," I said.

Tears started to run down her face. "Matt—I'm sorry... just let it go. I don't love you, I never did."

It was like she'd reached into my insides, grabbed ahold of my guts and twisted. I almost gasped. Red approached me closer. "Go away, little runt," he said.

I'd been trained from an early age to keep a hold of my temper. Papa didn't tolerate fighting or emotional outbursts. But this set me off. Without a second thought I let out a yell and punched Red in the face.

I felt his nose crumple under my first and he fell back, yelling in pain. I hit him with another blow to the face, then another, before he began to recover. Carlina screamed, "Matt, no!"

That just stoked the rage even more. Red had pushed me around and bullied me for years. He'd treated her like crap too, and now she was going back to him. I charged him, throwing punch after punch at his midsection. He doubled over and I kneed him in the face.

Red went down just as two of the pitchmen grabbed me, holding me in place. I struggled to get away from them as Red rolled away from us. Carlina was crying, and Red got up even as the two men started to lose their grip. They didn't lose their grip quickly enough—he charged, knocking me off balance and out of the arms of the pitchmen. I tripped over a generator and fell backward, narrowly avoiding hitting my skull on the pavement. Now the pitchmen were holding him.

I staggered to my feet.

"I'll kill you," Red shouted. "You. Are. Dead."

I just shook my head.

An hour later, both of us were standing with our fathers as Tom Neighbors, the general manager, dressed them down for not keeping us under control.

"This is your only warning, and I'm only giving you that because you're still a kid," he said, pointing a finger at me. "I don't care if your father could levitate up to the bar. You don't fight on my lot, understand?"

I nodded. "Yes, sir."

He repeated a similar warning to Red.

All I could see was Carlina. Crying. *Why was I so stupid? Why didn't I see it?*

***

A week later, I'd finally reached the point I couldn't handle it any longer. I'd spent days doing nothing but the trapeze and sleeping. I had to know. Why?

But when I went to the paddock, her father's trailer wasn't there.

What the hell? Urgently, I began to search around. Everything was as it should be in the area—except the missing trailer. I ran over to the paddock and shouted to one of the riders. "Where's Nick? Carlina?"

The rider shrugged. "Gone. Nick was fired."

"What?"

He shrugged again.

Fired. What the hell? He'd been with the circus forever.

Then the suspicion began to rise. My dad knew the fight with Red was over Carlina. He knew it.

I began to run back to our trailer.

***

I arrived just as Papa came out of the trailer, followed by Mamma. They were preparing to head to the arena for the show.

"What did you do?" I shouted. "She's gone!"

Papa's face twisted in anger. "And good riddance!" he shouted. "She's a whore! She used you then went back to that shit-for-brains Red. Her father was a drunk who was stealing!"

"That's not true!"

He grabbed my shoulders. "Matty, get a hold of yourself!"

"You had him fired!" My accusation rang out across the lot. A small crowd was forming.

"I did no such thing," Papa shouted. "Now get yourself under control. We have a show."

"Screw the show!" I shouted. "I don't want to be in your stupid show any more."

"Matty!" Mamma's voice was shocked.

Papa slapped me across the face. I was stunned, immediately shocked into quiet. I heard murmuring around us.

"I wish I wasn't your son," I said. My tone was bitter. "I wish you were dead."

He looked at me and shook his head, a gesture of dismissal. "We'll talk after the show. Go get yourself dressed."

He turned and walked away.

Those words were the last we ever spoke to each other.

CHAPTER FOURTEEN

CHUMMY, AREN'T THEY (MATT)

THE BEGINNING OF the meeting is almost a replay of the last one. Peggy Young is there first—I think she'll likely be early to her own funeral. She wears a flowered dress which was probably in style in the 1960s, but who cares about that? The important thing is that she is a tough old bird. When I arrive, she's standing in the administrative office on the third floor of the town hall, where the school department is headquartered.

Tyler shows up right behind me, then Dianne Blakely, who gives me a death glare as she breezes past the secretaries and walks straight into the superintendent's office without knocking.

"Chummy, aren't they?" Peggy observes.

"Huh," Tyler says.

"It pays to give these sorts of things attention," she says. Then she winks.

Tyler grins. If she wasn't 50 years older than he is, I think he'd be in love. We spend a few minutes talking strategy about the upcoming meeting, but we quiet as we hear footsteps coming up the stairs. It's Susan Greeley, the most reasonable of the school committee members. Her shoulder length blonde hair is done up in tiny ringlets, and she's wearing a sleeveless, formfitting burgundy dress. If it wasn't for the wedding ring, I would think she was out for a date.

"How are you all doing?" She looks perfectly friendly when she asks the question.

Of course it's Tyler who answers. Susan may be a couple of years older than he is, and married, but Tyler is still Tyler. "I think we'll all be doing a lot better when the strike is all over. We should make a deal today and go out for drinks and celebrate."

"You're right, we should. You all can come back to my place, and meet my husband. He loves to mix martinis."

Tyler sags like a slowly deflating basketball.

The office door opens, and Michael Barrington, the superintendent, waves. "Come in, everyone. I didn't realize you were waiting out here."

I'm sure he didn't. Peggy looks as if she's just sucked on a lemon.

Two minutes later we're all sitting around the table again. Barrington says, "Thank you all for coming today. Before we discuss the terms of our revised offer to the union, I need to make a couple of comments."

Peggy and I meet each other's eyes. New proposal. That's good news.

"As you all know, it's a violation of the law for the teachers union to strike. We're going to make a new proposal in an effort to resolve this issue, but I want to be clear that we intend to pursue legal action against the union. As you know, the last strike in the state, by the teachers union in Cambridge, resulted in a several hundred thousand dollars fine against the union."

I find it interesting that he opens the negotiation with threats. Everyone in the union is aware of the Cambridge strike and the fines that the teacher's union had to pay. That was part of the discussion we had in the first place, and we made a decision to go ahead because of the principle. All I can guess is that he's looking for a stronger bargaining position.

"That said, the committee and the town selectmen feel it's urgent to get the doors open again in the school system. We are prepared to make a compromise proposal. Are you ready to hear it?" At our nods, he continues. "First, the issue of the department heads. Our proposal is that we can proceed with eliminating the department head positions and replace them with curriculum coordinators as planned. However, we will do so by attrition—when a department head retires, only then will the position be eliminated. We will then allow the schools to examine the impact for two years, and revisit it the end of the two-year period."

Barrington continues with the details of the counterproposal. The school system would split the difference between what the union asked for, and zero, which was what the school committee had originally proposed. Health insurance premiums would still increase, but the school system would pick up an additional 15% of that increase.

Peggy, Tyler and I all maintain poker faces. Any proposal would have to be taken back to the union anyway, but I suspect that this compromise proposal will do the trick.

"The final change in our counter proposal addresses disciplinary procedures," Barrington says. "I think you all know that we've had some concerns about continued bullying at the high school. The anti-bullying task force made several recommendations earlier this year which addressed the need for more accountability on the faculty and staff. The committee has agreed that any new offer to the union must include these provisions."

Diane Blakely passes out the report from the anti-bullying task force. I'm familiar with the recommendations already, and I don't think there will be any issues as far as the union is concerned. Essentially what the proposal does is allows the superintendent's office to directly address issues in the classroom when the education or safety of a child is involved. The language is overly broad, but I think it will likely go through. I don't say anything, though. We'll let the union address that when it meets.

"I'd like to see more specific language in that provision," Peggy says. "It will be difficult to make a recommendation to the union when it's so open ended."

Barrington frowns. "In principle I agree, Peggy. In practice, we need to get the kids back in school. I think we can fine tune the language over time."

Peggy looks at him skeptically. "I don't see any reason why we can't get the language sorted out now."

Barrington almost rolls his eyes, and his impatience is visible. The sinks back into his seat. "What   are you looking for here?"

"We need some specifics. Under what circumstances does the superintendent's office get involved?"

Susan Greeley speaks in an annoyed sort of whiny tone. "It's for bullying."

"We know what it's for," Peggy says. "If it is for bullying, then there's no reason we can't be very specific about the language. As it stands, the wording in the proposal gives the superintendent's office carte blanche to intervene in any disciplinary matter. That's always been in the hands of the school principals, not the district."

Blakely and Barrington look at each other. Her expression is one of annoyance. Barrington shrugs. "I don't have any problem with revising the language," he says.

"Then let's get started." Peggy's tone allows for no defiance.

The process of going over the school committee's proposal is slow. All of us want to get back to work, so we go through it one sentence at a time. Peggy's insistent, and the more she raises potential scenarios, the more I think she's correct.

Despite everything, I feel like we are making solid progress. Shortly before we break for lunch, I have a moment that takes me aback.

Tyler makes a sarcastic comment about how the teachers will be grateful to me, because there would have been no strike without me and Peggy. Peggy mutters something, I don't know what. But for the barest second, the superintendent looks at me with naked malice. It's over so quick I doubt whether I ever saw it; his face shifts back into politician mode. It's disturbing. It's almost four in the afternoon when we finally wrap it up. The proposal is ready, we've all agreed on it, and now it merely needs to be submitted to the union for a vote.

The meeting breaks up, all of us coming to our feet. Tyler stretches and Susan says, "I've got to be going. The babysitters were expecting me home more than an hour ago." We all shake hands with her and begin to disperse. Downstairs and out the front door, Peggy stops me and Tyler. "That Michael is up to something," she says.

"What do you mean?" Tyler looks confused when he asks the question.

"It's out of character for him to give up this easily," she says. "Michael Barrington isn't a smart man. But he is one to carry a grudge. Matt, you and Tyler keep in touch with me."

A few minutes later in the car, Tyler sums up his feelings about Peggy. "I can't decide if that old bat is crazy or brilliant. Her warning made my skin crawl."

He's not the only one. Not only does the thought creep me out, but I suspect she's right. Barrington's already got a bad reputation within the school system, and he's been in office just a year. Let's hope he doesn't take out his resentments on us. "I think we ought to be careful, Tyler."

"You ain't kidding."

It's almost 5 o'clock when I get back home. I'm tired. Emotionally tired. I want the strike over, but I also can't help but wonder … what happens with me and Zoe when it's over? Over the last two weeks we've spent a lot of time together. Time that has meant a lot to me, and I don't want to give that up.

I should call her right now. I reach for the phone—I'm probably one of the few people left in America with a land-line—but before I can pick it up and dial, it rings.

Dammit! "Hello?"

"Matt? It's Messalina."

"Hey…" As always, I feel wary when my family calls.

"We got into Boston last night. I thought I should let you know."

"How's Mom?"

"She keeps saying that she's wondering if you're going to visit."

Lina lets the words hang there for a moment. I don't take the bait.

She continues. "Tony says you're not going to."

"What does Tony know?" I'm annoyed. And the annoying thing is that she knows her statement will annoy me.

"Does that mean you'll come?"

"Yeah. I'll come." The words come out of my mouth, but I instantly regret them.

It would be easy to make the excuse that my family's unconventional. And we don't observe the same conventions everyone else does. That we're eclectic, eccentric, maybe a little odd. None of that approximates the truth. In fact, we're inconsiderate of each other. Lina and I hang up without any of the normal courtesies such as saying goodbye.

HOW WOULD YOU KNOW (ZOE)

I let out a long sigh, then lean on the table, resting my forehead on my calculus textbook. Jasmine is in the bath. She needs it—she spent the entire day at Paul Armstrong's farm, taking lessons, but also assisting Paul with the other children. Jasmine's that good of a rider.

If only I was that good at calculus. Unfortunately, I don't get it at all. I stare at the textbook, I read the examples, I work the problems, and none of it makes the slightest bit of sense. I want to break something, I'm so frustrated.

Upstairs, Jasmine is thumping around and splashing in the bathtub. The tub is made out of metal, and the reverberations of toys banging against it sound throughout the house. Every once in a while, I can hear her singing. Mostly the pop songs that were hot through the summer, although sometimes she breaks into *Old McDonald Had a Farm*.

It's not too late for me to drop this class. I could take College Algebra instead, or even Math for Liberal Arts Majors or whatever they call it. Of course if I do that, I can forget about a sciences degree. Not that I've decided what I want to do, but I don't want to rule anything out. Not this early.

If I can't learn calculus, maybe I'm just not cut out for that kind of work.

I open up my laptop, and Google "calculus tutorial video," and check the results. There are quite a few. I navigate to the first one, and begin watching. I'm concentrating so hard, I don't hear the knock on the door. Of course, that's probably because Nicole knocks once, then just opens the door up.

"Hello!" she calls.

"I'm in here," I call back.

She wanders into the kitchen. She's still in uniform. "Hey, I just got off work a little while ago and thought I'd come by and see how you guys are doing."

I sit back in my seat. "You want a drink? Jasmine's in the bath, and I'm busy melting my brain."

Nicole tilts her head to look at the cover of my book, then twist her lips up. "Ugh, calculus.",

"It's evil. I'll be lucky if I pass."

"Really?" she asks. "I would've thought you'd have this stuff aced."

I shake my head. "I feel like such an idiot. It's not just the math. It's all of it. I don't remember how to do this stuff. I've got to write papers next week, this stupid book of poetry is giving me a headache, and calculus might as well be Greek. I don't know what I'm going to do."

"Have you checked into a tutor?"

I shake my head. "I don't have time for a tutor. I'll see what I can find online. Sometimes I think my dad was right, and I just wasted my life in the Army."

Nicole looks startled. Then her face shifts a little, she's incredulous. "I can't even imagine what you mean. Your dad didn't think that."

Maybe it's because this is a sore point. Maybe it's because I've spent so much time carrying it through my mind, so much regret that we were never able to clear the air. Her comment makes me feel a flash of anger.

"I think I know what I went through with my dad," I say.

"Zoe, most of the time you're right about people. But on this, you couldn't be more wrong."

I frown. "What are you trying to do, Nicole? I was pretty much at peace with it. I can't argue about this. You have no idea how awful it felt to know that my parents thought I was a failure."

"They didn't think that!" She says, her voice rising a little bit.

I stand up, walk to the cabinet and pull out two glasses. I fill them up with ice, tonic water, then a shot of vodka in each. I pass her one of the glasses. "I don't want to talk about this anymore. It's pissing me off."

Nicole shakes her head. "That's fine, but I'm telling you, you're wrong. Your dad never thought that."

Jasmine's voice comes from the doorway. "Never thought what?"

Damn it! Jasmine is standing there in her pajamas, her hair still pretty wet. I guess me and Nicole were so busy talking, I never even heard her getting out of the bath. Or I just wasn't paying enough attention.

"Don't worry about it Jasmine, it's something for adults."

"You're arguing about Dad," she says. "I want to know what it is."

"Jasmine…" Nicole leans forward. "It's okay, Jasmine. It isn't anything that involves you."

"I don't believe you," Jasmine says.

Another flash of anger. It's not any of her business. I don't care if she's eight. "Dad was mad at me for being in the Army," I say. "That's what we were arguing about. Nicole says that wasn't true."

"It's not," Jasmine says.

I sigh in frustration. "How would you know?"

"Because you're the only thing he ever talked about," she says, anger in her voice.

I shake my head in confusion. "Can we just drop it please?"

"Zoe…"

I almost growl in frustration at Nicole's word.

"*Please*. Can we just drop it?"

CHAPTER FIFTEEN

Papa, Come Back (Matt)

WHEN I GET in the car to drive to Boston, my eyelids feel heavy. I'm dragging.

It's because I didn't sleep well last night. I knew I would be taking this drive, and there's too much history, too much emotion, too much... everything... for me to take it lightly.

I've been having the dream a lot lately, especially since Lina showed up without warning. It's always the same, the smell, the noise, the moment when his hands begin to slip.

I blink and turn up the music in the car, trying to shut out the memory. How am I supposed to shut it out?

It all happened too quickly for me to ever understand or grasp. One minute Dad was flying through the air, on his fourth forward somersault, arms outstretched. My arms were braced, ready for him, and we locked our arms together. There was always that moment of panic when he was coming through the air. Was I strong enough to catch him? Would I slip, would one of us fall? It's not like it didn't happen. We observed all the safety rules, and Dad was a strict disciplinarian. You didn't screw around on the ropes, ever.

All the same, my uncle Mario was crippled in the same accident that killed his wife twenty years ago. A moment's inattention, or maybe just too much sweat on the catcher's palms—it doesn't matter how it happens. So Papa was rigid about safety.

That day, despite our earlier argument, everything was golden. Our hands came together in locked firmly, and dad looked into my eyes with the fiercest grin on his face. He always had that expression when he completed the jump. It's not like he didn't do them every day, his entire life was one long death-defying act. All the same, every single time he landed, his lips would roll back, his teeth glimmering light in my face.

As always we swung back, the pendulum force taking me and my father almost parallel to the ground. In that position as the catcher, I was upside down, my back facing straight to the ground, even as my father's stomach was to the ground. Our timing was perfect that day. We reached the top of the pendulum and started to swing back. It's difficult to describe the sensation, of swinging upside down and backwards so high from the ground in the dark, so quickly, while holding another human being. There's something remarkable about it. There's also something terrifying about it. You know where everyone is—there's no surprises—but all the same, if there was some obstruction in the way there would be nothing that could be done about it.

Of course it wasn't that. Nothing so simple that can be pointed to, like a dangling wire, or any other obvious issue. Instead, I just felt his hands release. We were at just about two-thirds of the way through our swing when it happened, when he started to let go, too early for his release. I couldn't tell what was happening – he still had the fierce grin on his face, but something was so obviously wrong, because he was letting go too soon and instead of a controlled back somersault out of my hands and back to the bar, it was a sickening slide as I began to lose my grip. We reached three quarters around the swing, and now he was completely sliding out of my grasp. I struggled as hard as I could but the centrifugal force was too strong. As we reached the apex of the swing I lost my grip and my father's already limp body went flying off into space.

I remember the gasp of the crowd, the anticipatory horror and shock of not knowing whether there had been an accident or if this was part of the act, but that ended very quickly. Before my father even hit the ring, I released my legs and fell straight to the net, evoking loud screams from the audience. I bounced in the net, rolled to the edge and swung down. It was too late. My father didn't reach the net—instead he went well beyond that, hitting the apron net like a limp sack, then falling to the floor of the arena.

Everything else that night is a haze. I was hysterical, and charged through the crowd to my father. I remember screaming, *"I'm sorry, I'm sorry, I'm sorry. Papa, come back!"*

There was no coming back.

***

I wasn't allowed to go to my father's funeral. See, Red was still angry enough to kill. So even as my father was being placed in the ambulance, Red found one of the investigating police officers, and told the whole story of Nick being fired after Carlina dumped me, and the screaming match between me and Papa right before the show began. He embellished the story—adding

one essential detail that the county prosecutor latched onto—
he told the police that I had shouted, "I'm going to kill you."

As Mamma wept, and Tony and Lina stood stunned, the
police handcuffed me and walked me away. I was seventeen
years old—old enough that the County police took me to the
jail instead of juvenile detention. Then I was trapped in a world
I'd never imagined. It smelled of oil and sweat, and was punctuated by the rhythm of doors crashing open and closed, of
prisoners rapping in their cells, and of the echoing boots of the
guards as they walked up and down the block. In the lockup,
there's only the barest distinction between those who are awaiting trial and those who have already been convicted. Those of
us awaiting trial wore orange jumpsuits—the convicted wore
gray. Otherwise, we were housed together, showered together,
exercised together and ate together.

It was Monday afternoon – three days later—before Mamma and Lina came to visit. The jail didn't allow visitors on the
weekend.

"Where's Tony?" I had asked.

"He's trying to find you a decent lawyer," Mamma said.

"The circus…"

Mamma shook her head. "They have a lawyer, but he does
contracts, not – not —"

"Criminal law," Messalina said.

"I don't understand why I'm here," I said. "Why do they
think I hurt Papa?"

"You and Papa had… that argument…" Lina looked sick
when she said the words. "That's why they think that."

Not long after, they left. Over the next several months
Mom and Messalina visited almost every day. The tour continued, but without The Flying Paladinos. Mamma took the little bit of life insurance money she received and stayed in Texas.

My life had a rhythm to it, a self-contained rhythm. The first three months, I was housed with Jim Dawson, a fry cook from Calhoun County who had been jailed for failure to pay child support.

"I'd have paid if I had the money," he told me more than once, "but I lost my job."

Jim was eventually released, replaced by Gerald LeDuke. Gerald was awaiting trial for murder. The first four nights he was in the room he writhed and screamed as he went through withdrawals from whatever had been his choice of drugs. The fifth night he came to and attacked me in a frenzy. I held him off, barely, before the guards finally took him away.

Then, one day in September, I met Howard Echols. Howard was a retired high school teacher, and came to the prison almost every day as part of a one-man ministry, an ongoing passion play of his own where he spent his days educating prisoners and struggling to make lives better.

"Where did you go to high school?" He asked me the first day.

I shrugged. "Central Florida, but mostly all over..."

He had paced back and forth, his face a caricature of agony. Finally he turned toward me, and said, "You're a smart kid Paladino. You could be just like the rest of these guys in here, in and out of jail for the rest of your life, if you're not careful."

"I'm not like them," I said. "I didn't do anything. It was an accident. Don't you think losing my father was enough?"

He had shaken his head. "Don't matter what's fair, Paladino. It's not about fair. It's about reality. If they convict you, you might not ever be able to get a job. And if they don't, you still might struggle. The only thing you can do is try to get an education."

At first it was hard. I had in fact gone to high school, but barely. I had taken the basics required by the school system, but the Florida Public schools cast a wink and a nod to the circus families who lived there a few months out of the year. And so in school I learned to read—just barely—and write. I learned basic math. I wasn't writing sonnets or plays, and my math extended to balancing a checkbook.

Howard changed all of that. He started with reading—Steinbeck and Hemingway, Fitzgerald and later Stephen King and other contemporary authors. I studied math, then algebra and geometry. Howard had discarded textbooks, donations that had been given to his tiny ministry from churches, parents and school systems around the state. He pushed me hard, but I also pushed hard. In November, I took the SAT. It was a specially proctored exam—they don't give the SAT in prison—but Howard had made it possible.

I'll never forget the day my score report came in the mail. Like all mail, the wardens office had slit the envelope open and read it. But I didn't look. Instead I rushed down to Howard's tiny classroom. We stared each other, and he said in a calm voice, "Open it."

I'd scored a 1225.

I was stunned when Howard suddenly sniffed, and his eyes went bloodshot, and a tear rolled down his face.

"Promise me you'll go to college, boy."

"I promise."

And I did. After nine months of waiting, I was finally released. The medical examiner's report, which had taken months to be released, made it clear my father was dead before he hit the ground. The prosecution had no case, and ultimately dropped the charges.

I never got in the ring again.

***

Traditionally, Americans think of the circus is taking place under the big top. It's embedded in our consciousness. But after many of the small circuses in America failed in the middle of the 20th century, fewer and fewer circuses actually operated in the country. And the biggest of those, Ringling Brothers, toured almost exclusively in large arenas. That's what I grew up with. As a teenager I performed in Madison Square Garden, at the United Center, at fifty other indoor arenas. I don't recall a single instance where I performed under a big top.

That changed for the Flying Paladinos after my father died and I left the circus. When I got out of jail, I immediately took my GED and passed it. Thanks to Howard, I'd already been accepted at three different colleges—Florida State, the University of Georgia, and Boston University. It wasn't a difficult decision for me to make. Aside from the fact that it's an excellent school, BU was the furthest away of those possibilities from Central Florida. That was all the motivation I needed. Mamma took on leadership of the troupe, with Tony and Lina in the starring roles. They recruited two new flyers from a circus in Brazil, but they didn't go back to Ringling Brothers.

When Mamma took charge of the troupe, she decided to go back in time. She signed on with the Binder & Mills Circus, a smaller outfit that actually tours under a tent. It's not quite like the old style circuses, however. For one thing the production values are very much 21st-century. But the star act—the flying trapeze—has changed little in the years I've been away from it.

When I get to the gate, I have to bang on the glass of the ticket booth for several minutes before the teenager inside takes any notice. He's sitting there reading a comic book and chewing gum, and obviously assumes I'm a local. Finally he stands up and saunters to the window, leans close and says, "Box office ain't open yet."

"I'm here to see my mom and brother and sister. My name is Matt Paladino."

The kid, who doesn't appear to be very bright, stares at me and chews his gum for a minute. Then he says, "Box office ain't open yet."

I lean close almost placing my face against the glass, and say, "I'm with the Flying Paladinos. Let me in."

He gapes. More importantly, he lets me in. It's a short walk from the gate to the big top. Tonight, this space, with its dozens of game booths, fun houses, and other entertainment, will be alive with people. For now, all I see are the barkers and carnies getting their things together.

The tent is different than I expected. For one thing, the circus I grew up with always had three rings. This one has only one, with plush theater style seating surrounding the ring. I can imagine that this will be a far more intimate show than anything I grew up with.

I don't have to ask where Mamma or Tony or Lina are. Everybody can see them. Tony and Lina stand side-by-side on one platform. Lina has a pained expression on her face. They both wear worn practice tights which will be replaced later with some glittering and showy uniform. Tony needs a shave, and looks annoyed but respectful somehow simultaneously. On the other platform is Mamma. Swinging between them are two catchers.

Mamma shouts, "You think you can do whatever you want, Tony? You think you run the show? I already lost my husband and one son. I won't lose another. You listen to me!"

Her words are like a punch in the gut. I know   what she means. She hasn't lost a son. But I'm not part of their life anymore. It's not just that I'm not with the circus, I haven't even showed up for holidays. I'm stricken with guilt. Why haven't I visited?

The answer is simple. Because every time I smell the oil or hear the creak of the ropes, I feel the sickening loosening of hands, I see my father slipping away, and hear the clanging of the jail cell.

"I'm sorry Mamma," Tony says, a sheepish expression on his face. "I just want to try the quadruple."

"The quadruple killed your father. And you know not to try new tricks without warning your catcher. You could have gotten somebody killed."

The quadruple killed your father. I suppose in some sense that was true. With each somersault in the air, the G forces increase. The coroner had speculated that Papa died of a heart attack. His body just couldn't take the stress anymore.

I coughed into my right hand, just as I hear Mamma say, "Do it again. And this time do it right."

She sounds just like Papa did. The two unfamiliar catchers start, one offset slightly from the other, as they swing in opposite directions. I stay quiet and watch. When the show is running, the lights will be down, spotlights on the family, music playing. None of that is happening now—instead, it's light, everybody is sweaty and dirty, and there are no smiles.

Lina steps off first, taking the bar with one hand and swinging out with the other hand extended, her pose casually deliberate. She makes it look easy, even though I know that the pressure on that one wrist and hand holding her up is intense. As she reaches the apex of the arc, she seems to slowly turn in a circle, bringing her body around in the other direction. Now she takes the bar with both hands and kicks her feet out, and she swings, much quicker this time, back in the other direction, just as Tony leaps to the other trapeze.

It's all gracefully done. Beautiful. Dad would have approved, I'm sure. On her return swing, Messalina lets go of the bar and does an easy double, her hands slapping against the wrists of her catcher. Tony is right behind her with a triple, then they both swing back to their own trapezes and return to the platform.

The catchers drop to the net, followed by Tony, Messalina, then Mamma, signaling that practice is over. I step to the edge of the ring and into the light.

Messalina sees me first. She stops at the edge of the ring, puts her hands on her hips, and murmurs "Matt."

Tony's eyes jerk to me. I can't tell if his expression is relief, wariness, or anger. His features seemed to smooth out as if he's trying to hide his reaction, but the slight downturn at the corner of his mouth is unmistakable.

As reserved as my two siblings are, Mamma is anything but. She lets out a cry, drops out of the net and runs to me throwing her arms around me. I return the embrace which lasts all of thirty seconds before she steps back and shouts, "Matty, why don't you ever come see me? What's wrong with you? You think you're too good to come see your mother?"

"No, Mamma. Things are just busy at work…"

"No excuses. You're never too busy to see your Mamma." She looks at me critically, eyebrows drawn together, and pronounces, "At least you haven't let yourself go to seed. I thought when you came you'd have a beer belly, but you stayed in shape. It's a miracle." A miracle? Mamma is always tactful. I remember the summer before my junior year, Tony, Lina and I spent a rare vacation at grandma's place in Fort Lauderdale. It was two weeks of amazing relaxation, playing on the beach, and sleeping in. The first words out of Mamma's mouth when we rejoined the tour were directed at Lina. "How did you get so fat in two weeks?" Mamma had said.

I don't think Lina ate for six months after that.

Mamma doesn't mean to hurt people—the opposite is true. She has a warm heart, and loves her children. She also has a thick skin, and assumes that everyone around her is the same. The wounds that my mother delivers are unintentional, careless. And I don't know if carelessly injuring someone is even worse than doing it deliberately.

After Mamma steps back, Tony approaches. "Matty," he says. Then he throws his arms around me. "I'm glad you came." Then he steps back, looks at Lina, and says, "Guess I owe you ten bucks."

Lina smirks.

"I had bet you weren't coming, Matty," Tony says. "She won."

***

Tony introduces me to the catchers, neither of whom speaks very good English. When we break off to go get lunch, it's family today. And that only serves to underscore how much things have changed.

When I was eight or ten, and we were with Ringling Brothers, a family-only lunch needed a big table. Papa would be there with both of his brothers and his little sister, Mamma of course, and her cousin Lucia. Lucia eventually got married, pregnant, and settled down just outside of Houston, Texas. Papa's oldest brother Mario lives outside Sarasota now, and spends his days drinking and reliving his days with the circus and mourning his wife.

My youngest uncle Matteo—my namesake—quit flying after Papa died. The only member of the family with a college degree other than me, Matteo moved to Manhattan and went to work for a venture capital firm. Nowadays, his involvement with the circus is limited to a hefty investment in Binder and Mills.

The act is smaller; the family is smaller. It's just Mamma, Tony and Lina on tour. Soon enough Mamma will retire and that I think will be the end of the Flying Paladinos. I don't know how I feel about that. Our family has been in the ring for five generations.

As Mamma hands out the takeout Chinese, she says, "Matty, you must tell us everything. Are you still teaching? First grade?"

"Third grade this year, and of course I'm still teaching. I actually love it."

"You never think of coming back with us?"

I sigh. "Mamma…"

"I can ask. You're my son. I'm glad you're happy, but you belong with your family."

"I belong right where I am, Mamma. I like what I do. I like teaching, I'm representing the union. I've made friends."

"You have a girlfriend?"

I have to struggle not to roll my eyes. "I'm seeing somebody. I don't know yet…" I trail off unsure what to say.

"You don't know what? Whether you like her? Love her?"

"I just don't know, Mamma. I care about her. It's complicated. She was in the Army, and her parents just died. Now she's taking care of her little sister."

Mamma looks puzzled. "In the Army? What did she do?"

"She was military police. She went to Iraq, Mamma."

"I want to meet this woman," Mamma says. "Does she carry a gun?"

"Mom! For Christ's sake! I don't even know if we're serious, it's too early for that."

"Not too early. If I don't like her you don't get serious."

I shake my head and laugh. "No, Mamma. That's not the way it works."

She shakes her head too, then picks up a fortune cookie in its plastic wrapper and throws it at me. It bounces off my forehead. Messalina laughs; Tony looks annoyed.

I shrug, and open up the package and crack open the fortune cookie. Happiness is an activity.

Well, that's helpful.

After lunch, Mamma says, "One more practice this afternoon."

Lina frowns. "Mamma, we never see Matty."

"And think about how your brother Matt will feel, if you don't practice and you break your neck tonight."

I shudder at her words.

"Go practice," I say. "I'll watch."

Mamma looks at me, a frown on her face. "You come up the platform with me. I won't have you sitting in the stands. Your brother has something he can loan you to wear."

I shake my head. "Mamma, I'm all done with that."

"You come up to the platform with me. You don't have to fly. Come stand with your Mamma."

Lina looks at me, one eyebrow raised, as if to say, Try to defy her.

I can't. I shrug. "All right."

It feels strange putting on tights. It's been years since I've worn them, years since I've been in the ring of a circus. Even if I'm only going to be standing on the platform for practice, it simultaneously feels right and wrong. Confusing.

You're going to be a catcher, Matty.

People's lives are in your hands. Take care of them.

Take care of your arms and your shoulders. Someone's life may depend on it one day.

And that of course turned out to be absolutely true.

It's strange. I thought it would be worse; thought the simple act of changing into tights would cause some kind of panic reaction. But it's fine. It boosts my confidence and I walk out to the ring with my family. Everything is fine.

Until I touch the ladder.

By the time I get there, Tony has already climbed up. The two new catchers are also up there.

I get one foot on the latter and freeze.

"It's okay, Matty." Mamma's voice is soft.

I shake my head. "No. It's not okay. It's never been okay." I have to force the words out over a leaden tongue, but I get them out. My heart is beating wildly and I feel a drop of sweat on my forehead.

Mamma comes close. "It wasn't your fault," she says.

"I know that," I say. But do I? I've lived my father's death a thousand times. I've lived that moment of losing my grip a thousand times. He had a heart attack. A stupid heart attack. People live through heart attacks all the time. They get chest pain, they collapse, they go to the hospital, they get repairs to their arteries. They get bypasses and stents. And often they live. Yes, heart attacks kill a lot of people. But there's a strong chance if you have a heart attack when you are around other people, that you'll be able to get to medical help time and survive. That is, unless your seventeen-year-old son drops you from the height of a small building onto a concrete floor.

"I tried to hold him." I can't look at her when I say the words. But my voice shakes.

"I know, baby." Her response is almost a whisper.

There are a thousand things I could say. But where do you begin? She nods, as if she understands   what it is that I'm trying to say, even if I don't. And she puts her feet on the ladder, and climbs up to the platform. I don't stand where I am for very long. My fear is irrational. It consumes. I don't want to go up there, and that's why I have to. I grip the ladder as Papa taught, set my foot on the first rung, and climb. With each step up the ladder my view expands until eventually the entire arena is below. We're no higher here than we were in the center ring of Ringling Brothers. It feels higher because of the intimacy of this venue. When I finally take my position, I see Tony on the other platform. He nods, as if in approval. I'm not going to go out there—that's already been established. But getting to the top of the platform is a breakthrough.

ANOTHER TIME (MATT)

It's not until I get back to my car much later in the evening that I realize I left my cell phone in the car. I have two missed calls from Zoe.

In the first message, she says, "Hey, Matt. We just finished up with the students for the day. Jasmine asked if we could go to lunch with you, so I figured I'd call. Call me back!"

The second message—according to my phone that one came in at 5 p.m.—she sounded a little wary. "Hey... Matt... Just checking in since we haven't heard from you today."

I guess I should have realized. We've seen each other almost every day for the last two weeks.

I start the car and leave the crowded lot, immediately finding myself in snarled Boston traffic. I'm stuck on a narrow one-way street which is going in the opposite direction of where I want to go... I'll have to wait until traffic clears enough to make it around the corner so I can turn around.

When I think about the last couple of weeks, I'm not sure how to feel. The time I've spent with Zoe has meant a great deal—but even more so, it's made me realize just how isolated I was. Sure, I hung out with Tyler, and that's been a lot of fun. Tyler's a great guy—but I'm starting to realize that I kept him at arms length too. Something... Maybe the fact that he reminds me a little of Red... has kept me from opening up. He doesn't even know I grew up with the circus. It's not that noticeable I guess, most guys don't talk about anything but get-ting laid and drinking beer anyway.

It's different with Zoe. It's easy... She probably knows more about me in two weeks than anyone else has learned in two years.

That's still precious little. Several times in the last week, I wanted to tell her about Papa, about the jail... but every time I try, my throat just closes up. The effort to do so has raised some disturbing dreams—more dreams about my father, and falling, than I've had several years.

I don't like those dreams.

I flip my phone open and dial Zoe's number. Usually I don't talk on the phone while driving, but it's not like I'm mov-ing anywhere anyway.

She answers on the second ring. "Hello?"

"Hey, calling you back. I'm sorry I didn't get back earlier, I just got your messages."

"Oh... I didn't realize. What have you been up to?"

Of course she would ask one question I couldn't answer. I fumbled for a second, then said, "I had some things to take care of." That's illuminating, Matt. The fact is, I'm a terrible liar, and I always have been. This wasn't a lie, but it certainly wasn't telling her anything.

"Oh... Well, I called you earlier to see if you wanted to grab lunch. Obviously it's much too late for that. Although, if you wanted to swing by..."

I hesitate. After an awkward two seconds, I say, "I'm actually in Boston right now. Just getting ready to drive home. It'll be... around eight?"

Her voice is rigid when she answers, nothing like the lyrical rich voice she normally uses. "I see. Jasmine will already be in bed by then. Another time. Are we still meeting for the fair? We'll see you at ten."

She didn't leave room for anything there. And I can't invite myself over. I'm disappointed—I'd planned on heading back to South Hadley by two or three in the afternoon, reasoning that I could still get back home in time to have dinner with Zoe. Well, I blew that. She'd made it pretty clear that I wasn't welcome to come over tonight.

And that only highlights just how emotionally attached I've become.

HE KNOWS HE SCARES ME (ZOE)

I hang up the phone softly. I'm an uncomfortable swirl of emotions right now, disappointment mixed with anxiety mixed with curiosity. It's not like I know Matt. And I've been down this road before, cared about somebody, depending on them, then having them suddenly get flaky. Chase stopped being reliable well before I found out he was going out with that other girl. We would have plans, then he would not show up. He always had good excuses—things with work, or he was sick, or a friend was in trouble and he had to help, or he had a toothache. I don't even remember all of the excuses. I do remember the feeling of disappointment. I don't like that feeling, and I have it right now.

I'll still give Matt a chance of course. But I don't like his evasiveness. I still don't know that much about him. And that bothers me a lot.

I walk to the back door and open it. Jasmine is in the barn—we let the horses inside just a little while ago, and she'll be busy getting them fed and put down for the evening. I assume a smiling face, jump down the stairs, and walk to the barn. Looking into the darkness, I see her on the top rail petting Mono on the snout.

"Hey, want to go to Chick-fil-A for dinner?" That's usually a winner, because she can play in the indoor playground there.

"Yeah!" She jumps down from the railing, and says, "Can I get a milkshake?"

I grimace. The thing is, I kind of want a milkshake, but I know that as the stand-in for Mom, I'm supposed to make her drink juice or something. Right? Isn't that what Moms do?

I sigh, then shrug. Why not? It's Saturday night, and I make her eat healthy most of the time. "Sure," I say. "You should leave some room for ice cream for dessert. I thought we'd head over to McCray's farm."

Her eyes widen, then she shouts, "Hooray!" Her shout startles the horses, and Mono lets out a near roar, throwing his head back.

I think he knows that he scares me.

CHAPTER SIXTEEN

AMHERST FAIR (ZOE)

MY ENTIRE CHILDHOOD, the Amherst fair was something I looked forward to. There are carnival rides, fun houses, all kinds of food, and other fun. It may not be as big as a state fair somewhere, but it's a lot of fun for the kids. Jasmine has been talking about it for days—she may not be in school right now, but enough of the kids that she sees at Paul Armstrong's farm have kept her clued in on what's going on around the area. We make a day of it.

It's about 10 a.m. when we take the minivan and pick up Matt at his apartment next to the post office. He looks tired, but cheerful, when he comes running out from the parking lot and hops in the van.

"Jasmine!"

"Mr. P."

I feel a tension when I look over at him and meet his eyes. He gives me a faint smile, and says "Zoe."

It's a 20 minute or so drive to Amherst from South Hadley. Along the way, Jasmine sings one of Taylor Swift's new songs at the top of her lungs. When she doesn't know the lyrics, she just makes up her own. Honestly, Jasmine's are better. And definitely funnier. The three of us ride north, laughing the entire way, and I'm glad, because it helps cut the tension from last night. By the time we get to Amherst, I've decided to let it go. He had things to do. I need to give him a chance.

When we get into Amherst we sit in traffic for a while, mostly cars stuck around the common, and we have to park a few blocks away. I'm a little startled when Jasmine slips in between me and Matt and takes each of our hands. I glance over at Matt and our eyes meet. I feel heat on my cheeks, and look away. The three of us walk up the street to the common.

A flash of memory takes me back to Dad talking to me about Amherst and the Common. It's a large green area with old trees. On one side, Amherst College, on the other side the town. The Lord Jeffrey Inn and the town hall are in between the college and the rest of downtown. Robert Frost and Emily Dickinson lived here, and Dickinson is buried a few blocks away. For a literature professor like Dad, this was very near the center of the universe.

Today, however, there's no rarefied poetry in the air. Instead, the common is permeated with the smell of cooking hamburger meat, fried dough, and cotton candy. Tents cover the common with vendors selling everything from Chinese food to knock-off handbags. Jasmine has no interest in any of that, though I'm sure she'll want the food later. For now, she starts to jump up and down in excitement when she sees the tiny roller coaster. It's a bite-sized coaster, the cars just big enough to hold two children. The line of cars is shaped like a snake, and colored bright green with big eyes on the front car.

"Zoe! Zoe! Can I ride it? Please? *Please?*"

Matt chuckles. I say, "Let me get some tickets, and we'll take you around to the rides."

For the next two hours, we move from ride to ride, attraction to attraction. Matt stops at the ring toss game, his eyes scanning everything ... the bottles, the stuffed animals, the none-too-clean barker. The grand prize is a three-foot-tall panda bear. Matt looks at the panda, then takes out a five-dollar bill and passes it to the guy behind the counter.

I shake my head. "I never do these, they're rigged."

He looks at me and winks. Then he turns back and lands a ring on the very first try. Jasmine claps with excitement, jumping up and down. That was uncanny.

He takes the second ring, studies the scene for just a moment, then tosses it. It lands on the bottle right next to the first. This time I clap with Jasmine, stunned.

There's no way Jasmine can realize just how difficult a feat that was.

From the sour look the carny is giving Matt, he certainly realizes it. Matt ignores him, instead staring at the bottles, his face screwed up in tight concentration. Several people are standing around us now watching, and they've hushed, realizing that someone is about to win the grand prize.

Matt tosses the ring.

I suck in a breath, then exhale as the ring lands on the third bottle right next to the other two. We break into applause, and the barker shakes his head, a wry smile on his face. He turns and takes down the huge stuffed panda, and hands it to Matt. Immediately several children begin to shout at their mothers, demanding a chance to try themselves.

Matt kneels down, and hands the giant bear to Jasmine. "For you," he says. She staggers back a little as she wraps her arms around it. It's taller than she is.

"Really?" Jasmine asks, her eyes wide.

"Of course," he says. Then he shrugs, and says, "I've already got a stuffed bear." As he stands up, I feel an unusual wash of emotion, and my eyes begin to water. She's had such a hard time, she deserves some good in her life.

Matt meets my eyes, and I smile, feeling electric tension between us. It's so intense I have to look away.

Please watch yourself (Matt)

The first week back at school is a small triumph. I'm greeted on the first day with congratulations and handshakes and smiles from everyone on the staff—the union won the contract negotiations and major concessions from the administration. That happened because everybody in the union worked together; but I was getting a lot of attention because I'd been one of the negotiators.

In the classroom none of that is an issue. My goal is to usher the kids back into complete normality as quickly as possible—we begin our first day back as if it's only been a weekend in between. The kids are ready to go—they've had a brief unexpected vacation. For the parents it's not quite so easy—child care, jobs and the sudden strike were not a good combination.

Jasmine is doing better. Of course she's still grieving and missing her parents, but the worst signs of that are fading. She isn't stuttering as much, she laughs in class, she plays with the other girls. I can't ask for more than that.

I didn't see Zoe on Monday evening—she was working on a paper for one of her classes, and I had a massive amount of paperwork to do related to the end of the strike. On Tuesday morning, as the kids are streaming into the class, Jasmine walks in, her eyes to the floor. She carries a small painted box filled with wildflowers of various colors. She sets it on the edge of the desk, and stammers out, "Fr–fr– from Zoe... and me." Then she blushes a bright red, turns and runs to her seat.

A smile spreads across my face. On closer examination, I see that the box is a small rectangular planter, painted on the outside in bright blue and green pastels. On one side in neat, feminine letters—probably applied with a Sharpie—are the words, "For our favorite teacher." Next to that, in Jasmine's large and shaky handwriting, "Mr. P." The rest of the planter is covered in hand drawn stars and flowers. What looks like glitter glue is smeared on the other side. The flowers are a mix of dandelions and some little blue flowers I didn't know the names of.

I look up at Jasmine. She stares at the desk, her face still red. "Thank you, Jasmine."

On Wednesday morning, I find a letter in my inbox in the main office. It's sealed... the return address is from the office of the superintendent. I tear it open, puzzled.

This is ... odd. The letter says, *Please report to the office of the assistant superintendent at 2 p.m., Wednesday, October 1.* The letter is signed by the assistant superintendent of schools.

I walk over to the front desk. Sarah Higgins, the school secretary, usually has a pulse on everything that's going on in the district. "Do you know anything about this? They want me down at the superintendent's office this afternoon."

She shakes her head. "It came in with the other papers from the office this morning."

"Thanks," I say. The strange part about the letter is that class is still in session at 2 p.m.. It's not that we don't have meetings during the day—we do all the time. Typically, for an appointment at the school department, they'll schedule it outside of class hours. I shrug. I'll know in a few hours what it's about. I go to see the principal to arrange for coverage in my classroom, then head back to class.

***

I arrive at the town hall at five minutes before two. The school administration offices are small—after all, South Hadley has two elementary schools, one middle school, and one high school. There's little need for the bloated bureaucracy that you might see in a large city school system. On the flip side, sometimes I feel as if I'm an outsider at the country club. Everyone knows everyone, and they've all known each other for their entire lives. As someone who's been in town just a couple of years, I'm often intimidated by that. Times like this more than any other. I knock on the door, catching the attention of the administrative assistant just inside.

"Oh, Mr. Paladino. Come in, the Superintendent is expecting you." I step into the crowded office, and try not to fidget while she picks up a phone and calls the superintendent.

A moment later, Michael Barrington opens his office door and bustles out. As always, he looks a little fussy, wearing a nice suit, which appears to be both new and expensive, but his tie is slightly off center and a tiny stain mars the collar of his shirt. He's clean-shaven, but has a visible shaving cut on his chin.

"Matt," he says. "Come in, come in." We shake hands and I follow him into the office.

Something feels off. I don't know Barrington well, but every time I've seen him, he has seemed both stressed and very serious. He frowns a lot, and his eyes often appear distant, as if he's worried about some indefinable future.

Today, however, his mouth carries the hint of a smile. His eyes are shifting everywhere. He sits down behind the desk and gestures to the seats in front of it. I take a seat.

"I suppose you are wondering why I called this meeting," he says.

I nod. "I am, actually. What can I do for you?"

"Matt... What can you tell me about Jasmine Welch?"

That's odd. "Well, sir, her parents were killed a few weeks ago in an accident. Her sister Zoe has custody of her. She's doing as well as can be expected."

"Is she receiving special education services?"

This is puzzling. It would be a trivial matter for him to look Jasmine up in the computer, to find out whether or not she is receiving any accommodations. There's no need to call me to the school system offices to answer these questions. I proceed slowly and carefully, mindful of Barrington reputation. "No, sir."

"She doesn't have an IEP?"

An IEP, or individualized education plan, is put in place to modify the curriculum to accommodate the needs of children with disabilities. I shake my head. "No, she doesn't have an IEP."

He frowns, deepening the crevices at the corners of his mouth. "I don't understand, Matt. Her curriculum was modified."

I shake my head. "Not really. She's been learning the same things, we just changed the order of some things and added some additional drawing components. She's been struggling with grief, so I've been trying to work with her in areas where I could reach her more effectively."

"Matt, I completely understand that your motives are... well intended. But you cannot just go around modifying the curriculum anytime you feel like it."

I stiffen, and feel my face heat up. "With all due respect Mr. Barrington, I made no modifications to the curriculum. And she's doing much better than she was, she needed help. That's my job."

"And the fact that you are dating her sister has no bearing on any of this?"

"Of course not." I feel anger rising, a tightness in my chest... "First, that's none of your business. Who I date is not the concern of the school system. And second, our job is to teach those students. I've done the most effective job I could with Jasmine."

The corner of Barrington's mouth jerks up. A smirk. "At the expense of the other children in your class. There's a reason we have specialists in special education, to help deal with these situations."

I'm furious now. This is bullshit. This has nothing to do with Jasmine or the other students at all—it's all about Barrington paying me back. The question is, what can I do about it?

"The students in my class have lost nothing, Mr. Barrington."

"Mr. Paladino, I'm afraid I'll have to be the judge of that."

I feel my pulse in my ears, my hands are twitching and I'm having difficulty not thinking of the thousand things I want to say. It leaves me paralyzed. We sit there in silence for a while... fifteen seconds? A minute? It seems like a very long time. Eventually, however, he breaks the impasse.

"I recognize, Mr. Paladino, that you are a gifted teacher, if a little unseasoned. For that reason, I've decided you won't be officially reprimanded. We'll simply include a brief note in your file about the discussion today, and your agreement that you will no longer modify the curriculum on your own."

My mouth runs ahead of me. "I'll agree to no such thing."

He raises an eyebrow. Naturally, I'd walked right into his trap. Technically I'm not authorized to make any changes to the curriculum. But the fact was, having Jasmine do the extra drawing didn't constitute a change. We may not have much leeway, but we do have some. This is utter nonsense. It has nothing to do with the curriculum. It has everything to do with my representing the union during the contract negotiations.

"Mr. Barrington, rest assured I won't be running around making changes to the school's curriculum. I'm not going to agree to sign off on any kind of official or unofficial notes or memo or anything else going in my personnel file." I plunge my index finger down against his desk. "This is nothing more than retaliation. It's inexcusable."

Barrington's face jerks into the barest of smirks; then he wipes it away. He's enjoying this. I should have realized… In the eighteen months or so since he became superintendent, Michael Barrington has already received a strong reputation for exacting personal retribution for even the slightest of offenses. It's highly unlikely that the union would've gone on strike if it hadn't been for that… but there is more to the process than dollars and cents and benefits and contracts. There is also the overall work environment, the tone of which has been extremely negative and is getting worse.

"If there's nothing else, I'll be going." I stand as I say the words.

"No, there will be nothing else." Barrington looks mildly amused as he says the words.

I turn to walk to the door, feeling my skin crawl a little at his attitude. I open the door to the office, and start to step outside, when I hear his voice again.

"Mr. Paladino… please… watch yourself."

Ass.

Secrets (Zoe)

"Are you going to burn dinner again?" I put my hands on my hips and turn around. Jasmine is in the doorway, surveying the scene. She's been out riding Mono for the last hour. Now she's in, presumably to get a bath and get ready for homework. The last couple of weeks have been very good for her, and I'm grateful that she has Matt as her teacher because he manages to draw her out in ways that I haven't figured out how to do.

Despite that gratitude, it's hard for me to push away a tendril of... anxiety? Concern? Matt was very evasive about Saturday. It's not that it's any of my business—it's not like we're even really dating. Or are we? We don't own each other. The opaqueness of his past, with his refusal to talk about his family, childhood, or anything prior to becoming a teacher in South Hadley, is disturbing. Who does that? People have lives. They have friends and family and experiences and just... life... that they talk about and share.

For Matt, that life appears to have begun three years ago when he arrived in South Hadley. Outside of that, I only know tidbits. He grew up somewhere in Central Florida. His father is dead. I don't know where the rest of his family is, or why he doesn't talk about them.

Right now I have other things to worry about. He'll be here in another twenty minutes, and I need to get dinner on the table. I turn around, and for a second I see the kitchen through Jasmine's eyes. To the left of the stove, the countertop is covered in a mess of flour and God only knows what else. I breaded chicken over there, and you can tell. It looks as if the Tasmanian Devil decided to fry the chicken, splattering salt and flour and chicken juices everywhere. I think the deep frying pan on the stove may be too hot, because the oil is giving off smoke. It's no wonder Jasmine asked if I was going to set dinner on fire again. I refuse to let domestic life defeat me. I'm acting *in loco parentis* to Jasmine, and I'm going to do the best job I can.

To the right of the stove, an open calculus textbook sits in front of my laptop. A YouTube video titled Introduction to Calculus Lesson Six plays on the screen. The narrator has an interesting voice and does her best to make it both interesting and theatrical. Unfortunately, I'm clearly not the target audience for this topic.

Here goes nothing. One at a time, I pick up the chicken with my metal spatula and gently lower it into the hot oil. Oil splashes everywhere and it begins to sizzle loudly. I feel a couple of pinpricks of heat along my forearm, tiny splatters of oil that hit me. I drop two more pieces of chicken in and look on, satisfied, as they begin to fry.

While the chicken fries, I turn my attention to the mashed potatoes which I load with cream and garlic. This dinner won't win any awards from the National Heart Association. Though it does have broccoli, so that's something. I take the bowl of vegetables—swimming in cheese sauce—and put them on the table. Two long stemmed candles sit in the center of the table, not lit, and three place settings are arrayed around them. It's almost ready.

The front door bell rings. "I'll get it!" Jasmine shouts unnecessarily as she runs down the hallway. I shrug, and continue cooking.

A minute later, Matt walks in the door. He looks tired, a little strained. He stops in the doorway, smiles, and says "That smells delicious. Kind of like home."

So fried chicken smells like home. Another tiny little factoid to place in my paltry Matt dossier. As he approaches he presents me with a bottle of wine—a Pinot Noir. I smile and point to one of the cabinets. "Glasses are up there. Do we need to chill it?"

"Already cold." Matt busies himself with pouring glasses of wine, as I get the rest of the food on the table. A second later, Jasmine comes into the room clutching a rolled up sheet of yellow construction paper. Her eyes drop to the floor, then jerk back up.

"I made this for you," she says, and hands it to Matt. I suck in a short breath, then catch myself and relax.

"Thank you very much," Matt says, as he unrolls the paper.

I pour a glass of milk for Jasmine, and bring it over to the table.

It's a crayon drawing, and a remarkably good one for a third grader. Mono, huge as ever, is on the left side of the paper. But there's something unusual. Jasmine always draws herself riding the horse. In this picture, she's not riding Mono. She's standing between a woman and a man. At first it looks like Mom and Dad, but then I realize it can't be. She's drawn a black beard on the man—it's Matt. The woman on the other side is me—yellow shoulder length hair, and the shirt even says Army. Jasmine stands between us in the picture holding both of our hands.

I cover my mouth with my hand, and my eyes water until I blink the tears back. I meet Matt's eyes—searching. Searching to know if he's going to be around, or is he going to break Jasmine's heart. I'm a big girl—I can fend for myself. Jasmine doesn't need any more heartbreak.

He seems to understand what I'm thinking, because he doesn't take his eyes off of me, even as he reaches for Jasmine's hand and mine. Finally he looks away from me, and towards my little sister.

"I think that's the most beautiful gift I've ever been given," he says. His voice chokes up as he says the words. His reaction looks sincere, but I wonder why he reacts so emotionally.

I hate it that I'm so distrustful.

As we sit down to eat, I find myself once again thrown into an uncomfortable role. It was my mother who always said things like, "put your napkin in your lap," and "don't put your feet on the dinner table." Now I'm the one in that role, and I find it more than a little bit strange when I tell Jasmine to please eat somewhere in the vicinity of her plate so it's not such a mess to clean up. Jasmine may be a third grader, but she eats like a four-year-old.

Through the meal she tells a long meandering story about her friend Hannah who has a brother in the Navy. "Hannah says the Navy is better than the Army because they have spaceships. I told her that's not true. Nobody has spaceships. Is that true Zoe? Does the Navy has spaceships?"

I shift in my seat a little, unsure what to say, but I finally land on, "Have, Jasmine. Not have. I don't think any of them have spaceships Jasmine. Except maybe the Air Force."

Jasmine huffs. "No." She drags out the word no. As if it were spelled nooooo. Her tone is sharp. "None of them have spaceships. Spaceships aren't real. That's what Mrs. Bates told us."

Matt raised his eyebrows.

"Who is Mrs. Bates?" I asked.

"She was the substitute this afternoon. When I got mad because Hannah said the Navy was better than the Army, Mrs. Bates made us sit in timeout for five minutes. I shouldn't have been sent to sit timeout. Hannah was wrong. She shouldn't say that."

That's a lot to take in. Why did they have a substitute this afternoon? And why did Jasmine care whether Hannah said anything about the Army versus the Navy... I didn't even care about that. "Sweetie, you don't have to worry about that. It doesn't matter what she says about that."

"It does! You were in the Army!"

I look at Matt in hopes of gleaning some clues from him about how to handle this—he's got a lot more experience with kids than I do. He doesn't offer any help. I look back to Jasmine. "Look at it like this. Who is better... Barbie? Or Dora the Explorer?"

I was taking a chance with that question. She looks at me with scorn on her face, and says, "Well, Dora, of course."

"Well, would you fight with Hannah if she said Barbie was better?"

Jasmine is puzzled. "No. That would be stupid."

"Well, this is kind of the same thing."

She shakes her head violently. "No, it's not! It's not the same thing at all!"

I try to hide my exasperation. It's never easy reasoning with a third-grader. "What would Dora do if Barbie stole her backpack?"

Jasmine looks at me as if I've gone stark raving mad. "Why would she do that?"

I close my eyes and count to ten thousand. Or ten. I'm not sure how much. "It doesn't matter why."

"Well of course it matters."

I fall back to the least useful response ever. "Eat your chicken."

Matt doesn't even bother to try to hide his amusement. His eyes are raised slightly, his lips curled up, his eyes flashing a hint of mirth as he eats silently.

"So where were you?" I ask.

"This afternoon? I had a meeting at the superintendent's office." As soon as he says the words, the mirth disappears from his face.

"Is everything okay?"

He sets his chicken down, and takes a drink of wine. He holds it in his mouth for a moment, clearly thinking about the question. He's silent long enough that I become uncomfortable. Eventually, he says, "I'm not sure. The whole situation was surreal. I got called in to meet with the superintendent, who wanted to talk about why we had modified the schedule for...." He doesn't finish the sentence. Instead his eyes dart to Jasmine.

That's weird. "Why did he do that?"

"That's the thing. I've never had the superintendent get involved in anything like that before. For one thing, it just wasn't that big of a deal. And for another it's usually the principal or the counselors or special education. I don't think it has anything to do with that... I think this was all about the strike."

"What are you going to do?"

He shakes his head. "I don't know that there is anything to do," he says. "It wasn't an official reprimand—I think it was more an effort of intimidation."

"Well, that's bullshit."

Jasmine giggles. "Zoe said a bad word." Silence descends on the room for a few seconds... then Matt smirks, letting out a tiny snort.

"Whoops," I say. "Sorry about that, Jasmine."

At 8 o'clock, after a cutthroat game of Uno, I take Jasmine up to bed. As always, she gives me a halfhearted, "Please, Zoe?"

It really is halfhearted. I can tell that she needs the rest.

When I get back downstairs, Matt's pouring us another glass of wine. I take the proffered glass and say, "How about we sit on the porch? We won't have many more good nights for that."

We sit down on the rocking chairs on the wraparound porch. The wood underneath creaks and groans—the house is old, and it's settled a lot over the years. Despite the creaking, it is sound.

We sit quietly for a few minutes. Fall is coming... it's already dark at eight o'clock. I find myself hoping for an Indian summer—the longer I can put off the snow the better. I grew up here and I'm no stranger to cold, but five years of being stationed in Kentucky, Iraq, and Tokyo have rendered me uninterested in snow. We'll have plenty of it by January and February, so with any luck at least November and December won't be so bad.

The deepest part of winter is always a bit of an ordeal around here. Horses can't stay in their stalls, regardless of whether or not there is snow on the ground. Every winter as far back as I can remember, along with shoveling the walks and driveway, we shoveled a path from the stables to the paddock. The horses know the land well, and even in deep snow they're generally okay. Before we send them out in the wintertime, extra care is required, when we change their blankets and harnesses and double the amount of times we have to clean and muck out the stalls.

On top of that, winter is just more expensive for horses. Up until the first frost, the horses live primarily on grazing, though we supplement that with hay. During the winter I'll be buying several bales of hay for each horse each day. That adds up to a lot of food—and a lot of money—very quickly. I've got enough for the short term, but there's this cold pit of anxiety when I think of that routine extra expense when I don't have a job.

"You've gone off a long ways, haven't you?" Matt's words jerk me back to the present. I take a sip of my wine, stalling for time while I compose myself.

"I was. Worrying about money and the horses and winter and Jasmine."

"That's a lot of worry all at once."

"Isn't that what being an adult is all about? Worry and responsibility?"

Matt winces. "I don't know about all that," he says. "I feel like there ought to be a lot more to life than that."

I shrug. "My parents seemed to have that... more... they knew what they loved and wanted to do. I've never had that... I'm seriously clueless about my future."

"Maybe you don't need to worry about all of that right now," he says.

"I'm twenty-four, Matt. It's time for me to figure out what I want to do when I grow up."

He snorts. "Good luck with that. I don't think anybody knows for sure."

"What about teaching?" I ask. "How did you get into that?"

He stares out into the growing darkness, seeming to compose an answer in his head. Just before the silence becomes interminable, he says, "I had a teacher who inspired me. He made a real difference in my life, at a time when I needed what he had to offer. That's why I ended up focusing on education. Honestly, I wanted to teach high school. Jobs were scarce when I graduated, and when I got an offer in South Hadley, I took it."

"You didn't look in Florida?"

In a slow, thoughtful tone, he says, "If a hurricane were to wash all of Florida away into the Atlantic Ocean, I'd be unlikely to shed a tear."

Wow. That drives home the fact that there's a great deal I don't know about Matt Paladino. What is it about his past that makes him so evasive? What is it that makes him so angry?

"I don't suppose you're going to tell me why you feel that way."

He shrugs, and says, "Not much to tell. Florida is a cesspool. There's no funding for schools. Kids don't get textbooks, and the teachers barely get paid. In Florida, I could do better waiting tables."

I'm sure all of that is true. I'm also sure that it's only part of the story.

"Have it your way, Matt." I don't even bother to hide my annoyance.

"You know, for someone who pushes so hard for me to open up about my past, you've said   nothing about your time in the Army."

Now my annoyance flashes into anger. "That's because it was a vicious, traumatic experience. I don't like to dredge it back up."

"You don't say?" His eyes are gentle, but I feel as if he's laughing at me. Caught in my own trap. I ought to know well, that war is hardly the only traumatic experience. Look at Jasmine... She went off to camp one morning and returned an orphan that afternoon. She'll probably be in therapy for a decade. I probably ought to be. Maybe it's wrong for me to push Matt so hard.

All the same, secrets bother the hell out of me.

CHAPTER SEVENTEEN

You can shove your support (Zoe)

I'M NOT READY for this.

The small conference room in the Student Union feels crowded even though there aren't that many of us in here. Part of that is the lack of windows. Part of it is the oversized table that's out of proportion to the room. At the head end of the table is Craig Stills, the Director of Veterans Services at UMASS. He has a fierce grin on his face, like a wolf that's just taken down its prey. I'm sandwiched in between Craig and Nicole, who showed up in her uniform. Me and Nicole are the only women in the room. At the end of the table opposite Craig are two men, both in their early twenties, both looking as if they are uncomfortable in their own skin. Hair cropped extremely short, I would expect either one of them could change back into uniform this afternoon and look wholly in place.

Across from me, slumped in a chair with his eyes closed, is a man with disheveled looking hair that's well past his shoulders. His tangled blond beard is overdue for a trim. His skin is weathered, giving him an overall appearance that seems out of sync somehow. I can't quite place what's wrong, until I look at his hands. No age spots… His hands look young. He looks like he's twenty, but his eyes make him look fifty.

When Craig clears his throat and says, "Let's get started," the man across from me looks up and meets my eyes.

That's when I realize I was wrong—he's not young. His eyes make him look a thousand years old.

"I think we'll all introduce ourselves first," Craig says. "I'm assuming you don't know each other. I'm Craig Stills, Director of Veterans Services. You've all come to my attention—one way or another—that you're combat veterans. While I'm sure there are more on campus, we'll start with this group and maybe grow over time. Long story short, I was an Army Sergeant until late 2005, when the insurgents decided it was time for me to medically retire."

As Craig probably expected, his grim humor evokes chuckles around the room. "Anyway… After a year of physical therapy and recovery, I got my Master's in social work at NC State, then came to work here."

Craig points at me. Why we can't go around the table in the other direction? Whatever. "I'm Zoe Welch. Military police, one tour in Iraq, then I was stationed in Japan for a little bit more than a year. I just got home a few weeks ago."

Craig smiles and says, "You don't have to talk about it, obviously, but there are some unusual circumstances around your life now. Do you want to say anything?"

No, I want to punch him in the face.

I sigh. "My parents were killed in an accident a few weeks ago. I have custody of my eight-year-old sister. I'm trying to figure out what I'm going to do—I didn't have a plan for when I got out of the military because I was planning on staying in."

Craig gives me a warm smile, and says, "Welcome home, Zoe." His words make me choke up a little. Now I want to punch him even more.

"Nicole?"

Nicole grimaces. She elbows me in the side. "Me and Zoe were best friends as kids and enlisted together. We were in Iraq together. I got out of the Army before she did. Now I mostly police up drunken frat boys and investigate stolen laptops and dormitory sexual assaults… in other words, I'm a UMASS cop."

Craig says, "Nicole won't tell you, but I will. She was awarded a Bronze Star for valor."

Nicole tries to waive it off. "It was just for showing up."

I interrupt. "That's bullshit Nicole. You saved our lives."

She rolls her eyes.

"Mike?" Craig directs the word at Tom Cruise look-alike at the end of the table. He seems to sit at attention. Clear complexion, dark brown hair, light blue eyes and a cocky grin. His striking appearance is marred by his obvious arrogance.

Or is that just me reading my own bias into the situation?

"Mike Palmer. Infantry, Afghanistan and Iraq. I'm a junior here majoring in engineering."

No… I'm guessing my assessment was correct.

The next man speaks without prompting. Like Mike, he has a formal, almost rigid look about him. Extremely dark skin, with very short cropped hair, he's wearing a polo shirt with the creases ironed so sharp you could cut yourself. He'd look more at home in a business meeting than on campus here. "I'm Terrell Palmer. Marine Corps. Civil affairs. I did four tours in Iraq."

My mouth drops open. It's not that I didn't know people that served that many tours…it's just that I didn't know anybody who'd served that many and come out of it without being a little crazy.

Of course, it was pretty early to tell anything about Terrell.

Finally it's the turn of the guy across from me. He lets silence weigh the room down for a few seconds before speaking. Finally he said, I'm Luke Osmond. I was a sniper."

Luke says nothing more. I'm not the only one who notices. Craig looks at him, raises an eyebrow, and says, "That's it?"

Luke shrugs. "Ain't that enough?"

I guess so.

"I called you all together because I believe there are particular challenges associated with being a combat veteran returning to college—over and above what others might face. I want to give you guys a chance to network… And maybe lean on each other a little. Sometimes it's hard to find people who understand what language we're speaking."

Luke snorts. "Who would want to?"

"I don't have any problems readjusting," Mike says. "I'm happy to help anyone who is having trouble." As he says the words, he eyes Luke.

"We'll see how things develop," Craig says. "Don't rule out how much or what help you may need in the future. I'll tell you a fascinating fact that I learned last year. During the Gulf War? There was a surge of PTSD diagnoses among World War II veterans. The same thing happened for Vietnam veterans during Iraq. Sometimes this shit sets in a long time after the fact."

Mike smirks. "Like when people are looking for a check from the government?"

Craig frowns.

Luke shakes his head. "I get it. You're one of those jerks who thinks he knows everything."

Mike freezes. Then in a conversational voice, he says, "And you're one of those crybabies who sits on the street begging for money saying 'poor me' aren't you?"

Always helpful, Nicole blurts out, *"Motherfucker."*

"Gentlemen…ladies… that'll be quite enough." Craig says. "Maybe we should stick to topics that have to do with supporting each other."

"You can shove your support up your ass." After he says the words, Mike gathers his bag and walks out, leaving the door ajar.

A weird silence settles over the room after his departure.

Nicole stands up, walks to the door and closes it. "He's kinda mad."

That evokes a choked laugh from Luke.

Terrell says, "Looks like he needs this group more than anyone."

"Maybe," Nicole quips. "Support groups can't cure being an asshole."

The four of us remaining in the room look at Craig as if to say, "What now?"

Luke actually asks it. "What now?"

Craig says "We continue as planned. This isn't for everybody. Not everybody needs it, and even less people want it. It's up to you guys. I called this group together for you—if you think you can use the support, here it is."

Nicole gets a wry smile on her face. "Well, I'm staying for all the drama." The rest of us laugh.

Craig says, "Why don't we get started with you guys telling us a little bit about your biggest challenges since returning to school."

Luke says, "That's easy. It's being around all these people."

I understand that. I honestly thought I was going to go insane in Tokyo sometimes. I grew to tolerate the crowding, and even to love the city, but I never felt entirely comfortable.

Craig asks, "What is it about the people that bothers you?"

"I guess there's some diamonds in the mix, but most of them are over-privileged, immature kids. It's all about partying and getting drunk and getting laid and who gives a shit about anything else. When I tell people I was in the Army they look at me like I said I was from Mars. As far as they're concerned I might as well be."

"How does that make you feel?" Craig asked.

"Sometimes I want to go back. Or at least get away from here. Honestly it was a little easier on the streets. Get something to eat, something to drink, you're good to go. At least until winter comes. Now it's all complicated. I hate that."

It takes me a minute to make sense of what he is saying. *It was easier on the street.* Was he homeless?

Nicole, who dropped her verbal filter in the toilet years ago and never got it working again, leans her head back, eyes narrowing a little. "Wait a minute... I thought you looked familiar. You used to panhandle over near the Starbucks." It wasn't a question.

Luke shrugs. "I played guitar some. Sang a little. I entertained people for a dime."

"I remember. I wondered what had happened to you."

"I guess I decided dorm life was better."

"That's not a hard call to make," Nicole says.

I catch myself wondering what Luke looked like when he was still in the Army. Before he had the scraggly beard and long hair and cheap secondhand clothes.

"How did you end up homeless?" I ask.

"Wasn't one thing. It was 109 of them."

Nicole shakes her head, and I get a sinking feeling, and it's obvious that Terrell knows what he means. He mutters, "Shit."

Nicole is still struggling, so I let her off the hook. I lean over and touch her on the shoulder. "He's saying he had 109 kills. He was a sniper." The room goes grimly silent. Nicole croaks something.

Luke says, "Not trying to kill the vibe guys. But you asked. I ended up homeless because I couldn't work. I can't work because I can't sleep. And I've got a little bit of an anger problem. Fucking Army threw me out. They said I had a personality disorder. Yeah, I had a personality disorder. Who wouldn't after shooting all those people?"

Personality disorder? "What does that mean?"

"Means they threw me out with the garbage. No veterans benefits. At least not until Craig helped me out. Anyway, I don't want to talk about my bullshit anymore. What about you?" He looks at me as he asks the question. "You lost your parents?"

He asks the question as if he thought I did it.

"It was an accident. A stupid freaking accident. They were killed by an oven."

Nicole says, "You don't have to —"

Luke stares at me. His eyes are uncomfortable.

Then he asks the craziest question I ever heard. "What kind of oven?" He has one eyebrow scrunched down as he asks the question.

I shake my head just the barest of shakes. "I…it … it was a commercial oven. It hit my Dad's car." I realize how weird that sounds, and I wave my hands a little in confusion, then say, "It was flying. I mean… it… the truck turned over. The oven flew out…"

Nicole looks horrified.

Terrell has an expression more appropriate for a Marine—incredulous near—amusement. He leans forward, and says, "Your parents were killed by a flying commercial oven?"

Luke nearly chokes himself. "That... is the craziest thing I've ever... what the hell?" He's obviously struggling to suppress... laughter?

Terrell mutters, "Oh my God."

That's all it takes. I don't think anybody outside of this room would understand what happens next. I don't even understand. Luke lets out a choked cry and loses it, exploding into the most inappropriate laughter ever. Immediately he looks ashamed of himself and he clamps his hand over his mouth and squeezes his eyes shut. Then Terrell bursts into laughter.

Nicole is going to set them both on fire.

But then, before my best friend can rush to the rescue, I do something that appalls even me. I start laughing myself. I can't stop. It rumbles up from my chest until I have to scream, and tears roll down my face as I both laugh and cry.

Luke has sort of gotten ahold of himself by now. "Christ, I am so sorry," he says. I shake my head urgently, unable to speak. Then I fall into mild hysterics again, but this time there is less laughter and far more tears.

"Shit," I mutter. Then I hiccup. I force down another burst of hysteria. Luke looks at me gravely and says "You don't have enough laughter in your life."

This is too much for Nicole, who was already outraged. "Fuck off!"

He raises his hands as if he were being arrested, and says, "Of course, officer." Then he turns to me, and says, "I'm sorry if I upset you."

I shake my head and hiccup again. I need to get it together. "It's fine. You didn't do anything."

"Except make fun of your parents who died," Nicole says.

"Sometimes you gotta laugh at death," Terrell says. "Seriously. Fuck death. Fuck war."

Craig, who has been silent most of the last little while, says, "I can get behind that. Zoe, how is your sister adjusting? And how are you adjusting to being... her guardian?"

I shift in my seat and find myself shrugging. "She's slowly doing better. A lot of nightmares, and she started stammering. I think she's got a lot of anxiety. Mono has helped, and so has... her...uh...uh... teacher." I swallow, aware from the heat rushing up my face that I'm blushing a little.

Mr. Deadeye Dick head across the table from me doesn't fail to notice. He raises an eyebrow and smirks a little. "Mono?"

"Jasmine's horse. The thing is... I'm looking for a therapist for her... but I'm not sure how effective talk therapy is going to be for a kid her age. I don't even know how effective it would be for me. Sometimes, when you see the way people heal when riding—it's amazing."

All of them stare at me with quizzical looks on their faces. Except for Nicole, who nods.

Luke asks, quietly, "Tell me more."

I shrug. "I can't explain it. They're like... thousand pound toddlers. Horses just do what they want. They'll break things, get into things, eat anything in sight. Part of taking care of them is learning how to communicate with your whole being. With people you can spin a web of words and make that a lie. You can't do it with horses... they take in far more information from your body language than anything else, so it kind of forces honesty. You basically have to love them."

Craig asks, "You've heard of horse therapy?"

I shake my head. "What's that?"

"It sounds like what you are talking about. I haven't heard a whole lot about it other than the fact that it exists, and that there are some people in the Valley specializing in it now. Maybe you should look into it?"

Huh… that's something that would've never crossed my mind. And did he mean, look into it because I need therapy? Or did he mean, look into it as a potential career option? Or for Jasmine?

Or maybe all three. As the meeting breaks up and I say goodbye to Nicole and the others, then drive back to South Hadley in the minivan, my mind keeps turning over the thought. Maybe I should consider getting a degree in psychology. I've always wanted to help people—it's one of the things I occasionally liked about being military police. If I were to go in that direction, I could stay right where I am on our land… Right where Jasmine needs to be… And not have to worry about some career dragging me away—it's something I could do right here.

Crazy to think that after all the times I resisted getting involved with horses, I might get back into them voluntarily.

CHAPTER EIGHTEEN

HOW TEMPORARY? (MATT)

"**M**ATT, I'M SORRY. I don't have any good way to break the news. I don't have any choice but to suspend you."

The words, delivered by Lauren Blunt, the principal and my boss, are like a blow to the head. I feel my cheeks heating up, my ears red, and my lips are like putty. Everything is slow, and details are painting themselves vividly in my mind. The slightly wilted flowers on her bookshelf. Her once-fashionable yellow suit.

"You can't." Not the most effective argument I've ever made. I'm so stunned I have a hard time gathering my thoughts enough to say anything.

She frowns and shakes her head. "Matt, it's not up to me. Just between you and me, this is … it's wrong. But it's out of my hands."

A wave of exhaustion sweeps over me. What is this about? Why?

"I don't understand," I say. "You're going to have to give me something here, Lauren."

She shakes her head. "There's no good reason, Matt. What the superintendent's office cited was... you were late three times this year. And they're claiming you modified the curriculum without approval for Jasmine Welch. I've never heard of anything like this."

I shrug. "It's because I represented the union."

She nods, her expression sad.

"What am I supposed to do, Lauren?"

"This is temporary," she replied.

"How temporary?" My tone is a little sharper than I'd intended.

"If Barrington wants to push this, drag it out, it may be the whole semester."

I suck in a breath. "That's crazy."

"I know, Matt. I'm just preparing you for the worst."

"The worst," I say, bitterly. "Barrington wants to make my life so miserable I quit, doesn't he? That's what this is all about."

She closes her eyes. "Matt. Please don't make this any harder than it has to be. I'll do my best to get you back as quick as I can. I promise."

I stand up. My head is heavy and I'm stiff with regret.

"I guess I'll see you around," I mutter. I've gone to so much effort to keep my past hidden, afraid something like this would happen. It turns out I needn't have bothered—my involvement with the Union screwed me up first. I don't know what to say to her, so I turn away.

She calls my name as I open the door, but I don't answer. I walk out of the office, letting the door swing shut behind me.

The afternoon passes in a fog. After the kids are gone, I walk to my classroom.

On the back wall, two months worth of artwork are displayed in a riot of color. I easily spot Jasmine's work, along with all of the others. I can't understand this. It's not just that I'm angry about the suspension. It's not the job at all. It's the kids.

This is my third year teaching. And it's only now, standing in this empty classroom, that I realize that I've fallen in love with this job. I've fallen in love with the crazy, whacky, silly kids. And having it taken away feels like losing Papa all over again.

At that thought, I feel tension settle in my body. I jerk open the drawers of the desk and take out my personal items. Notebooks. Pens and pencils. Charger for my phone.

I swallow. A photo of Zoe and Jasmine is in the drawer. I put my belongings in the box.

I feel a buzzing in my pocket. The phone, silenced during the school day. It's probably Zoe—I take the phone out of my pocket.

Messalina.

I flip the phone open. "Yeah?"

"Matt."

"Hey, Lina. What's up."

She sighs at the other end of the line. "I already know you're going to say no. Mamma made me call."

"What is it?" I ask.

"Gianni sprained his wrist. Bad one. He's going to be out of practice for two weeks."

"Who is Gianni?"

"He's our catcher, Matt. You met him when you were in Boston?"

"Ah, yeah. I remember."

Her tone is bitter. "I don't normally set myself up for rejection. Mamma—Matt—she asked me to ask you if you would come practice with us. Just for the weekend, give him a chance to get it back together. We're in New London this weekend."

New London is about ninety minutes south. I swallow. I don't answer.

"Matt? You there?"

I tap my foot nervously. Before Dad ... died—I used to love it. The thrill. The crowd. My entire body is shaking with rage.

Suspended.

My throat is dry. "I'll do it."

"Matt, it's only for a weekend, it won't—what?"

"I said, I'll do it."

She coughs. "That's what I thought you said. Are you sure?" She sounds concerned. Ironic, considering that she's been hectoring me to come tour with the family during the summer.

"Yeah," I say. "A couple days away is what I need."

"I'll come get you."

"You don't need to, Lina. I promise I'll come."

"No." Her voice is firm. "I mean... it's not because I don't think you'll come. I'm in Brattleboro, I'll be driving by your place in a couple hours anyway. I'll pick you up on the way."

"Okay," I say. "See you then."

"Matt?"

I don't respond. She finally says, in a quiet tone, "Thanks."

THERE. OVER THERE. (ZOE)

"Listen, I'm sorry to do this again, but I won't be able to meet tonight."

His voice sounds oddly stiff. "What's wrong, Matt?" I ask.

He breathes for a second, then says, "I'm sure you'll hear about it from Jasmine. I've been fired. Suspended. At least temporarily. But that's not—I need to go deal with some family stuff, okay? I just can't make it tonight."

His voice is rough as he says the words, his tone heavy with sadness. My heart hurts for him.

"It's okay," I whisper. The words come hard. I want to know what's going on. I want to know why he's so evasive. But I've been telling myself for days that a huge part of relationships is trust. It's not just that I want to trust Matt—it's that I have to if we're going to make it as a couple. So I continue speaking. "Do what you've got to do, then you can tell me about it later."

As I finish saying the words, I wonder if I mean them.

We hang up. Stood up again. And the babysitter will be here in twenty minutes. I stand there in the kitchen, arms crossed, mentally paralyzed somehow. Then I pick up the phone and dial Nicole's cell phone.

"Yeah," she answers.

"My plans just got cancelled. How about dinner? Drinks?"

"You betcha," she said. "Where?"

Matt and I were planning to eat in Amherst. I hesitate, then say, "How about Yarde Tavern."

I like the food at Yarde. I do. I'm not suggesting there because Matt lives in the apartment above the restaurant. Seriously, I'm not.

"Okay," she says. "Are we drinking?"

I know she takes the question seriously. Yarde is walking distance to my house. "Yeah," I say. "You can crash here."

"I'll see you in half an hour," she says.

"Perfect."

It would be in character for me to worry about what was happening with Matt. To question myself; question him. My normal *modus operandi* is to assume that I've done something wrong, and also to assume that Matt is hiding something.

It doesn't help that he obviously is hiding some things—things about his past. It bothers me, often. I've told myself that I need to let him tell me in his own time.

In the meantime, I have things to do. If Nicole will be here in half an hour, and the babysitter in 20 minutes, I have to get busy. The horses have already been fed and lead in for the night. Jasmine is watching television—I pass her as I head up the stairs.

When I was in high school, preparing for a date sometimes took hours. It still takes a while, but one thing the Army taught me was how to get myself together quickly. In fifteen minutes I showered and dried my hair, and I'm just finishing getting dressed when the doorbell rings. That will be Megan, who sat for Jasmine a couple of times before.

I'm just finishing putting on my mascara when I hear the front door open and close with a near slam. That would be Nicole.

I head downstairs and see that Jasmine and Megan are already playing a game of Uno. Nicole has joined them for a hand, which hopefully won't be long. I'm ready to go.

Megan looks up at me, brushing her pink hair out of her face. "Not going out with Matt tonight?"

She'll probably never admit it, but Megan blushes every time she says Matt's name. I shake my head. "He's busy with some family stuff."

Of course, I know nothing at all about his family.

"Maybe we can see him tomorrow," Jasmine says.

"I hope so." There's little else I can say.

I lean against the door frame and watch the game proceed. Jasmine has three cards left. Megan and Nicole each have a fairly sizable handful. They aren't letting her off easy—Jasmine is just very good at that game. Megan has a frown on her face as she stares at the yellow nine at the top of the deck. With a wince, she drops a yellow Skip card on top. Jasmine shakes her head and smiles, and lays down a yellow +2.

I step out of the room as Jasmine says, "Uno," and walk into the kitchen. For a second I think about calling Matt. I'm worried about him. If I call him, am I too clingy? Too needy?

Too distrustful?

I close my eyes, take a breath, and put the phone away. As I do so, I hear loud groans from the other room. I walk back in—it's clear that Jasmine won the game.

"Ready?" Nicole asks.

I nod. I turn to Jasmine. "I'll be home late. You'll behave for Megan?"

Jasmine rolls her eyes. "Well, of course."

I shake my head, a smile on my face, and lean down and hug my little sister. "Sweet dreams," I say. Then Nicole and I head out the front door.

It's chilly outside. Not cold, not yet. I can feel the first hint of winter. I tighten my coat around me, and begin walking. It's about a third of a mile from my house to the restaurant. Walking means we don't have to worry about finding parking, or about driving. It's dark, however. As we walk up the slope toward Mount Holyoke College, I'm uncomfortably reminded of the dream I had a few weeks ago. The dream of being chased. The dream of my father.

I must've betrayed something, because Nicole asks, "You okay?"

"Yeah," I say. We walk in relative quiet. Traffic is light along College Street tonight, though the night is punctuated by the occasional car passing us. I can hear the wind blowing in the trees, and the air carries the faint smell of fertilizer from somewhere in the distance. We reach the campus, on our right, and a long row of large houses that face the campus across the street. Mixed with the houses is an old observatory and the Gaylord library.

By the time we've gotten that far Nicole has reached her limit of silence. She begins to tell a story, stringing together a series of unlikely events which took place on campus. Nicole's stories are so often filled with exaggerations and outright inventions, I find myself not listening that closely. That is, until she mentions Tyler.

"… At that point, Tyler stood up on the table and shouted, 'sit down!'"

I shake my head. "Tyler? Matt's friend?"

"Haven't you been listening?"

"I missed something obviously. Why was Tyler there?"

Nicole doesn't answer right away. Her silence is… odd. I looked over at her, and even in the light of the street lamps I can see that she is flushed red.

"Wait a minute… Were you out on a date with Tyler?"

The silence drags. "No. I… I don't know. He's such a dick. Why would I go on a date with him?"

"I don't know, Nicole. You tell me."

"Well… Yeah. We were out on a date. What's the big deal?"

I just smile.

We're in luck. The patio at Yarde Tavern is packed, but there's one small table in the back corner. This will likely be the last time we can sit outdoors for a meal this year. Almost as soon as we sit down, a waitress takes our drink order and disappears.

"All right, fess up."

Nicole laughs and rolls her eyes. "There's nothing to say. We went out for dinner and drinks. I thought it might be fun.

"Well, was it?"

She gives the tiniest of nods in response.

"Come on, you gotta give me more than that." This time Nicole laughs. "Fine," she looks around the patio for a minute, as if she were trying to find some description of what happened. After a few seconds of floundering, she says, "I know he's a huge dick. But not completely. He's actually kind of a sweetheart. He showed up with flowers." She leaned close to me, and says in the quietest of voices, "Zoe, I ... like him... a little."

For Nicole, that is practically a declaration of love.

I start to ask another question, but she interrupts. "Enough about me. I don't want to talk about it anymore, it's too soon. What's going on with you? How's your semester going?"

I sigh. "I'm starting to get it. The math. It's just been too long, but it's starting to come back."

She grins. "I knew it would, you've always been crazy smart, Zoe."

I shrugged, squirming uncomfortably. "I don't know, I guess."

"No guessing."

"I never imagined I would find myself in college at UMASS, living here and raising Jasmine. Everything is... different."

"I know. You are making the best of it."

"I've had a lot of help. You. Matt. A lot."

Her change of expression is so sudden, that I freeze. Her eyes narrow, her face twisting into a frown, and she reaches out and grabs my wrist. Heart thumping, I whisper, "What is it?"

She whispers, "There. Over there."

I twist around and follow her gaze. A tall, lanky woman in a miniskirt with multicolored hair is walking to a newish looking car.

Matt walks beside her. They stop, say a few words to each other and he gets into the passenger side.

Blood rushes through my head, making my ears ring. The brake lights of the car light up. I'm frozen in place. As I sit there in disbelief, the headlights turn on and the woman drives off with my boyfriend.

CHAPTER NINETEEN

IS MISTER P OKAY? (ZOE)

"**Z**OE, I THINK it's time to slow down on the drinks."

Nicole and I moved to the bar some time ago—I'm not sure how long. "Don't be silly, I'm just getting started, this is only my second drink." I hiccup.

Nicole smiles and shakes her head. "No, that was drink number four."

I wave at the bartender, a woman vaguely in her twenties wearing a stretchy black outfit with her hair up in a ponytail. I can tell a man manages this restaurant, because all of the servers are young, female, and they all wear extremely tight shirts with low cut v-necks, obviously a required uniform. Fucking typical. "I'll have another," I say waving my finger vaguely in the direction of my martini glass.

"And that's the last one," Nicole says. "I don't feel like cleaning puke off my shoes."

I laugh and sit up. I point out the waitress's boobs to Nicole and ask her, "Why are men such dicks?"

Nicole chuckles. "That's just how God made 'em." She gives me a wry smile. "They aren't all that bad. You just had a run of bad luck."

Bad luck. No one has this kind of luck. Two boyfriends in a row cheated on me and got caught red-handed. That's statistically improbable.

I start to say that, but then realize that in my current state there is no way I'll be able to pronounce improbable. Or statistically. I feel a sudden urge to cry. "I thought he was different. I thought…"

"I know honey. If it's any consolation, I'll put the word out to my friends on the force. Old Matt is going to get a rash of speeding tickets."

I smile at the thought. "You're my best friend."

The bartender appears with another apple martini.

"That's why you're going to listen to me when I tell you that it's time to go in a few minutes."

"Do you think it's me?"

Nicole shakes her head violently. "Stop. You know that it's not you. Everything else aside, Matt was secretive from the very beginning. I don't know what he's hiding, but I do know that this is all him. I refuse to let you beat up on yourself because he's a jerk."

I take a too large drink of my martini, and say, "I never thought anyone could hurt me as bad as Chase did. But this is worse. Because it's not just me. Jasmine's involved too, and she's going to be devastated. I could kill him."

Quietly, she says, "You never did tell me what happened with Chase."

Damn it. I blink, trying to force back watering eyes. "I just didn't want to talk about it, Nicole."

"I think you should. What happened?"

"The same old thing." I shake my head, feeling desolate. "Everything was fine. Then he started making excuses. Not showing up. Canceling dates. Then I caught him."

Her eyes narrow. "Caught him?"

I nod. "He took his date to the same theater I went to one night. Tiny little Japanese girl."

"Asshole!"

"That's what I said, isn't it?"

She nods, a grim expression on her face. Her voice low, she asks, "What are you going to tell Jasmine?"

Helpless, I shrug. "I've got no idea. He said something about being suspended at work, but I don't know what to believe. Oh God," I say. My stomach is twisting into painful knots. "I'm going to have to see him at parent-teacher conferences and school functions. I'm going to have to pretend…"

Nicole grimaces. "No way. Jasmine needs to go into a different classroom."

I shake my head. "I don't know. She's attached to him."

Fervently, she says, "All the more reason, Zoe."

I feel queasy. Suddenly I don't want to finish my drink. I don't want to talk about it anymore. I want to go home, curl up in bed, and not come out until all of this goes away. I think back to earlier in the conversation. Nicole saying not all men are like that. I look at her for a second, then say, "Name one man—just one—who isn't a complete ass."

Nicole laughs uncomfortably. "Are you kidding me?"

I shake my head. "Think about all those dickheads we knew in Iraq. I'm sure they were all gentlemanly with their wives at home, but if one more swinging dick grabbed my ass I was going to pop a cap in his."

Nicole snorts. "Well, of course those guys were assholes."

"I'm serious. Just one. Name one guy."

Her expression is befuddled. Finally she shrugs and says, "Your Dad."

If Nicole had punched me in the face it wouldn't have hit me as hard as those two words. Tears spring to my eyes and run over before I can stop them.

"Oh, shit, Zoe. I'm sorry."

"Let's go," I say. I need to make a rapid departure before I cry even more. We have to pay the bill, and the bar is getting crowded, and it takes several minutes before we finally get out of there. Several humiliating minutes, because I can't stop the tears from running down my face. I can feel the men and women at the bar sneaking furtive looks at me. God knows what they are thinking. It's probably easily transparent that I'm crying because of a stupid guy.

It's more than that.

I'm not just crying because of Matt. I'm crying because of Chase... because of my parents... because of the war... because of me.

**

We stumble back to the house, with Nicole half supporting me. I'm embarrassed. Getting drunk because of a guy? Weakness. About halfway home, I have to stop and bend forward, afraid I'm going to puke. I manage to hold it down, and after a minute or five I say, "I'm okay. Let's go."

At the house, Nicole handles explanations for Megan. I have no idea what she tells her. I go upstairs and lay down in my clothes on top of the sheets. My head is swimming. I feel myself drifting to sleep. My entire body jerks in a tiny spasm.

When I open my eyes, it's nighttime and I'm back in Iskandiriyah in Iraq. I'm dreaming. Maybe. It's two in the morning, and the town is quiet except for the occasional dog barking. Nicole is at the front of the column with the first squad, and I'm in the back with the third. We're the only women on the patrol, and Lieutenant Anders insists we stay separated in case of an IED or a suicide bomber, lest they kill both of us. Even here, on patrol with an infantry unit preparing to arrest a suspected insurgent, we're treated differently.

This was a last minute mission. As is often the case, a tip from someone—possibly an intelligence agency, or an informer, has directed us to a small walled compound in the town.

Lieutenant Anders signals us to halt. For a few seconds he confers with the Sergeant, then gives a hand signal to don our night vision goggles. It's cold out, and the air has a weight to it. In a minute, maybe two, Anders will give the order to storm the compound. I'm just getting the goggles in position when loud shots ring out in the darkness. Anders goes down, a bullet in his shoulder, and his screams jerk me into instant wakefulness.

I struggle against the weight on my body, then realize it's nothing but blankets. I'm in my room.

Jesus Christ.

If there was ever any sign I shouldn't drink much, it's that dream. I'm chilled, my body drenched in sweat, and my heart pounds in my chest. I struggle to remember. I'm home and I'm safe. I'm home.

Then it hits me. I may be home, but my parents are dead, and I'm all Jasmine has left, and Matt is cheating on me with some anorexic bitch with wild looking hair.

I start crying. Now that is a sign that I should never ever, ever, drink.

***

When I stumble downstairs in the morning, Nicole is already awake, and looking far more chipper than I feel. She and Jasmine are at the kitchen table, Jasmine with a cup of hot chocolate, Nicole with coffee. Jasmine is chattering about something. I can smell the coffee, and I pour myself a cup in hopes of shaking away some of the cobwebs.

"Morning," Nicole says.

Jasmine continues her story. Something about school, and the other girls in her class. I slip into my seat and struggle to follow along. I missed the beginning, and none of it makes sense. Jasmine finally shifts randomly to a different topic. And not one that I'm prepared to address.

"Is Mister P coming for dinner? Can we have spaghetti? And ice cream? Chocolate? Or maybe strawberry."

I meet Nicole's eyes. She's expressionless.

Shit. Shit. Shit.

I swallow, trying to drum up the courage to tell my eight-year-old sister the truth.

Jasmine's no fool, and for an eight year old, she's remarkably perceptive. She stops talking and looks back and forth between me and Nicole.

"Jasmine…" I start to say.

"He's not coming? Did something happen to him? Is Mister P okay?" Her voice has an edge of panic in it. I'm stunned at first. Why *wouldn't* she be afraid of losing someone else? God I wish there's a way I could break this to her without breaking her heart.

"As far as I know he's okay. He—he called me yesterday and said he has some family business to take care of this weekend, and had to cancel. I don't know when he's going to be back."

Jasmine's voice has an edge to it as she responds. "But he will be back, right? Everything's fine, isn't it? Zoe? Is everything okay?"

I can't stop the tears that spring to my eyes. "Oh, Jasmine."

"Tell me the truth," she demands.

I close my eyes. Then I lie. "I just don't know right now. I don't know when he'll be back."

I just can't tell her that outside of school, we'll never see him again.

WHY DID YOU COME? (MATT)

The pounding of a fist on the cheap paneled door awakens me at 6 am on Saturday morning. For a few seconds I stare around in shock at the unfamiliar surroundings. I'm in a tiny one-person bedroom in one of the touring trailers. A thin mattress rests on a hand-built plank bed. A small shelf with a pole underneath accommodates clothing. Even though I've never been in this particular room, it is all too familiar. I spent much of my childhood living in campers little different from this. I shake the fog out and stand up just as the door trembles under another fist.

"I'm up!"

"It's about goddamn time." The welcome from my brother Tony makes me feel all warm and fuzzy inside. On the tiny shelf are two sets of practice tights. If I'm going to do this there is no point in screwing around. I go ahead and dress for practice. Once I'm finished, I leave the tiny room and walk down the equally narrow hallway to the crowded living quarters.

Lina sits at the table, her hands wrapped around a steaming mug of coffee. Across from her, Tony is unapologetically occupying two thirds of the table with his newspaper. It's spread across the table, a disheveled mess. A quick look shows me that it's the Hartford Courant. Mamma is at the tiny stove. In a black cast-iron pan, eight strips of bacon are sizzling, their scent flooding the room with the savory smell that makes my mouth water. On the griddle next to that, she's cooking pancakes.

"Good morning," Mamma says.

She steps away from the stove, and wraps her arms around me. She smells like childhood. "I'm so glad you came, Matty." She breaks off the embrace and goes back to cooking. I pour myself a cup of coffee, then slide into one of the seats.

"Why did you come?" Tony asks. His tone seems to indicate he'd have been just as happy if I hadn't.

I look at my brother, studying his face. He barely responds when Mamma upbraids him for his words. I don't understand why Tony is so hostile to me. We were close once. All of that changed my senior year, or what would have been my senior year. He never visited me in the jail. We've barely spoken a word to each other since.

"I guess I thought it was time," I say.

"So are you like a tourist? You're gonna come around for a few days, then drop out of our lives again?"

Messalina says, "Give him a break, Tony. What's your problem?"

Mamma says in a sharp tone, "You don't use language like that at my table."

Tony starts to say something else, and Messalina interrupts him. "I mean it, Tony. Stop it."

Tony sits back, annoyance on his face.

In as careful a tone as I can muster, I say, "I don't want to fight with you Tony." He snorts.

I sigh. There is no point in engaging in this right now. It's clear that Tony's not interested in anything I have to say. And the truth is, I don't have anything to say. I don't know why I'm here. Why now?

There were a lot of reasons I never came back. I wanted to go to college. I wanted to leave behind that life. A life with no stability. There's a lot to be said for a life on the road with the circus. But almost all of it is negative. No stability. No normal friends—everyone I knew and saw more than a few months in the winter, were also transients. On top of that, no matter how careful we were, no matter how much we focused on safety, accidents did happen. You can do everything you want to try to prevent them, but there's still some level of luck involved. After all—my dad might have lived through the heart attack if he'd been sitting in an office somewhere instead of flying through the air.

No point in dwelling on all of that. I'm here now. After breakfast, Mamma announces that we'll begin practice immediately. I'm still in good shape but that's still a long way from being able to catch and hold a person flying through the air. Even though I'm only standing in for the weekend ... I want to do it right. If only so I can show Tony.

After eating, I step out of the trailer and take out my phone and dial Zoe's number. If it was anyone else, there's no way I'd call this early in the morning. But Zoe's usually up well before five. My call goes unanswered—in fact it doesn't even ring. Maybe she forgot to charge her phone. I start to dial the house phone, but at that moment Tony and Lina come out of the trailer. They're dressed for practice.

I send Zoe a text to let her know I'll be out of touch most of the day and that I'll check in at lunchtime.

Five minutes later, we're standing around the practice lot. It's cold out, but we'll be warmed up soon enough. The rigging and nets are set up outdoors in the parking lot, forty feet high. This all has an incredibly familiar feel—Mamma has continued

Papa's years of precision in how the nets and rigging are configured. Any one of us could walk on to any lot in America and find our setup to be the same. The objective, of course, is to take advantage of unconscious reflexes. Not having to worry about the location of the apron or the safety lines meant that we can focus on the act, each other, and above all, safety.

Mamma motions for us to gather around her. Her eyes dart from Tony to Messalina to me. She purses her lips, then says, "It's finally time all my children were together again. The flying Paladinos were once the premier trapeze act in America. We headlined Ringling Brothers. Your father was the first flyer to ever perform a quadruple. And the three of you are part of this family."

Tony groans a little and mutters, "Mamma, come on. We know all this."

"Did I ask you to open your noise hole, Tony? You listen!"

Tony freezes. I feel like I'm twelve.

"We're not what we once were, and we never will be again. Your father, God rest his soul, is gone. But we do have this chance to shine."

Tony mutters, "Until Matty quits again."

I feel a surge of rage, and start to open my mouth, but Messalina beats me to it. "Shut up," she hisses at Tony.

Mamma continues. "Matty has a good career, Tony, and I'm proud of him. You need to stop. He won't be with us anymore, except these few days, and that's fine. We have this chance. And I want to make it count."

Tony doesn't exactly acquiesce, but he does stop talking.

Mamma continues. "We'll do matching stunts. Classic trapeze, Matt and Tony catching. We'll start with the basics, since Matty hasn't been in the ring."

Tony murmurs, "Neither have you Mamma, pretty much."

"It's time then isn't it?"

I try to hide my unease. Mamma is in great shape for fifty, but I've already lost one parent in the ring. I also know that no one on earth could dissuade her from this course.

"I'd like a few minutes to get the feel again before we attempt any catches. I don't know how my timing is."

"Go."

I walk to the ladder and stare up into the rigging. My heart begins to thump in my chest, but I swallow, place my hands on the ladder, lift one foot and begin to climb. My anxiety is much higher than it was when I was up in the rigging with Mamma a couple weeks ago, when I knew I was only going to stand on the platform. Now, I'm planning to do the one thing I said I would never do again. When I reach the platform, I wipe my hands in rosin, then reach up to the chalk bag and dust my hands carefully. Then I reach up and take the bar, lift high, and swing out.

My stomach lurches as I go into free-fall and swing at the end of the pendulum across the lot and back up into the air. At the top of the swing I jackknife my legs up, pull my body straight, and flip over so I'm facing back toward the ground. Then I swing my legs in front of me and begin the descent again, this time nearly twice as fast.

As I swing back down at the lowest part of the arc, I realize that I'm completely comfortable. It's been years since I've been in the rigging, but everything feels very familiar. I flip again as I reach the top of the swing, then come back down. The air whooshes in my ears as I build up speed, and on the end of the fourth swing I let go of the bar, flip myself over and position myself in the catch trap. Then I swing back down, arms outstretched and feet in the ropes. I swing all the way back up, testing the feel and my stability. This is the essential point. When I'm in the trap, I have to be absolutely stable. At the height of the swing, I'll be taking hold of a hundred pound weight moving at two G's. I could lose my grip on Mamma or Messalina, sending them flying off into the net or the apron.

That's exactly what happened after Papa had his heart attack.

At the end of the next swing up, I let go with my legs again and flip up, grabbing the bar with one hand. I let myself swing with one hand all the way back up the arch again, flip over, and do a high arching dive into the net.

That dive always elicits screams from the audience, no matter how much they know that there are nets underneath. At the last second I roll into a ball, and bounce on the net. A second later I'm on the ground.

"Looks good," Tony says. "But your right foot wasn't wrapped properly, you'd lose it if you'd caught someone that way."

Mamma nods. "He's right. You need to practice that."

I nod, taking the criticism in stride. People's lives depend on this being correct.

We practice for hours. From the beginning, I'm focused on re-learning the basics. Timing. Positioning and grip on the ropes. Getting the feel of the catch trap again. By the time it's close to noon I'm trembling. I need to eat, a lot and as soon as possible. Mamma looks at me and says, "One more time before lunch, Matty. This time I want you to catch me."

I freeze up at the words.

The pain starts at roughly the center of my rib cage and slides upward along my sternum toward my throat. I have to remind myself to breathe.

"Matty. You are ready to do this. Your father's death was not your fault."

I stare at her, barely understanding. I can smell the heat of the lot in Texas where he died. I can hear the voices of the animals at the lot. I can see his red angry face as I shouted at him, *"I wish I wasn't your son! I wish you were dead!"*

I'd do anything to take that back. Anything in the world.

"Matty?" Messalina's voice breaks through my concentration. I look up, almost startled, and say, "I'm ready." I can't look at them. I turn away and climb up into the rigging.

Everything seems to move in a painful ragged slow-motion. I keep thinking of the possible problems. What happens if I'm too slow? If I only get a good grip with one hand? Or if I slip? Am I strong enough to hold her? Will I have to compensate for loss of strength because of her age? These thoughts race through my mind even as I take hold of the bar and swing out over the lot.

The already cool air chills me when it blows past my sweat. I swing forward and back, forward and back. On the third time as I'm about to reach the apex of my return swing I call ready. She drops into her swing the same time I start to descend.

We hurtle toward each other, and at the right moment she launches into space toward me. It's all happening in incredibly slow detail. She flips forward in an easy double forward somersault, extends her arms, and our hands and wrists slap together.

Instantly my hands closed around her wrists, taking her weight as we swing into the return. We are face-to-face, and like Papa always used to have, she has a grin on her face. In addition to that grin, her eyes are wet with tears.

With a graceful arc, we return back to the center and she releases with a half twist, perfectly reaching the bar and swinging back up, even as I drop to the net. I'm breathing again, but I feel oddly numb, even as Messalina runs over to congratulate me. After all, it's the first time I've caught someone since the day my father died.

I realize that right now the only person I want to talk to is Zoe. She doesn't know anything about this part of my life.

Somehow doing this... it's time to tell her. About my Dad. About the time I spent in jail. All of it. We break for lunch, and instead of going in directly to eat, I retrieve my phone. One missed call, one message, both from Zoe. I decide to listen before I call her. I have a dumb smile on my face as I dial into my voicemail, but the smile erases itself instantly.

Her voicemail is clear, cold and direct.

"Matt. I've had it with your secrets and lies. Don't call me again. Don't come here. I'm having Jasmine switched to a new class, and you goddamn well better stay away from my sister. I don't want to hear from you ever again. Goodbye."

I listen to the message with mounting disbelief and shock. *That's not possible.* I sink down, my back against the trailer, in shock.

No. I dial her number, but something strange happens. It doesn't go to voicemail, and it doesn't ring. Instead, it clicks to silence. I try the home number, but get an automated message, "The caller you are trying to reach is not accepting calls at this time."

She's blocked calls from me?

I don't understand! I know I cancelled at the last minute last night—and didn't give a very good excuse. But ... seriously? I close my eyes and press my hands against my temples, trying to shut out the suddenly blooming headache.

CHAPTER TWENTY

MY BOYS (MATT)

O N SUNDAY NIGHT, I had to tell my mother and siblings the truth.

"The thing is, I've been suspended at work. The superintendent was angry I represented the union, and even though we won, I'm getting the backlash."

Messalina and Mamma looked shocked. Tony stays expressionless.

"So… That's why I'm free for at least another week. Maybe longer. I don't know."

As is custom with my family, we eat a light meal for dinner… There's no performance for another week, but it's an ingrained habit to not eat much food before going into the ring. Heavy meals are reserved for lunch and after performances. Because it's Sunday, Mamma has no plans to regroup for practice tonight after dinner.

When I walk out of the trailer, it's already dark. Winter is on its way, and along with the darkness I feel the chill in the air. For the hundredth time that day, I take out my phone. No messages. No texts. For the first time in my life, I regret not having a smart phone. Maybe Zoe has updated her Facebook or Instagam or whatever else it is she uses. I don't know which ones, because I don't use them. First, I don't have a smartphone, and second I don't need students... or their parents... friending me online.

I wasn't alone amongst my peers in refraining from social media, but I also wasn't in the majority. It wasn't just a question of students and their parents to be honest. If anything, my lack of Facebook or Instagram is merely a symptom of my greater social isolation. I go out with Tyler for drinks every once in a while, but that's it. I'm not part of a larger community. I don't go to church, or social clubs, or family events.

Somehow, without my even realizing it, Zoe and Jasmine have broken me out of that isolation. Now, with Zoe not returning my calls, I feel it like a stab through the gut.

Uselessly, I dial her number again. The automated response: the caller you are trying to reach is not accepting calls at this time.

In other words, she's blocked calls from me.

Earlier today I even tried her from Lina's phone. Zoe answered, I started talking, and before I could get half a dozen words in, she'd disconnected.

I don't understand why. I know there's been a couple of weekends when I broke off our dates with no warning, but this seems drastic as a response. Then again, sometimes responses just don't make sense.

On Monday morning, instead of waking up and heading to school, I get up and practice with the family. It has a rhythm that is so deeply familiar, I fall right into it. Warm-ups, followed by crossovers, followed by the more difficult stunts and finally running through the whole routine twice. Mamma runs the practice like a drill sergeant, her emphasis on safety as intense or more than even my father's had been.

On Monday afternoon, Gianni comes by the rigging. His right arm is in a sling. Tony's face darkens, and he drops to the net followed by Mamma. A few moments later, the rest of us gather around.

"So what's the news?" Tony asks.

The response is a head shake. "Doc says I have to take at least a month off the ropes."

"A month!" Tony's eyes flash with anger. "We're playing in Springfield this weekend. You have to be ready by Friday."

Mamma interjects. "Hush, Tony. If the doctor says he's not ready, he's not ready. I will not have somebody killed because of a foolish accident." She glowers at Tony as she says the words. "If we can't perform the show, we can't do it. I won't risk our family's safety."

An uncomfortable silence falls over us, and I realize that Messalina is looking directly at me.

I had only agreed to practice with them as a fill-in to help through the weekend.

I have nowhere to go this week anyway.

I don't need to be at work. Zoe apparently wants nothing to do with me. Until I get things sorted out at work, I am free.

I roll my eyes up to the sky. "I can stay through the week."

Mamma immediately responds. "You don't have to do that, Matty."

"It's fine, Mamma."

Mamma's face softens. "I'm glad you're with us."

Messalina says, "Me too."

Tony scowls. Then he stomps off.

That is it. I've had it. I don't necessarily expect to be greeted like the prodigal son, but the barest of politeness would be appreciated. I start after Tony.

Messalina grabs at my arm. "Matty, let him go."

"No. I want to talk to him."

I shake her hand off and follow him. He doesn't make fifteen feet before I grab his arm and spin him around.

"Keep your hands to yourself," he snarls.

I back off, holding my hands slightly in the air. "I just want to know one thing, Tony. Why the hell are you so hostile to me? What did I do to you?"

"Fuck off,"

I sag in frustration. "I don't get it. The least you can do is have the courtesy to tell me why you're so pissed off."

"It's not enough that you're a self-centered jerk?" He demands. "You were Papa's favorite. *Matty, you're going to be the catcher. Matty, you're the steady one.* But then when Papa died, you flaked. Go off to college, do something else and leave the rest of us to work with strangers." He makes a fist, extending his index finger and poking me in the chest. "I've been here every day. And you know what? We don't need you. Go back to your girlfriend and your stupid job."

The verbal attack staggers me. "Tony… It's not like I left voluntarily. They threw me in jail."

Tony's face works in anger. "You think I don't know that? All we heard before that was you screaming at him. Telling him to stop trying to control your life. Telling him to butt out. Telling them to go to hell. Is it any wonder people thought you killed him?"

I hear a gasp behind me, Mamma's voice. "Tony, you know that's not—"

I hold up a hand flat behind me to signal stop. "No, Mamma. Let him say it. Do you think that's true, Tony? Do you think I killed Papa?"

Tony slams his palms against my chest, knocking me back. I stagger trying to keep my footing. His next words come in a choked shout. "No! He died anyway. We lost everything. He was gone, we left the big top, everything fell apart. And you didn't bother to come back and help us put it back together. The minute you got out of that jail, you ran away. I want to know why."

A maelstrom of emotion floods through me. There are a thousand things I could say, and there's nothing I can say. I struggle to articulate a sentence, and he shouts at me again. "Why? It was bad enough that we lost Papa, but we lost you, too. Why?"

The words are ripped out of me. "Because I was ashamed. I was so damned ashamed. The last thing Papa ever heard me say was, *I wish you would die.* He didn't hear me say, I love you. That's the last thing. I couldn't save him! I tried! I couldn't hold on, he was a dead weight and I lost him!"

I'm horrified as the last words come ripping out of my chest.

I don't see the fist coming. I hear a howl of rage from Tony, then my vision goes black. This time I'm knocked off my feet. Almost before I hit the ground, Tony shouts, "I'm sorry!"

As he shouts the words I can hear anguish in his voice. He drops to his knees next to me and grabs my shoulders and says, "I'm sorry. I didn't mean to hit you. I didn't... I'm sorry I hated you. It wasn't your fault. It wasn't your fault we lost him, but I hated you anyway."

I'm shocked by the words, but not nearly as shocked as I am by the tears which are freely running out of his eyes now. Tony grabs me by the shoulders and throws his arms around me. In a rough voice, he whispers, "Forgive me, brother?"

I feel an overwhelming flow of grief as he asks the question. Not just grief. Exhaustion. Love. Release. Grace.

I whisper. "Of course I forgive you. Can you forgive me?"

He nods, unable to speak.

Then I feel another set of arms around me. Mamma. "My boys. I'm so glad you're home."

I'll be there (Matt)

Tomorrow morning, the circus is packing up and moving to Springfield for three nights. Despite my extreme reservations, I've agreed to perform with the family. The reservations are no longer emotional... merely practical. I've been out of the ring too long. But for the last six days, we've practiced the routine to the point of perfection. I can still catch. I can still fly. I'm sore as hell. I'm exhausted. But I'm doing it.

I've tried to reach Zoe all week with multiple calls. No luck.

I'm going to have to go in person. She told me to stay away, but I won't do it without at least some kind of explanation. I deserve that much. On Tuesday I debate just leaving and going to see her. Instead, I decide to give her a few days to cool down. She can't sustain this kind of rage. Can she?

After dinner, Mamma says, "We'll practice one hour after dinner tonight. I want you to get a lot of rest. We'll move in the morning, go through the routine twice tomorrow afternoon when the big top goes up, then perform tomorrow night." I nod. That actually sounds fine.

I stand up from the table and stretch, and that's when my phone rings.

That's odd. The caller is Peggy Young. I answer it immediately. "Hello? Peggy?"

"Why didn't you tell me what was going on with this bullshit suspension?" She launches into the question without any preamble.

I sink into a seat. My mother gives me an odd, concerned look. "I don't know... I think I needed a few days away. And besides, what's the point?"

I can hear the anger in her voice. "What's the point? The point isn't just you, Matt. It's that the superintendent can't just retaliate against people who speak up. He's abusing his power, and you are letting him."

I wince. "I don't know about all that..."

"I do. If you let him get away with this, Matt, then someone else will be next."

I sag in my seat. There's no doubt in my mind that she is correct about that. "I've been taking care of some personal business for the last several days. Maybe I've been avoiding it... What can we do about it?"

"How long is your suspension supposed to be?"

I shrug automatically, even though she can't see me. "I don't know."

She mutters something under her breath that sounds suspiciously like a string of curses. "I'll fix him. Meet me at the superintendent's office tomorrow. 11 o'clock."

I think about it for a few second. We're not due to practice tomorrow until two in the afternoon—I could get to South Hadley in the morning, meet with her, then it's twenty or so minutes back to Springfield. "Hold on a second," I say. I set the phone down and say to Mamma, "I'm going to need to go home tomorrow morning. I'll meet you guys for practice in the afternoon."

She nods. "Do what you have to do Matty."

I put the phone back to my ear. "I'll be there."

CHAPTER
TWENTY-ONE

HOW DO YOU HEAL FROM THAT? (ZOE)

IN MY DREAM, the phone rings off the hook. It must be Matt calling, or Chase. Nicole is across the alley from me, crouched close to the ground with her rifle against her chest. Her helmet is slightly askew, the night vision goggles raised up so that I can see her eyes. The exposed skin at her neck and face is dirty, and there a bloodstain on the sleeve of her uniform.

"Turn it off," she whispers, the words coming out like bullets. "They'll hear."

I try to turn it off, but I can't. It rings again. I wince and so does she. Inside the house next us someone is shouting—the squad is in there clearing the house. They don't want us in there – not because we're women, but because we're *police*. I hear a thump followed by a scream. I can hear scrabbling in the sand down the alley, but I can't see anything. Someone is coming.

The phone rings again.

Terror rocks through me as I hear an explosion of movement at the end of the alley, followed by the distinct sound of a Kalashnikov firing. Nicole and I drop to our stomachs and return the fire, but then she's gone and I'm alone in the alley with my rifle and the insurgents. Tracers fly back and forth, then a window that wasn't there a moment ago opens up on the side of the house. My father leans out, a disapproving frown on his face, and he says, "If you'd gone to college like I wanted, then you wouldn't be in this situation."

His face accuses me.

That's when I hear Jasmine scream. Where is she? I search the darkness but she's nowhere to be found. The screaming seems to come from outside the alley beyond the insurgents. I pick up my rifle and charge toward them firing blindly. One falls, then another, and the others back away, then somehow I'm through them without getting hurt and I'm on College Street near the Village Commons. Matt is there, sitting at the table in front of the Yarde House, and he's whispering in the ear of the Japanese girl Chase was with. I stop in place, staring at him in shock, not understanding how she can be here. Then Jasmine screams again and I can't stay here. I turned away from that and run toward the sound of her voice.

My eyes pop open and I am wide awake. My phone is plugged in on my nightstand, screen lit up and alarm sounds coming from it. I roll over and press snooze. Then I lay on my back.

Oh, that was a *nightmare.* I lay there struggling to breathe.

The nightmare is still clear in my mind. Running through the sand. I shake my head to shut out the dream. I have too much to do to allow myself to indulge in such things.

I sit up, planting my feet on the floor before I start to fall back asleep. I dress in a pair of tough jeans and a flannel shirt, then head downstairs and start the coffee pot. Once that's going, I slip outside and walk in the cold darkness towards the barn.

As soon as I slide the door open, the horses begin to snort. Mono whinnies and paws at the floor, then snorts again.

"All right, all right, relax."

The horse responds with another loud snort, then kicks the side of the stall with a loud bang.

"Hey!" I shout. "Knock it off!"

Mono snorts again, but stops kicking. I load three bales of hay on the back of the tractor, then ride it out onto the pasture, breaking the hay up into small bunches that I spread across the fields. The horses will still graze on the grass, but now that the first frost has come and gone, there's little nutritional value left and their diet has to be supplemented. As I'm finishing spreading the hay, I glanced toward the house and I can see that Jasmine's light is on. In the last few weeks we've fallen into a routine. She'll come downstairs and join me in the barn in a moment, leading the horses into the pasture while I muck out the stalls.

Once that's finished and the horses are out in the field, both of us head inside and shower. Jasmine barely speaks a word this morning. She's barely spoken the entire last week, and when she has she's stumbled and stammered over her words. Losing Matt was a giant step backward in her recovery.

At least I'm hoping to divert her tonight—Nicole bought tickets to the circus. Thank God she's not bringing Tyler. Just us three girls. Thank God for good friends.

As I shower, my mind runs back over the dream. My father leaning out the window and chiding me that I should have gone to college instead of joining the Army. Some days, I don't think much about how my dad felt about my choices. Others, I try not to care—I made the decisions I felt I needed to. On the worst days, I think about my father and his disappointment in me and it breaks my heart that I can't do anything to change it. I remember how awkward and non-communicative he had been at my basic training graduation. He'd barely looked at me.

Someday soon I need to just clear out the garage. Not even look at his things because God knows what I'll find in there. After all, my dad was a prolific diarist. I don't think I could stand to read his thoughts about me not going to college. And what's so damned frustrating about that is that now that I am going to college—and I'm starting to think I might do okay—he's not around to see it.

I need to stop dwelling on this, I have too much to do. Instead, I head downstairs and scramble some eggs. When I was in school I never paid much attention to breakfast, mostly cereal and toast in the mornings. The Army taught me that breakfast makes a bigger difference in my day than anything else. So I've made a habit of making a good one for me and Jasmine. When she gets downstairs two plates are at the table with strips of bacon, eggs, toast and jelly. I savor the taste of my coffee for a moment before I begin to eat.

Jasmine doesn't say a word through the meal. I try to engage her—asking her about school yesterday and what they have planned for today. She shrugs. "I don't know. We—we have a substitute every day now." We continue to eat in an uncomfortable silence until it's time for her to go outside for the bus. As she throws her backpack on, she says "You—you—you…" She screws up her face in frustration, then bursts out "You don't have to wait with me. I'm old enough to catch the bus by myself."

I glanced out the window. The sky is pink, the sun barely up. "I know. I like to." She opens the door and walks out front, slamming it behind her.

I sigh, then open the door myself and step out onto the porch. She's already halfway to the end of the driveway. I stand in the porch and watch her. I don't know how much damage the break with Matt has done, but I do know that Jasmine was already too hurt to begin with.

As the bus arrives, I shout, "Have a great day Jasmine. I love you!" I wave.

She doesn't reply or look at me as she climbs up the steps of the bus. I stay there on the porch for another minute or two, then head inside to get my keys and books and head to school. Before I go, I gulp down the last few swallows of coffee and put the cup in the sink.

Before I get in the car I double check that the gates to the pasture are securely closed. Paul has agreed to check in on my horses through the day while I'm in class. In return, I'm letting him use our lower pasture for his horses. He's been needing the space because of his expansion, and I need the help because I can't go to school and take care of the horses at the same time.

A few minutes later I'm headed out of South Hadley and over the notch, a two-lane road through the woods and over a mountain headed to Amherst. School has been going better, except for calculus. Even that was better until this week, but I'm certain I blew the test on Wednesday. It's been a week since I saw Matt leave his apartment with that woman, six days since I broke up with him over the phone and blocked any communications from him.

I haven't cried.

Well, except when I was drunk. To be clear, I suppose I could cry. I allowed myself to let down all of my defenses. I allowed myself to trust him. And like always: when I trust, I get kicked in the teeth. So, I refuse to cry.

He doesn't deserve my tears.

That said, I was a mess this week. I couldn't concentrate, I did a half-assed job of studying and when it was time to prepare for my calculus exam I just stared at the book, the numbers and letters swimming around in front of me.

Maybe Nicole is right. I should just join the force, drop out of college, and start earning a living.

For that matter, I bet they'd make me go to college if I was a campus cop anyway—former MPs might get a leg up—but they expect officers to have degrees. And I don't want to spend my career chasing drunks and writing parking tickets. Nicole tells a lot of great stories, but the common thread of them is that she is a babysitter for 30,000 over-privileged kids.

It's with that in mind that I decide to buckle down and focus. When I get to the campus, I adjust my frame of mind and head to class.

The little room in the student union is more crowded than last time. Terrell is there, along with two other guys I don't know. One introduces himself as Mark Perez, a former Air Force enlisted man who was detailed temporarily to the Army for two tours in Iraq. The other man is older, in his late 30s.

"Nick Conti," he says. "Retired Sergeant Major." We shake hands. I ask Craig if Luke is coming. He frowns, and gives a minute shake of his head. "I don't think he's going to be here. He's not been to class in a week."

Nicole and I meet each other's eyes. A mix of thoughts run through my head all at once. I've got enough problems without taking on someone else's issues. More than enough problems. On the other hand, I had instinctively warmed to Luke, and his haunted stare left me deeply concerned. I mean—I have nightmares about the war. I freak out sometimes, and find myself feeling weird and disconnected and randomly angry. What I experienced in Iraq wasn't anything like the trauma he carries around every day. I can't imagine what goes on inside his head.

"Why don't we get started," Craig says. "I think this is going to be everybody."

Like last time, we go around the room and introduce ourselves. Craig begins the session by prompting us with questions about our experiences in college since returning from the military. I find myself drifting off periodically. Thinking about Jasmine, and how she has begun stammering again; her listless behavior since last Saturday morning.

I think about Matt. I don't understand how he could live that way. I knew he was secretive about his past, and assumed there was something there that he was ashamed of. But I never expected that he was cheating, when our relationship had barely even begun. I never expected that he was lying to me when he said he had urgent family business. I never expected he was going to break my heart or Jasmine's.

I find myself thinking about Luke Osmond. *109 reasons,* he had said.

How do you heal from *that?* I couldn't even imagine the struggle and pain he must go through. It made my problems with Matt feel trivial. I remember Nicole saying that she had seen Luke panhandling in front of the Starbucks in Amherst. I have a little bit of time after class before I have to head back home. I decide to go see if he's there.

ARE YOU GOING TO EXPLAIN? (MATT)

I get back to South Hadley at 10:35 in the morning, driving Messalina's car. Too much time to stand around waiting at the superintendent's office, but not enough time to go check on Zoe or take care of anything else. So I park the car near the town hall, and walk up the street to *The Egg and I*, a small diner just a couple of blocks away. I grab a used newspaper off a small stack near the door, sit down and order a cup of coffee. While I wait I scan the headlines.

It's the local weekly, and there's not a whole lot of excitement in there. Coverage of the high school games, meetings of the South Hadley Falls Association which is trying to rejuvenate the area, other similar stories. On the editorial page, however, it's a different story. A half page editorial covers the recently ended strike. I scan through it and I'm shocked by the hostility of it. I look back to the byline—Lauren Blakely. I should have realized. Now I read the editorial more carefully. She points out, truthfully, that the strike itself was illegal. Most of the rest of the first half is drivel, but when I get to the next-to-last paragraph, my mouth sets in anger. I'm mentioned there, described as a union organizer who was recently suspended for incompetence.

Anger is not the word to describe my response.

I'm still steaming over the editorial when I walk into the town hall at 11 am . Peggy Young is standing in the lobby and gives me a warm smile when I step inside.

"Hello, Matt." Her smile fades almost instantly. "What's wrong? Oh, wait. You've been out of town, haven't you? You must have just seen the pleasant editorial."

"I'm going to sue Lauren Blakely."

She shakes her head. "There's no need for that. We're going to walk out today with everything we want."

"I don't see how you can say that with such confidence."

She gives me a mysterious smile. "That's because you aren't from South Hadley. I'm guessing you've never lived any length of time in a small town."

I shrug. "I've never lived for a long time anyplace."

"What you need to understand, Matt, is that we all know each other's secrets. Some of us... even know yours." She taps her fingers on her forehead as she says the words, then she starts up the stairs.

She can't possibly mean what it sounds like she means.

I stand staring after her dumbly, until she calls down from the first landing. "Coming, Matt? You're not going to let an old lady beat you up the stairs, are you?"

Shaken out of my daze, I start up the stairs after her.

Barrington's office is the same as it was a week ago. It's quiet, and the receptionist in front of the office politely bars the way. "Mrs. Young... Mr. Paladino... I'm afraid the superintendent isn't seeing anyone right now. Can you make an appointment?"

"Well, aren't you sweet? Rest assured, young lady, he'll see us now. Go tell him who's here."

The receptionist is startled by the response. She stands up and does as Peggy says.

Six seconds later, we are ushered into Barrington's office. Peggy merely smiles, as if she expected nothing less. I'm certain if it was just me they'd keep me cooling my heels for the next week.

"Please have a seat, Mrs. Young. Paladino."

Peggy gives him a contemptuous look. "That won't be necessary, we won't be here long enough."

I don't say anything.

Barrington is startled by her statement. He raises his eyebrows, and says, "Well then. Let's get to it. What can I do for you?"

Peggy says in a calm voice, "You can reinstate Matt Paladino effective immediately."

Barrington's eyes widened.

"Why ever would I do that?"

Peggy grimaces. "I had hoped not to dredge your past into it, Michael. You've been a little power mad since you took this job. But don't think I don't remember you as a 10th grade bully in my class. I remember well. So here's what I'm going to insist on. You are going to reinstate Matt. You are going to stop retaliating against teachers in this school system. You are going to put it in writing that you will not involve yourself in disciplinary matters anymore."

Barrington frowns. "You've finally gone off your rocker.. Why would I do any of those things?"

Peggy smiles. She reaches into her purse and removes an 8.5 x 11 envelope. She passes it to the superintendent.

He frowns, tears open the envelope, and begins to look through the papers it contains. He reads the first few words, then blanches. Instantly he stuffs the papers back into the envelope. Face pale, he looks up at Peggy.

"Where did you get this?" The question comes out in a hiss.

Peggy shrugs. "The question isn't where I got it, Michael. I've had those papers for many years. The question is, what am I going to do with the original?"

"I ought to have you arrested for blackmail, you witch."

"I'm sure that would make for entertaining headlines. *Superintendent presses charges against teacher who reveals sexual assault.* Yes, I do think that has a nice ring to it."

His face flushes red. *Sexual assault? What?* I stare back and forth between the two of them, feeling like a spectator in someone else's drama.

"I was *seventeen*," he says.

She shrugs. "All the same, I suspect parents in this district would want to know that the superintendent of schools once assaulted a girl at a drunken party."

"First, that's not what happened. Second, the charges were dropped, and you know that. *You know that.*" His voice is taking on a desperate tone.

Peggy leans forward, hands touching the edge of his desk. In a low tone, she says, "I know that your family pressured the police to drop the charges, and with their money, they were able to do it. I know that Lynn was threatened with having her name dragged through the mud because she'd gotten drunk and found herself in a dangerous position. I know that even if you were never formally charged, you were as guilty of rape as if you'd knocked her down in an alley."

Her voice drops to a low, dangerous tone. She says, "I know I've got nothing to lose. I can retire any time, and you can't take that away from me. And I know you were exactly the wrong person to be in this job. I'll be damned if you'll do any more harm to this school system."

With that, the battle is over. Barrington sinks into his seat. His eyes have an unfocused look, almost as if he were drunk. He waves a hand and say, "Fine. You win." Then his eyes shift to me with a humorless gaze. For a second I think he's going to give me a threatening look. Instead, his eyes just slide off of me as if I weren't even there.

"Matt can come back to work?"

Barrington shrugs. "Report to work on Monday, Mister Paladino. I'll send an email to Mrs. Blunt."

We leave the office without any further interaction. As soon as we step into the hall, I blurt out, "How—"

She holds up a hand and says, "Wait."

I shut up, and follow her down the stairs and out of the building. When we reach the front door, I look at my watch. It's ten after eleven. Ten minutes, and my whole life just changed.

"Are you going to explain?" I ask.

She smirks and slightly shakes her head. "I told you Michael was a... a problem... in high school. His family bought his way out of all manner of scrapes. In the winter of his senior year, the football team had a party and he had sex with a girl who was too drunk to say no. The charges were dropped, his record was clear. But ... the poor girl. She transferred to Belchertown High School, but it followed her even there. This was the 1980s, and date rape was neither uncommon nor was it typically prosecuted. I'm sure you can imagine, it would ruin Barrington's career if that came out in public today. "

"That was a big gamble."

"No. Not a gamble at all. I knew precisely how he was going to react."

I give her a smile. "For what it's worth, I'm grateful."

"It's worth a great deal, Matt."

With that, we part ways. Peggy headed back to the high school, and me ... well, I've got some business I need to take care of. I drive out of the Falls and up to College Street and pull into Zoe's driveway.

No one home. Of course not. Zoe's probably in class, and Jasmine's at school. I scrabble around in the car, searching for some paper. Under the seat is a flyer from the circus's appearance in Boston. I stare at the blank back of the flyer. I'm going to write the wrong thing. I'm going to mess this up.

No. No, I'm not. I write a long note on the paper, then fold it. I step out of the car, walking up to the front step of the house and on to the porch. The wood creaks under my steps. I take the folded note and slip it into the crack in the doorjamb. There's no way she'll miss it.

Finished, I walk back to the car. I'm breathing heavily. Time to head to Springfield: I've got a show to get ready for.

ALL THAT DRAMA (ZOE)

An hour and a half later, I walk up the sidewalk in the center of Amherst, a small stretch in the center of town featuring old shops and restaurants. A frequent location for homeless panhandlers is the bench near the Starbucks—as I walk toward it, I see that Luke is there.

He looks even more unkempt than he did at our first meeting a couple of weeks ago. His eyes are bloodshot, his hair tangled, his knuckles scraped raw and red. He sits on the bench strumming a guitar. I walk toward him.

"Zoe," he says, his tone warm. "This is an unexpected visit."

Without asking I sit down on the bench next to him. "I heard you had stopped going to class, and you weren't at Craig's veterans meeting today."

He shrugs. "What's it to you?"

His breath stinks of bourbon.

I shake my head. "I don't know. I felt like I should come see you."

He reaches into his pocket and passes me a metal hip flask. "Drink?"

I shrug, open the flask, and take a sip. Then I pass it back to him.

He takes a sizable swig of the drink. Then he screws the cap on and puts it away. "I needed to get away from things for a little while. I got into a little spat with one of the guys in the dorm."

"What kind of spat?"

He shrugs. "Bullshit kind. He was behaving like a 19-year-old. Dickhead. I lost it on him. He got all up in my face, and I shoved him up against the wall. And for a second there I considered choking him."

"That's not good."

"Yeah. Scared the crap out of him. Scared me even more. I needed to take a walk for a few days."

Impulsively, I say, "I get it. If you need a place to stay short term, we've got a little bit of room."

He smiles and strums a chord on his guitar. "No thanks. I pretty much decided to go back to the dorms in the next day or two anyway. I'm gonna see if I can switch to a single next semester. Then at least I won't have to put up with other people's bullshit."

"That seems like a good idea."

He leans forward, resting his arms on his guitar, and scowls at me. "So why do you look so screwed up?"

I ignore the question. Instead, I asked him, "So... what's your plan?"

He nods slowly. "I gotta keep trying. You know? A big part of me wants to give up. Get a drink or five and to stay the hell away from everybody. It doesn't matter how far I run, or how much I drink, I can't make their faces go away."

I shudder. My problems aren't his problems, but I know that there are things I'll never be able to forget, no matter how hard I try. You can't unsee certain things.

We sit in a companionable silence for several minutes as people walk by on the sidewalk. All kinds of people... young and old, rich and poor, every ethnic group. One of the things I love about Amherst and the Valley as a whole is that it has the feel of a small town... farms and horse camps all over the area... the Five Colleges give the area a cosmopolitan feel that normally you would find in a big city. A few passersby give me odd looks. My companion is filthy, unkempt. Undoubtedly it looks strange.

Who cares?

"Something's on your mind, Zoe. What is it?"

I shrug. "It's stupid."

He weighs a hand vaguely. "Who's to say what's stupid? What's wrong?"

I don't know why—maybe it's because he's clearly as messed up as I am—but I feel comfortable talking. I open my mouth to say that Matt cheated on me, but something completely unexpected comes out. "Do you ever wonder if your parents were proud of you?"

"Sure they are," he says with a snort. "Dad loved to congratulate me on my kills. He gets to brag about me at work. My son, the mass murderer. He doesn't know what it's like to serve in a war. He doesn't know what it's like to hate yourself, to look in the mirror and see nothing but death. So he can be proud of me, but for the wrong reasons."

I nod slowly. Then I find myself telling him about my father and mother, and their disappointment that I joined the military instead of following in their footsteps. I wander back and forth in my story, telling him about the summer nights sitting with my dad in his garage, about my deep respect and love for him, and how devastated I was when my mother said, "Your father is so disappointed."

The story comes out in a jumble, a confusing mess of half incomplete sentences and interrupted words. It's a wonder he can follow any of it, but as I wind up, his eyebrows draw together and he says, "Wait a minute. Did your father ever say he wasn't proud of you?"

I blink. Then I take a breath and say, "No, not really. He asked a lot of probing questions when I told him I wanted to join. He made it clear how he felt."

"Your friend—you said she argued with you, that your father didn't feel that way."

I'm defensive. "Why would she know?" In the back of my head, I think: *Nicole grew up in my house. She knew my dad as well as I did.*

He stares at me and says "Are you sure it's not you?"

How am I supposed to answer that? And... *what if I'm wrong about my dad?*

The idea seems crazy to me. After all, this isn't something new. I've known my dad was disappointed for a very long time. When I think back to the weeks after I made the decision to join the Army, it's always my mother I picture. Dad was there... but it was mom who expressed their collective disapproval. Could I have just been wrong? The truth is I have no idea what he thought. I've been terrified to go into his office or the workshop, and suddenly that decision seems very shortsighted.

I look at Luke, dumbfounded, realizing that I haven't spoken in at least a couple of minutes.

"You look as if I struck a nerve." He raises his eyebrows as he makes the statement.

"You did." I slowly stand up. Then I nod and put a hand on Luke's shoulder. "Thanks."

His mouth quirks up in a smile. "Glad I could help. Whatever it is."

"Will I see you at the next meeting?"

He considers for a moment. Then he says, "Yeah. I think so. Can't miss all that drama."

CHAPTER TWENTY-TWO

That's not possible (Zoe)

WHAT IF I was wrong the whole time? The thought runs through my head all the way back to the house. I've been accused more than once of being too quick, of being someone who rushes to judgment. I barely notice the drive through South Hadley until I pull into my driveway and park the car.

Everything looks the same. The peeling paint, the decaying wood on the porch. An orange flyer, probably for a Chinese restaurant or something, has been folded and stuffed in the front door of the house. But it's not the house I'm looking at. It's the detached garage, straight ahead, a small white painted building which hasn't been opened since the end of August.

I step out of the van, my feet crunching on fallen leaves. I need to rake the yard.

I walk toward the garage, my mouth full of dust. It would be ironic, now that I've gotten up the courage to go in (maybe) if the lock stuck and I couldn't get in. The side door is solid on the bottom, with nine panes of dirty looking glass on the top half. I can barely see through the glass, and it's dark in there, and the door isn't going to open itself no matter how long I stand here.

I dig for the key, feeling my heart beating in my chest. Then I slide the key in and unlock the door.

I take a deep breath. *Come on, Zoe. You've battled insurgents in Iraq. You can do this.*

Somehow this is worse. I open the door and switch on the light.

The first thing I notice is that it feels empty in here without the Austin Healy. That car was in here my entire life, slowly transforming from a wrecked, rusted-out hulk to a polished, beautiful work of art under Dad's loving hands. As always, the garage is a study in chaos. Arc welder piled on a table, tools everywhere. I push my way past the shelves which contain hundreds of random tools and parts and walk toward his desk.

It's dusty. I feel my eyes water at that realization. No one's been in here in a long time, and that makes me sad.

I sit back and just look. Above the desk—a Classic Cars calendar, stuck now forever on the month of August. Books—some automotive related, some English literature—scatter the desk in small piles. To the left of the calendar, a mosaic of photographs decorates the space above the desk. It's hard to look at them.

Me and Dad, his arm casually thrown over my shoulder, the Pioneer Valley spread out behind us. We were standing on top of Sugarloaf Mountain when that was taken.

Another one. Mom laying on a hospital bed, looking sweaty, exhausted. Dad is there, and so am I. In the picture,

I'm holding a newborn baby—Jasmine—and my face is messy with tears.

A picture I've never seen before. It was the day I came home on leave from Iraq. In the picture, I can see Dad's eyes are red and watering as his arms are wrapped around me. I remember that moment. I'll never forget it. I'd walked out of the security gate at Logan and there they were. Mom cried out my name, but Dad ran to me wordlessly and threw his arms around me and wouldn't let go. It was the first and only time I ever saw my father cry. He hadn't been able to stop, and Mom and I both found ourselves trying to help him calm down.

Other pictures. Me cheerleading. Me in the school play. A letter I wrote from Japan is tacked to the wall.

I'm having a hard time holding back tears. I miss him so much. I miss both of them. A tear runs down my face, then another; then I am crying and can't stop.

That's when I hear the sound of the school bus. I sniff, trying to hold back tears. Jasmine can handle getting off the bus, and she'll see the door open here.

I don't want her to come in. Not until I've had a chance to sort myself out. So I wait.

On the desk, against the wall behind the other books, is a leather-bound journal.

A journal.

"Zoe? Are you in the garage?"

I twist around in the chair and face the door. Jasmine's standing there. She's holding the flyer that was on the front door and looking confused. "Are you o—o—okay?" she asks. Her face twists in frustration as she stumbles over the word.

"Yeah," I say, sniffing. "I'm okay. I just … I need a little while. Can you get your snack sorted?"

She nods. "Yeah. Then I'll go check on the horses."

"Thank you, Jasmine," I say. I know it's irresponsible of me. I should get up and get her her snack, and have her start her homework, and act like a parent. But … for now… I can't.

Her eyes go back to the orange flyer again, an odd expression on her face. Then she walks out. Whatever. I'll deal with her later. We're going to have to have dinner early if we're going to make it to the circus on time. I might just take her out to dinner somewhere. I am not in a mood to cook.

I reach for the journal, hesitating just a moment. I'm violating his privacy.

No. He's gone. It's okay. I close my eyes, saying a half prayer, then I open the book.

My eyes fall on the words in the middle of the page: *"Only three more weeks before Zoe's deployment is over. I want to thank God that she's almost home, but I'm afraid to do it. Three weeks is still a long time in a dangerous place. Please protect her."* Chills run down my spine as I read the words.

I flip to another page, later in the book.

We got a letter from Zoe last night. I think something's wrong— she doesn't say so in the letter, but there's no mention of Chase, and there was a tone of melancholy in the letter. I'm afraid something may have gone wrong between the two of them. I'll ask her about it when she comes home, it'll only be in a few weeks. Missed her terribly at Christmas this year. Jasmine has been asking when Zoe is coming home—it's been almost a year.

Another one, this one almost four years ago:

I got into a verbal altercation with Donna Tumbler during the Symposium on 16th Century Poetry. She made some kind of a sneering comment about two of the visiting students from UMASS who were wearing Army ROTC uniforms. I'm afraid I was uncivilized in the tongue lashing I gave her. But her attitude appalled me. Young men and women like Zoe are putting their lives on the line every day while people sit back here bloviating about their political opinions. It makes me sick.

That one is a shock. I never imagined my Dad thought that way.

Tucked in the journal, several years old, is an article from the Town Reminder—about me and Nicole. **South Hadley Soldier-Cheerleaders Head to Iraq.** I laugh at the headline. Side by side photos on the front of the paper show me and Nicole during our junior year, cheering at the football game, and three years later in our Army uniforms.

I can't believe Dad saved that article. It's ridiculous. The article was ridiculous. Soldier-Cheerleaders. Sexist. Plenty of guys from South Hadley served, but they sure didn't get headlines like that.

But seeing it there in his journal puts a lump in my throat. That's not the only article—I flip forward forty or fifty pages, where another newspaper article is taped in place.

Oh my God.

It's about the firefight. The firefight, the night Nicole earned her Bronze Star. This looks like the Boston Globe, which makes sense. I remember the reporter wandering around the FOB in the days right after that fight. I scan through the article.

South Hadley residents Nicole Banks and Zoe Welch, both military police, were attached to the platoon during the ambush. First Sergeant Randy Wilson said, "Sergeant Banks's quick action saved several lives, and I expect to nominate her for a medal. Technically they aren't in the unit—they aren't even infantry—but they do everything the men in our unit do, and they do it well. Before this deployment I've always been against having women in Combat Arms, but I've changed my mind."

The two women were cheerleaders at South Hadley High School, and according to sources at the school, Welch was accepted to more than one exclusive college.

Jefferson Welch, chair of the English Literature department at Mount Holyoke College, said about his daughter's military service, "I couldn't possibly be prouder of Zoe. And I couldn't possibly miss her more."

Jesus. I can't. For the first time in weeks, I break down again in tears. After several minutes of sobbing, I page randomly through the book again. Then I stop. What?

This entry is from three years ago.

I received the strangest email from Howard yesterday. It seems that a boy he met at the jail in Texas is applying for a job at South Hadley High School. The guy, named Matt Paladino, who Howard somehow got into Boston University—was a circus performer who was apparently unjustly accused of murdering his own father. He's trying to start his life over as far away as possible from where he grew up.

I've assured Howard that I'll talk with Peggy Young, who is chairing the selection committee for the new applicants.

What?

I—

That's not possible.

I scan through his journal again. To last August, at the beginning of Jasmine's second grade year.

There it is. Holy Christ.

In the funniest turn of events, Howard's protégé Matt is to be Jasmine's second grade teacher. I met him in person for the first time during orientation today. He keeps his past close to the vest— I've heard nothing of it during the three years since he came to work here. He's a nice young man and quite smart. Of course I didn't tell him of my involvement in his hiring here.

Without thought I reach out and boot up Dad's computer, a six year old iMac that slowly cranks to life.

No password. I open up Google, and hesitate over the keyboard. Then I type. Matt Paladino. Circus. Murder.

The first hit is an article from the Bradenton Herald. **Circus Flyer Cleared in Father's Death.** I read through the article. Matt Paladino of the Flying Paladinos with the Ringing Brother's Circus. Oh my God. His father had a heart attack during a stunt? While Matt was holding him in the air?

Paladino, now 18, was held in the Travis County Jail for nine months while awaiting trial. He was released without charge yesterday. District Attorney Dan Mullins cites witness description of an argument between Paladino and his father immediately prior to the senior Paladino's death as the primary reason for suspecting Paladino of his father's murder. When asked why it took nine months to clear the high school senior and release him, Mullins argued that budget cuts have created a backlog in the prosecutor's offices and the courts.

I go back to Google and this time type in "Flying Paladinos." Photos of the circus family. A wikipedia article. Another accident, several years before his father died.

The photos. Oh my God. There's the woman. The woman he got in the car with.

Messalina Paladino.

Matt's sister.

Sudden terror shoots through me. I can't believe I was so judgmental. I can't believe I didn't even give him a chance to explain. I need to talk to him. I need to talk to him right away.

SIS. I NEED YOUR HELP. (MATT)

Fifteen minute break. I stand near the ring, sweating and staring at the floor. Tough practice. We have one hour to go, then we'll rest up before the show.

My phone, sitting on the chair next to me, rings. I pick it up.

Holy Crap. It's Zoe. I snap the phone open. "Hello? Zoe?"

"Mister P?"

I swallow and gasp. "Jasmine?"

"Hi, Mister P. I just got home from school, and I ... I saw your note."

The note. Why hadn't Zoe gotten it first? "Isn't your sister home?" I ask.

Jasmine says, "She didn't come in the house. She's out in Daddy's garage. I think she's crying."

I close my eyes. Christ. I want to be there, right now. "Do you know why?"

"No, Mister P. But ... listen ... can you come here? I've heard her talking with her friend. She's mad at you. She thinks you are in love with another girl with funny hair. "

"A girl with funny hair? What?"

As I say the words, though, I see Messalina walking back toward the ring. Then I put it together. I'd cancelled, with terrible excuses. Had Zoe seen me leaving with Messalina and assumed I was going out with another woman?

That would explain... a lot.

"I don't know. You're not with another woman are you?"

"No, Jasmine. No. Never."

My phone chirps. Battery must be dying. The battery on this flip phone lasts forever, but I haven't charged it in days. I don't even have a charger here.

"Can you come here? Like tomorrow morning? We're going to the circus tonight, but Zoe will be here in the—"

"Wait. Jasmine. You'll be at the circus? You mean in Springfield?"

"Yes. Nicole got the tickets. I can pretend I'm sick if tonight's better. I want to see the circus, but I want you to come see us more. I will. I'll pretend."

"No," I interrupt. "First, you shouldn't lie. And second—I think you can do both. I'll see you tonight."

"Really?" She asks.

"Yeah. I promise."

The phone chirps again. "Jasmine, I gotta go. Battery is about to die on my phone. I'll see you."

"Will I see you at the circus? Or at home af—"

The phone cuts off.

They're coming to the circus.

I stand up. Messalina's approaching. "Sis. I need your help. Bad."

Would you let him? (Zoe)

Damn it. His phone must be dead, or turned off. It went straight to voicemail. I try one more time. Same thing. I start to leave a message, but my throat closes. I just... I need to hear his voice. I need to talk with him, not at his voicemail.

I can't believe what I've seen here. I shake my head in ... relief? Shock? Amazement? No wonder Matt was so secretive. I start to stand up.

Jasmine's at the door. I start, then reach behind me and touch the power button on the computer. It shuts down, but not quick enough.

"Was that Mister P? On the computer?"

I sigh. "Yeah. Yeah. I miss him."

Jasmine looks wary. She asks, "You do? I thought you didn't want to see him again."

I sniff. "Maybe I was wrong, Jasmine. I ... I don't know." I don't want to promise anything to her. Not until I talk to Matt. Because he might not want me back after I cut him off like that.

"What are you doing?" She asks.

I turn toward the desk. Then I start to cry. God damn it. "Just looking through some of Dad's things."

She walks forward and touches my hand. "Don't cry, Zoe."

I shrug. Then I sit down and say, "Sometimes there's nothing else I can do. Come here. Take a look at this." I point at the picture of me holding Jasmine when she was a baby.

"Do you know who that is? The baby?"

Jasmine shakes her head.

"That's you," I whisper. "You were ... ten minutes old then. Mom and Dad let me hold you, and I sang you a little song."

Jasmine's eyes water. "Can I sit in your lap?"

"Oh, honey. Of course." I pull her up into my lap and put my arms around her.

"I miss Mommy and Daddy," she says.

"I do too," I reply. Now I'm crying. A lot. So is she.

"I miss Mister P too. Do you think... if he came back... would you let him?"

I pull her to me. Then I whisper, "Yes. Yes, I would. I miss him too, Jasmine."

CHAPTER TWENTY-THREE

QUIT FREAKING OUT (MATT)

The crowd is alive.

It's a feeling I've not experienced in years. The roar, the rising and falling breath, the wave of noise that crests just as the spectacle opens the performance.

From my position at the top of the rigging, I've been scanning the crowd, trying to see Zoe and Jasmine. This is a smaller, much more intimate venue than when I was growing up playing for Ringling Brothers. The Binder & Mills Circus usually seats less than a thousand. You would think that in the much smaller crowd, I'd be able to see them, but so far no luck.

"Quit freaking out, Matt. I'm sure they'll be here if she said they would." Messalina's words come out harsher than I think she intended. Of course I could be wrong. Maybe she meant them that harshly.

"But I don't—"

"Shhhh."

She's beside me in the rigging. Our opening is one that will startle the crowd. Tony and Mamma are on the platform across from us, facing us across the ring. Tony and I will go first, getting into catching position. Then Mamma and Messalina will jump off, swing into position, then launch into their first tricks. They cross next to each other, of course, but to the audience it will appear they're hurtling through the air straight at each other. From there it's a fairly classic trapeze routine, but tightly synchronized, ending in dual triples, Mamma and Messalina side by side. That is rare as hell.

This weekend will likely be my only performance as an adult with the Flying Paladinos. I want it to count. At the end, I've got my own little performance planned, provided everything falls into place like it's supposed to.

Then I see them. Around the fifteenth row, fairly high in the steeply tiered seats. Jasmine sits in between Nicole and Zoe. She looks excited, pointing around the room. I know she can't see me up here in the darkness, but she will soon enough.

I CAN'T BE SEEING THIS (ZOE)

"Look at the tigers!" Jasmine shouts and points.

She's been doing a lot of shouting tonight. In fact, I've rarely seen her so excited and talkative. I lean forward, looking to my left at Nicole. Nicole crosses her eyes and bursts into laughter. Jasmine is bouncing now.

To be fair, it's been a lot of fun. I haven't been to the circus in years—the last time, I was about Jasmine's age, actually, when my parents took me to see the Ringling Brothers circus in Boston. It occurs to me that I might have seen Matt that night—I vividly remember the trapeze artists. Who knows? I can't even imagine. I almost regret not having had the opportunity to see him perform before he left the business.

What a horrible tragedy. What a way to lose a parent.

Not so different than having a parent killed by a flying oven.

True. We have freak parental deaths in common.

Jasmine showed me the note when we went back inside. She'd given it to me sheepishly, as if she felt bad because of looking at it. It was something.

The note, handwritten in a terrible scrawl that was barely legible—embarrassing, really, for a teacher—was his message:

Dearest Zoe:

Please don't tear up this note or throw it away or incinerate it or dump it in with the horse manure. At least not until you read it.

There are things in my past that I'm ashamed of. And I've been very secretive about them. Not because I wanted to lie to you, but because I didn't want you to look down on me.

There are things I've been afraid to say.

Please give me a chance to say them. I promise you, if you want me to go away after that, I will.

With love,

Matt

With love, he wrote. Neither of us have said the words "I love you." But it was true. I do love him. And if I can ever figure out a way to get ahold of him or see him again, I'll tell him. And I'm going to beg for forgiveness. I look at my watch. It's 9:15. Show will be ending soon.

That's when Jasmine screams. It's a different scream than I've heard from her, and Nicole and I both look at her in shock. She goes silent, but is pointing. Up, up into the ropes and rigging in the darkness near the ceiling.

Oh my God.

Matt is up there. He's wearing black tights and a bright, sequined silver tunic.

My brain tunes into the loud voice of the barker. "Performing with us tonight for the first time since his father's tragic death in the ring, the world famous Flying Paladinos are rejoined tonight by the amazing Matteo Paladino!" The crowd bursts into applause as spotlights swing toward Matt.

"I can't be seeing this," Nicole says.

"You can," I say.

The crowd bursts into applause as Matt and another man— his brother, I guess—take hold of bars and swing out toward each other, the spotlights flaring off their sequined shirts.

"I guess we know where he learned to ride a horse," Nicole says.

"At the circus!" Jasmine shouts, bouncing up and down in her seat. She's clapping and cheering, and—she's crying too. Happy tears, but tears. That makes me wipe my eyes, damn it.

Both of the men on the trapeze do sudden flips or something, and the next thing I know, they are hanging by their feet, arms outstretched in front of them. Music suddenly begins playing, melodic classical music, and the two women—Matt's sister and mother swing out toward each other, then go flying straight at each other. Someone in the crowd screams and hundreds of the rest go silent with a great intake of air.

GOT HER! (MATT)

Got her!

Mamma's grip and mine are tight as we lock arms together. The crowd goes insane. I don't know if it was the trick, or the scare of Mamma and Messalina almost hitting each other, or if they know how my Dad died, but the crowd is with us, screaming and applauding. Mamma smiles up at me and mouths, "I'm proud of you," as we swing back. This is the most dangerous part. I have to release her at the precise moment so she can grab the bar that is even now swinging on its own back and forth. If I let go too soon she'll miss it entirely and fall to the net. Too late, and the bar might smash her across the face.

Release.

I let go and Mamma does a back somersault and catches the bar and swings away. The crowd roars again as we get into position for the next trick. Tony and I will be swinging Messalina back and forth between us, which the audience will love, until Tony lets go and swings at the end of a chain, me holding Messalina's ankles as she holds Tony's hands. Then we'll swing back up and he'll go back to the bar. We've done it a bunch of times in practice, but this is the real thing.

We launch into it. Vaguely I can hear the announcer telling the audience the history of my family as we begin tossing Messalina back and forth. Five generations of trapeze artists since the 19th Century. Tragedy struck the family in each generation—right up to the death of the Antonio Paladino.

Papa. Jesus. The announcer is talking about my retirement from the ring after Papa died and how this is my first time back. I want to punch him in the throat.

But I have more important things to do. As I come up from the last swing, Messalina reaches up and grabs the bar tossed down by Mamma. As she swings back up to the platform, Mamma appears to jump right over her and me, into Tony's waiting arms.

I forgot how much I love this. I love teaching too. And I'll never give it up. But this is family.

Then we head into the finale. Almost time. That is, if Tony and Messalina pulled off my plan.

NO TIME! (ZOE)

The crowd goes insane after Matt and his family finish their act. A standing ovation, probably helped along by the announcer's storytelling, which struck me as exploitive.

"Did you know any of that?" Nicole shouts at me over the crowd.

"I just found out this afternoon!" I reply.

She shakes her head in wonderment. "Why the hell didn't you tell me?"

"No time!" I reply.

Jasmine is waving. At Matt. Oh my God. He sees her and waves back. The crowd can't tell, but I can. Because he looks right at me, and his eyes are sad.

Down on the floor, the announcer begins to introduce the next act when three clowns come running across the ring. One chases the others with a big wooden paddle and Jasmine laughs in delight.

But then the lead clown breaks away and runs straight for the announcer, who looks shocked. The clowns are running around him now, and one of them grabs the microphone and runs with it. The crowd busts into laughter as the announcer gives chase. They go around the ring once, but the other clowns run interference.

But then—this can't be what normally happens. The clown throws the microphone, which swings end over end toward the ladder up to the trapeze, where Matt's sister catches it. She twists and tosses it up higher, where Matt's brother catches it, then he turns around and throws it all the way across the ring.

To Matt, who is now sitting casually on one of the trapeze poles, using it like a swing.

The crowd laughs and applauds as the announcer bunches his fists at his hips and shouts something at Matt.

Matt looks down at the announcer and smiles, then shakes his head. He looks back up. Right at me.

He opens his mouth and begins to talk.

SHE'S NODDING (MATT)

It's hard to see Zoe's expression with the spotlights shining in my eyes. Is she angry? Jasmine looks … hopeful. Nicole skeptical. The rest of the crowd is clueless of course.

I take a deep breath. "So, does this thing work?"

My voice bursts out the speakers. "Oh good, it works." I clear my throat. "This isn't part of the show. And I'll probably get fired for this."

"You're right you will!" shouts the barker. I wave at him again and he shakes a fist. The audience, still not sure if this is actually part of the show, laughs. I look out at Zoe.

"The reason I have the microphone is that there's someone special in the audience. Two special girls actually. A little girl named Jasmine, who lost her parents in a terrible accident back in the summertime. And her big sister, Zoe, who is taking care of her."

My stomach hurts. But I have to go on.

"See, the thing is, you all heard the story of what happened to my Dad. What they didn't tell you is that me and Dad had an awful fight right before he died. And for a while there, they thought I'd done something horrible. And I went to jail, until they realized that it was just a heart attack. And…I was… ashamed. Of all of it. Of the circus, of… of my life. Especially of going to jail. So I came here, to college; then to work. But I didn't want anyone to know."

"You're going to jail again if I have anything to say about it!" shouts the announcer. But now Anthony Rubio, the owner of the circus, is there. He grabs the announcer by the arm and whispers something urgent to him.

The crowd is utterly silent. Captivated almost.

"Anyway," I say. "I've only got the mic for a couple minutes. But while I have it, I need to say a couple of things. And here they are."

Zoe is staring at me, dumbfounded. Her hands are clenched into fists in her lap. I don't know if she is happy or if she wants to kill me. But I have to say it.

I take a deep breath. "Zoe, I'm sorry. I kept my past a secret. I didn't tell you where I was going when I went to practice for... this. When I went to meet my family. I ... I was super secretive."

I take a deep breath. She's nodding. She's nodding. And Jasmine has the biggest smile on her face I've ever seen. Even Nicole is smiling, though it looks like she might crack.

I take a deep breath, fall over backward and plunge to the net. The crowd gasps, goes silent again as I roll into a ball and land on my back, a perfect landing Papa would have been proud of, though he would have chided me for going to the net holding something.

I roll out of the net and onto the ground. I'm facing her from below now, approaching the first tier of seats.

"See, the thing is...." My voice sounds loud to me down here coming from the speakers. Also the crowd is ... holding their breath?

She covers her face, peeking out from between her fingers. A spotlight shines on her. "The thing is," I say. "The thing is... I love you. I hid my past because I was afraid you would ... I don't know. Think I was crazy. Or worse. But I don't care if you think I'm crazy."

As I speak the words, I am walking up the stairs past the first few rows, until I'm level with her. Nicole slips out of her seat and into the aisle, out of the way. Jasmine is staring at me crying. Zoe is still hiding her face. "All I care about is … will you forgive me?"

Hushes silence. She peeks from behind her hands and meets my eyes. Hers are flooded with tears.

Then she nods. "Yes," she mouths.

I turn and throw the microphone back toward the announcer, who catches it in an extended hand. Then I turn back to Zoe and take her right hand. She stands up.

"I love you," I say again.

"I love you," she replied. "I do."

"I really love you," I say.

"Forgive me?" she asks.

"Always," I reply.

I pull her to me and lean forward. When our lips touch, the thousand people at the circus erupt into cheers. It's a long, long kiss. When we step back to breathe for a second, I reach down and pick up Jasmine. "And you, little girl," I say. "Will you forgive me too?"

Jasmine nods her head and throws her arms around me, burying her face in my neck. I meet Zoe's eyes again. They're brimming with tears. The spotlight moves away as the announcer begins speaking again. Thank God. I lean forward and kiss Zoe.

"I love you, Zoe. Will you be mine?"

She replies in a whisper. "Always."

The applause of the crowd fades in my mind as we kiss again.

EPILOGUE

THE STORY WAS in the next day's paper, and overnight, Matt became somewhat of a local celebrity. Not only was he the great looking third grade teacher who had taken on the school administration and won, but he also had an amazing story of tragedy and vindication.

And he was mine.

In the weeks after our reunion, his past came up a lot. He only performed with the family over that weekend, but it was enough. He was being talked about on the local radio, and the local weekly, the Town Reminder, did a story. A cover story, featuring a huge photo of the two of us kissing in the stands at the circus.

I took some ribbing about it from the other vets in our group at UMASS. But that was okay too.

Matt went back to teaching third grade. And I went back to school. Zoe stopped stuttering the day we got back together.

I still miss Mom and Dad. I always will. I go visit their memorial occasionally, but I don't drag Jasmine there, except on Easter. She doesn't need that much sadness in her life. She finishes the third grade with flying colors.

Tyler and Nicole are dating. Seriously dating. I wouldn't believe it if I didn't see it, because he's a giant jerk. But I kind of love him all the same.

I still see Luke and the other guys on campus regularly, and we've had Luke over for dinner a few times. You can see the pain behind his eyes, but he's moving forward.

I've decided I'm going to major in psychology, specializing in horse therapy for children. Little kids like Jasmine can't voice their pain and grief the way adult can, but you can't bullshit a horse. I've seen how Mono helped Jasmine recover, and I want to help other little girls like that.

So nowadays, life is pretty good. I go to class, Matt goes to work, Jasmine goes to school. We spend our lives together.

Matt showed up on Christmas morning. I was expecting him—we'd planned on spending Christmas together. But I wasn't expecting Jasmine's weird behavior. Instead of running for the door screaming "I'LL GET IT" at the top of her lungs, she hung back and waited for me to get it.

So I did. And there was Matt, dressed normally except for a silly Santa Hat. But then he did something crazy. He got on one knee, and opened up a stupid box, with a stupid ring inside, then said, unbelievably "Zoe ... I want to be your husband. I want to be Jasmine's stepdad. I want... I ... will you marry me?"

I cried.

Then I said yes.

THE END

ACKNOWLEDGEMENTS

Joanne Huff and Laura Litterer at Full of Grace Farm in Hadley, Massachusetts. Thank you for letting me come out and learn a little about horses, including sweeping stalls and watching you both give lessons. What I got right in the story came from them. The mistakes are my own.

To an amazing group of beta readers: Dimitra Fleissner, Kelly Moorhouse, Kirstin Papi, Kirsty Landar, Laura Wilson, Michelle Kannan, Rebecca Tyndall, Sally Bouley, Sherry Brannigan, Tanya Spence Hall. Most of you have been through several books with me by now, and I can never express how grateful I am.

To Andrea, for reminding me that the English language needs hyphens, and for being the most amazing partner and future wife anyone has ever had. I love you with all my heart.

www.ingramcontent.com/pod-product-compliance
Lightning Source LLC
Chambersburg PA
CBHW071104250626
47159CB00002B/593